A WILD EDEN

SCOTT SHARPE

A
Wild
Eden

HUB CITY PRESS
SPARTANBURG, SC

Cover design: Meg Reid
Book design: Kate McMullen
Editor: Betsy Teter
Proofreader: Kalee Lineberger
Cover: "Woodwall with Coat Buttons" © mblifestyle / Shutterstock
"Treehouse on the Lake" © daizuoxin / Shutterstock

Printed in East Peoria, IL by Versa Press

Library of Congress Cataloging-in-Publication Data

Names: Sharpe, Scott, author.
Title: A wild eden / Scott Sharpe.
Description: Spartanburg, SC : Hub City Press, 2019.
Identifiers: LCCN 2018060589 / ISBN 9781938235573
Classification: LCC PS3619.H356654 W55 2019 / DDC 813/.6—dc23
LC record available at https://lccn.loc.gov/2018060589

The South Carolina Novel Prize is sponsored by Hub City Press,
the South Carolina Arts Commission, the College of Charleston, the South Carolina
State Library and South Carolina Humanities.

chapman cultural center

Hub City Press gratefully acknowledges support from
the Chapman Cultural Center in Spartanburg, South Carolina.

HUB CITY PRESS
186 W. Main Street
Spartanburg, SC 29306
864.577.9349 | www.hubcity.org

For my parents, Roy and Bonnie Sharpe,
who provided a Wild Eden for this wayward son.

CHAPTER ONE

The preacher had scarcely cleared his throat when a backfire broke the solemn and a noxious haze drifted through my father's funeral. Zell Branham, the local farrier, stumbled from his truck and over to the graveside. I smelled the whiskey seeping from his pores from the far side of the hole. Zell ran a hand down his beard and studied the gathered mourners out the corners of his eyes, as if he was hoping nobody had noticed his arrival. But at six-foot-six and closer to three-fifty than three hundred pounds, he blocked a lot of sunlight. Mama's friend, Miss Ida Mae Sanders, jostled her way over to stand beside the big man. On her tiptoes, she snatched his hat from his head and stuffed it into his ponderous gut. He colored up and she nodded smartly to the preacher, as if to let him know all was screwed down tight and he could proceed with his funeralizing. Her own hat appeared to be fashioned from road-kill peacock and flea-bit fox fur. She was five-foot-nothing, but whatever she might've lacked in her dimensions, she more than made up for with her zealous prosecution of etiquette.

A group of women, most pierced and tattooed, huddled together, staring defiantly at the black-clad, ink-free, unpierced, geriatric group that made up the better part of the bereaved. My father's longtime attorney, Lawrence T. Ramsey, stood hoe-handle straight between Zell and the inked women, his eyes fixed on the heavens, as if he was thinking deep and celestial thoughts. With his sanctimonious bearing, Larry looked more hellfire TV preacher than genteel Southern attorney at law. I half expected him to start laying down the brimstone or healing one of the women of some sin transfused into their blood by Satan's vile ink.

Dad's graveside service was far from the dignified affair I would've expected. More carnival than funeral, he might've said. I was surprised my straight-as-a-plumb-line father had even known anyone with neck tattoos, much less pierced lips, noses, or eyebrows. Far as I knew, he'd never strayed much from his thin views. I couldn't seem to reconcile the departure of it all. My baby sister, Magnolia, caught my eye, turned to look at the array of funeral goers I'd been studying, then shook her head—Maggie's way of letting me know she was just as mystified.

Hell, what did I know anyway? Surely nothing substantial about my father. Dad and I hadn't ever had a real conversation. He'd kept his distance from me, and I'd returned the favor with interest. We'd had an unspoken, ongoing contest where we tried to out-ignore one another. That battle had always finished in a draw. And I remember him always watching me when he thought I wasn't looking—watching me as a body might scan the horizon for a crop-killing storm.

But he'd gone and left me without answers to questions I had always meant to ask. I'd come up with the short end of the stick again. I'd danced to that tune far too often.

The earliest grievers escaped the worst of the sun under frayed green awning, paper fans working against the South Carolina heat. Latecomers spilled out onto the sun-murdered grass covering the field of the dearly departed. Flower sprays stood behind and to the sides of Dad's polished pine casket. Their sick-sweet fragrance didn't begin to cover the scent of the fresh-dug earth or the stink of so much collected death.

Family, friends, and strangers braved the heat to pay their respects to the great Tom Parker. Most of the tattooed women wept for Dad. My mother took my hand and squeezed it. I looked at her hand grasping mine, then up to her careworn face. Even on the day she buried her husband of thirty-seven years, she glanced at each of her five children to see how we were coping. She'd always been like that. She was surely their marriage's better half.

The preacher spoke his flowery words, but I'd stopped listening. As he finished, he glanced at his watch then prayed briefly but fervently, Bible clutched against his heart, right hand in the air. Then he walked over to my mother and whispered to her. She nodded, patted his shoulder, and managed a sad little smile. He whispered to each of my mother's children in turn. I said nothing in reply. The preacher's tired trivialities were wasted on me. Or maybe I was just pissed off at the whole world and not in the mood for any of his sympathetic bullshit.

The mourners milled about and spoke to our family for a few minutes before drifting away like afterthoughts. As she was leaving, one of the tattooed women looked at me and nodded. She seemed to know me, but I didn't know her. What's more, I couldn't imagine my father knowing her—at least well enough to draw her to his funeral.

Finally, only the Parker family remained, three generations strong. We were quiet—not altogether normal for us—but not overly weepy. Dad's health had been declining for a few years, so his passing hadn't snuck up on us.

My brother, Bill, and I escorted Mama to the long black car and made sure she was comfortable inside. We kissed our wives, hugged our three sisters and our children, and sent them all on their way to the funeral home and the Parker farm. Poor Mama was too spent to notice Bill and me not leaving with the rest of the family. Though I'd not told her my intentions, my wife, Sara, would know why I wasn't leaving just yet. She took Bill's wife by the hand and whispered something, her eyes never leaving mine. Kathy glanced at Bill and nodded to my wife. Sara looked at me once more before she disappeared behind tinted windows. Her smile, however joyless, fortified me for the grim work ahead.

We watched the cars carry away our family until the last taillights dipped below the hilltop. When they'd disappeared, Bill touched my arm and we approached the grave. Like me, my brother was all business when there was a job to do. But unlike me, Bill could leave the past in the past. Took a hell of a lot to push him too far. I could hold onto a grudge with a death grip.

The cemetery workers had already removed the carpet of artificial grass covering the newly turned earth, leaving a gaping wound in the ground. They'd disassembled the steel frame and the cables used to lower the casket into the suffocating hole. One scampered up out of the grave after wrenching the vault lid into place. Still others were folding and carrying the chairs, lined up neatly for loved ones, to a van. They eyed Bill and me with interest, a deviation to their otherwise routine day. The funeral director, who had remained at a respectable distance, approached us with a practiced, sympathetic smile upon his face. "Gentlemen, it might be unpleasant for you to remain while we cover the deceased," he said. His hands were clasped against his chest as if in prayer, as if he didn't realize we were beyond all that.

Bill grunted. I said to Mr. Elton, "We'll cover our father. Just give us a couple shovels and a little piece of clock."

He was clearly thrown off kilter, but his smile didn't miss a lick. He said, "That won't be possible, Mr. Parker. The participation of the deceased's kin in covering the final resting place is strictly against our policy. Our insurance would not cover any medical treatment should you be injured. Only cemetery workers may perform this final task. Now I assure you, gentlemen, we will take good care of your daddy."

"That mean no?" Bill asked. He'd removed his suit jacket and was looking down at his veined forearms as he rolled his shirtsleeves. The hint of a smirk puckered my brother's lips. He knew

I could be a stubborn ass when the spirit moved me, or when a pompous know-it-all son of a bitch, like Phineas J. Elton, Jr., told me I couldn't do what I'd a mind to do.

I looked Elton full in the face. "We appreciate the care you've given our father, sir, but you will make an exception to your policy today. Shovels?" I glanced at Bill and he nodded, likely glad I'd used words instead of other means. My brother knew I had a history of talking with my fists. He'd posted bail often enough.

To his credit, the funeral director pointed to the workers leaning on their shovels nearby and grinning at their boss. Elton's watery smile faltered, then faded to nothing, and he retreated to the funeral van's relative safety. He lit a cigarette and pretended to supervise the loading of the chairs and equipment. Bill tossed me a shovel he'd taken from the workers. Slowly we blanketed our father with fragrant, sandy loam. The thump of the dirt softened to a sigh as the vault and any chance for answers disappeared forever.

With Dad tucked away, I admitted to myself that his burial was not the first time I'd said goodbye to him. I'd lost my father many years before, when I'd needed him most. But nothing profitable could come from ruminating on the past. I wanted—hell, I needed—to put miles of blacktop between him and me and get on with the job of living.

After we finished, Bill and I watched Elton and company drive out of the cemetery before we began the trek home. We walked in quiet for a time, and then he said, "I could drink a beer." Leave it to my brother to think of beer after burying our father, but his comment coaxed the intended grin from me. I was inclined to agree, but thought we'd best get to the farm to check on Mama. I said as much and Bill nodded. Several cars and trucks stopped to offer us rides, but we declined each with our thanks, preferring to hoof the extra mile. The shovel work and the walk home were but small tributes to our father. He'd taught us, by example, the value of work. Tom Parker had been a first-rate teacher in that one respect.

Passing old man Arnold's hay field, I remembered the smell of fresh-cut fescue, sweet and green, waiting on the sun's kiss. All of Tom Parker's kids had worked nearly from the time we could walk. Money had been tight early on, and we'd pitched in while Dad's cabinetry business was still young. He was determined that no bank would ever get a toehold in our family land, the only wealth we had. While many of our friends had spent their summers at Myrtle Beach, swimming in Cedar Creek, or making crafts at Camp What-the-Hell, I'd walked beside the hay wagon pitching seventy-five-pound hay bales up to my sisters, with Bill driving our old Ford 8N. By the age of fourteen, I could toss the hay with one arm up to their feet, where they had but to grab each end and swing it atop the stack. We dug hundreds of post holes and strung miles of barbed and hog wire, often working as the light faded away to the south and west. We mucked stalls, delivered hay bales and sold corn by the roadside. On occasion, we were afforded a little time to hunt and fish and play, but chores had always come first, and cash money was king. Dad had never heaped praise on us, but I'd always hoped he was proud his kids could do a real day's labor. We worked, fought, and played hard. Bill, our sisters, and I had grown up strong and free, with just a touch of the wild to flavor us.

As we walked home, I was struck by how little I'd known about my father those last few years. It's hard to know a body when you're gone, and I'd been four hours away in Atlanta. We'd never been close anyway, but our formal relationship had reached new levels of quiet in the few years before he'd passed. I knew he'd worked hard, feared God, been a good man. But his life had appeared to me a pitiable quilt, patches of mediocrity and tedium sewn together by unskilled hands. When I was a boy, other than taking us fishing a few times, Dad had seemed to have no time for anything besides work. Either at his cabinet shop or on the farm, he'd always been in motion, always working. Because of heart problems, he'd been forced to retire from cabinetry a decade before, and I couldn't imagine how he'd occupied his days without orders to fill.

At one time, he'd been one of the most sought after cabinet makers in South Carolina. But had he taken any joy from his work? Or was it just a means to put food on the table? Surely if you do something that well for so long, you must love it. I was sure he'd enjoyed his horses and his farm, but they'd become mostly hobby years ago, when his cabinetry business took off. He rode less and less, as his health waned, but still kept a few gentle geldings around for his grandchildren. My father had always been a mystery to me, but that was understandable given our distance, physical and other.

As we rounded a bend in the road, my parents' farm came into view—Parker's Knoll. No matter how many times I'd seen it, I was always struck by the farm's humble beauty and balance. The rail fencing and tree-lined drive drew the eye up to a farmhouse painted the color of aged tatting, trimmed in black, and topped with shingles the shade of the sky just before a thunderstorm. The land rose to meet the house. Rolling pastures and groves of oak and pecan trees sprawled around it. A barn, horse paddocks, sundry sheds, and farm buildings spread out behind the house like a strutting tom turkey's tail feathers. Dad and Mama had raised us kids on that farm, and we'd claimed the surrounding land as well. Our playground was five thousand acres of pines, hickories, creeks, and ponds. We had a big back yard, even if we had to trespass a bit.

I'd lived there until I'd turned eighteen, then left to try marriage and college, returning on occasion to visit but never again to live. The marriage had stuck, but I'd failed like a son of a bitch at the University of Georgia. Even so, I couldn't abide living under Dad's roof once I felt I knew everything about everything. So I stayed away while Sara finished her degree and I found work.

And trouble.

I started fighting for any reason: a sideways look, an accidental bump. Whiskey and anger would flow through me until I lost control. I don't know why I did it, and it didn't matter who it was directed at. Hell, I can't recall a single face. I'd come home bruised and bloodied or spend a night in lockup. Bill would drive to Atlanta to get me out and try to smooth things over with my wife. On our seventh anniversary, a drunk grabbed Sara's wrist and demanded, "Dance with me, bitch." It took four men to pull me off of him. He spent a week in the hospital, and I spent a week in the county jail. When I got home, Sara's anger had reached its boiling point. She said, "Stop the bullshit, Jack, or we will leave you for good. I swear to God we will."

"We?" I said.

"Me and this child inside me, you idiot." She left and didn't return for two weeks.

It was a hell of a way to find out you're going to be a father, but I stopped the hard drinking and fighting that day.

Bill and I made our way up the long gravel drive and stepped up onto the deep back porch, where friends and kin entered Mama's house into her large kitchen. She'd been watching for us from her sink window. She opened the door and smiled at her sons. "You boys hungry?" Bill kissed Mama's cheek, slipped into the house, and commenced eating. When I didn't move, Mama walked over and hugged me. "Your daddy all squared away, son?"

"Yes'm. Reckon he's at rest now."

She pecked my cheek. "I'm so glad you're home, Jack." I knew I should offer comfort to my mother or an explanation of my absence since Christmas. But I couldn't find the words, so I just hugged her back.

The house was full of friends, family, and food. Mama called them the three Fs of funerals. Every room was filled with neighbors and kin, and every horizontal surface was covered with plates, platters, and bowls of fried chicken, sweet corn, mashed potatoes, and an intriguing variety of casseroles. At least a dozen desserts—cakes, pies, and cobblers—crowded the sideboard, sweet and medicinal.

My appetite had departed and I couldn't face a houseful of sympathy yet, so I slipped out and took a looksee around the Knoll.

A hundred years old or better, the barn still stood strong and steadfast, solid as a kept promise. The pine had hardened over the years, becoming like bedrock; it would've been nigh impossible to hammer a sixteen-penny nail into one of those massive beams. The building had weathered countless storms, a few tornados, and Hurricane Hugo in eighty-nine, all but minor inconveniences. Hell, that old barn would likely stand till Judgment Day.

Years before, Dad had divided its use between the original intention and his furniture and cabinet shop. I stood in front of the shop's door. His shingle hung above it, Parker Cabinetry & Hand-Crafted Furniture. As I stepped inside, the smells of sawdust, linseed oil, and wood stain whispered to me of a solitary man who'd spent the better part of his life working there, coaxing the wood to its most satisfactory potential. He'd spent countless hours crafting cabinets and furniture pieces, both useful and beautiful in their own quiet ways. The workshop was neat and orderly, every saw and plane and chisel in its proper place, the floor swept clean of sawdust and inspiration.

Although he'd been retired for at least ten years, Dad had still spent much of his days out there. Mama had once told me he'd left the house each morning and returned each evening, as if he'd never retired. Nobody knew what he did out there each day, and my family had left him to tinker about undisturbed. I fear pity was our collective motive. Dad would talk about horses or politics or weather, but never about why he went out there each day or how he spent all that time alone. In the few times I visited with him, I'd never pressed him, and he'd never volunteered any reason.

Leaving the workshop, I walked around to check on the horses in the barn's stalls. They were quiet but for an occasional soft nicker or snuffling blow. I felt a pang of pity for those geldings. My father had loved his horses and given great care to their needs, fairly doting on them. I wondered if they would receive the same level of care without him. Likely Bill, the dependable son, would assume those duties, as he had his own horses and lived close by. He'd fed them earlier, and they were all set for the evening.

The barn was near the tree line, at the rear of my parents' property, with vast woodlands beyond. They owned a hundred acres and most were cleared and in pasture. But a grove of massive trees stood between the house and barn, a tad to the north. Maybe forty or fifty southern live oaks were grouped together over several acres. The understory was a choir of graceful dogwoods, fragrant gardenias, and spring-bright azaleas—a perfumed cathedral of color in the warmer months, alive with birdsong.

All eight of Dad's grandchildren were gathered under the largest oak. They were looking up at something in the tree's branches, all hushed and still, as if they were having their own private funeral for their grandfather. I walked over and peered up into the oak feeling like an outsider. The beginnings of a sizable wooden framework were bolted to the trunk and larger limbs.

Without lowering her eyes, my sister Audrey's daughter, Izzy, said, "Papa was building a tree house for us." Izzy was both precocious and shy. I'd not heard anything about a tree house, but I imagined she was fancying herself sitting in it, books piled around her in tottering towers, the summer breeze soughing through the branches, chickadees crooning. She was a romantic, our Izzy, and she'd lost her grandfather and her haven-to-be all in one wretched bundle. She looked over at me and tried a smile. I thanked her for the information and walked back to the house, trying to picture my sensible, aging father climbing a tree, but the image seemed too outrageous for my mind to latch onto.

A few mourners had left, yet still the elderly and lonesome remained, those seeking the solace found in such commiserative gatherings. I made the rounds and spoke to as many folks as possible. I'd never been skilled in the fine art of small talk, but social niceties were expected of me, and I made the effort.

Everyone had a story to tell about Tom Parker, how he'd helped them in some way or another. The neighbor to the south, Don Marchant, told how Dad had taken one of Don's horses to a vet in Kentucky renowned for his treatment of the mare's particular ailment. My father had driven through the night to deliver the horse, stopping only for fuel, food, and coffee. Then he'd returned to collect the mare once she was healed two months later. The neighbor was old, much too frail for the rigors of pulling a heavy horse trailer, so Dad had just jumped in and helped out.

Mama shrugged and said, "Tom was always helping folks like that, especially after he retired. Said it kept him young. Your father was a compassionate man." When I asked her about the tree house, she smiled and told me Dad had collected lumber for a few years and had worked on the plans since he'd retired. "Didn't he ever mention it to you, Jack? He was working on it when his heart gave out." Throws you off plumb to learn new information about somebody you thought you had fixed. My father had always been so damn practical, never prone to folly. Mama's words were more proof I didn't know anything about him.

Still, I was curious about the tree house, about my father's motivations in building it so late in his life and with his declining health. But him working on it when he died gave me an odd peace. For many years, he'd made his living working with wood. It was fitting he'd died working with it too. He'd been consistent if nothing else.

Mama suggested we should tear down the framework, and Bill agreed. "It could be dangerous. One of the young'uns might get hurt swinging on it," he said between forkfuls of blackberry cobbler.

I nodded. "Maybe."

Sara, the kids, and I were staying at Mama's house. My sister, Lauren, and her family were down from Greenville and doing likewise. And even though Bill lived only a couple miles to the north, and Audrey and Maggie both lived in nearby Columbia, we were all sleeping in our parents' house. Mama had been adamant. "I want all my children under my roof tonight."

When everybody had settled for the night, I crawled into bed beside Sara and asked, "Did Wren or Lily mention anything to you about a tree house?" Our daughters kept in close contact with their South Carolina cousins through various electronic means. They were usually the first to know Parker news.

Sara looked up from the book in her lap. "Lily said something about it a few weeks ago during supper. Don't you remember? I think Tara told her about it. She said your daddy was building it for the grandkids." Tara, Bill's daughter, and my Lily were as close as any sisters.

"Why do you think Dad would begin something like that at his age and not bother to tell me? I could have helped. I build houses for God's sake."

Sara looked up again and frowned at me. "Besides you, your daddy was the most independent, introverted man I've ever met. Not all that surprising, is it? You two were so much alike. Maybe he did tell you about it and you forgot. And he wasn't that old, Jack."

Dad and I were nothing alike, and I was a touch put out at her tone but smart enough to keep it to myself. "But why now? I don't understand. He should've known better. He'd had heart problems for years, and that kind of work is far too strenuous. I can't believe his doctor didn't kick up a fuss."

Sara placed her book on the nightstand with a sigh. "Well, he was retired and probably didn't have much else to do. Tom was used to working hard, so maybe he was trying to stay active."

A knock on our bedroom door kept me from further grumbling. My mother's muffled voice said, "You two decent?"

Sara winked at me and said, "One of us is. Come on in, Lizzie."
Mama entered holding a white envelope clutched against her robe.

"What you got there, Mama?" Something about her expression gave me a twinge of trepidation.

"This is for you, Jack." She handed me the envelope and took a half step backward. "It's from your daddy. He made me promise to give it to you if something happened to him. He said you were to open it when you're alone." She turned to leave then turned back. "Goodnight, son." She kissed my cheek and wiped off an imagined lipstick smear with her thumb. Then she was gone.

I sat on the edge of the bed staring at my name written in my father's hand. I'd never received a letter or note from him. When I was growing up, Mama had always signed my birthday cards for them both. Why would Dad do something like this?

"Open it and find out." Sara stared at the envelope. Reckon I had asked that question out loud.

"Mama said I'm supposed to be alone. And I don't think I can handle it tonight anyway." I set the envelope on the nightstand and crawled back under the sheets.

"Honey, don't worry yourself. It could be instructions concerning the Knoll or his business dealings. Try not to dwell on it."

"Right. Why couldn't he just talk to me?"

"That's a two-way path, Jack. Try to get some rest tonight. It's been a trying day for us all, and we have to leave early in the morning." She kissed my cheek, turned off the lamp, and was asleep within a minute. I was still sitting up in bed, an open book in my lap, in the dark, wondering what had just happened.

I fell asleep hours later, with the sense that my father's green eyes were fixed on me.

Wanting something from me he'd not had the nerve to ask whilst alive.

Maybe accusing me of being the sorry-ass son everybody knew me to be. I was sure that damnable letter would prove me out.

13

CHAPTER TWO

Jack,

*I would like you to execute my will. Larry Ramsey will
call you to arrange a meeting. You also have power of
attorney for as long as you and Larry feel it's needed. He
has all the paperwork ready. I don't want your mother
to have to worry about anything, Jack. Take care of my
Lizzie. Take care of my family.*

Dad

Alone in my home office, three days later, I read my father's
words for maybe the tenth time, looking for a hidden meaning, any encouragement, a sliver of emotion. I'd looked on
the back, turned it upside down, held it up to the light, and thought
about sprinkling lemon juice on it. But still I found nothing past
a business transaction, cold and efficient. No secret message from
old Tom. Even his final order, take care of my family, left me on
the outside. Why did he think he had to tell me to take care of the
family? Did he think so little of me that he figured I'd abandon my
own mother, my sisters, and brother?

When we'd left South Carolina, Mama had seemed fine and strong. Still, I thought maybe we should be closer to her with Dad gone, to keep an eye on her, help her out around the Knoll. I'd considered moving back home a number of times over the previous seventeen years we'd been gone. Just never was able to reconcile myself to living that close to him again. A body could only take so much frost. But that hindrance was gone.

Sara and I had both grown up on homesteads east of Columbia, in an unincorporated part of lower Richland County—the sticks. Both of our daughters were born in Atlanta, where we'd ended up, and I was reluctant to disrupt their lives. But my girls were strong and independent, like their mama, and I was beginning to think maybe they'd have enjoyed living near their grandmother and most of their first cousins.

As a home builder, I could work anywhere. I had a good reputation around Atlanta and figured I could make the transition to the Columbia market with little more than a hiccup. The universal need for my skills afforded us a certain portability. Could be that's what had attracted me to building years before. Maybe my business's relative transferability meant I'd always kept moving home in the back of my mind.

Other than reading Dad's letter over and over, I hadn't accomplished a damn thing that morning, so I rose to stretch my legs, picked up a photo album from the bookcase, and thumbed through the old pictures. The photographs were all from around the time I was seven to nine years old. My middle sister, Lauren, was a toddler and my youngest sister, Maggie, wasn't even a twinkle in my mother's eye. Mama was striking in those photos, a true Southern beauty. Dad only appeared in two pictures in the entire album. In the first, he led a horse while Bill and I sat grinning in the saddle. I would've been about seven years old and Bill five. My father walked toward the camera smiling, his hand raised. In the second photo, he stood beside Mama with us kids arranged before them. I was maybe nine in that one. Dad's hand hovered above my shoulder, but he didn't look toward the camera, nor did he smile. I wasn't sure which troubled me most—that he was in so few photos, his clear brooding distraction in the second picture, or the fact that I'd never noticed either before that day.

As I lit the grill for hamburgers that evening, I asked Sara, "Would you like to move back home—not just talk about it, really move home?" We both still referred to South Carolina as home, although we hadn't lived there since we finished high school. The girls called it home too, though they'd both been born in Georgia. It would be an easy change for Sara. As a painter she could work from any-where, traveling to Atlanta for the occasional showing if need be.

"I'd love to be close to both our mothers, but are you sure about it this time?" Her first reaction was to question my resolve. We'd been down that road more than a few times.

"Well, yeah. I reckon now's as good a time as any. I'd feel better if we were closer to Mama."

"I think it's a fine idea," she said. "Why don't we talk to the girls about it tonight?"

Our youngest, Lily, was excited about the prospect of living close to Tara, but Wren seemed less than eager. She was involved in sports and clubs at school. She had good friends, and I knew she'd miss them. She was trying hard to play it up. I suspected she was trying to score sympathy capital to be used later. In the end, everyone was on board with the decision to move.

Although the idea had been mine, I began to have second thoughts straightaway. I kept them to myself.

After supper, while the girls studied their lessons and Sara painted, I went for a run. For me, running had always been a relax-ing experience. The sweat and the repetitive strides were a balm to me. But for as long as I could remember, I'd had a recurring dream where I was running and frightened of something unknown. I'd had that nightmare since I was a little boy, maybe seven or eight.

Because of it, the first few minutes of my run always caused me a measure of anxiety. But the ill feeling quickly faded, like mist before the sunshine, as I cranked out the miles.

When I called Mama at six the next morning, she'd been up for an hour. I asked, "Mama, what do you think about our moving home?"

She chose her words cautiously. "What a lovely notion, Jack. I think you should do whatever you feel is right for your family."

We chewed the fat a few minutes longer before hanging up. Her less-than-excited reaction was curious and bothered me more than I cared to admit. I'd have thought she'd have been thrilled to have two more granddaughters close at hand, not to mention her first-born son and daughter-in-law. I'd made a habit of keeping people at a distance regarding personal decisions, but I found myself wanting approval and enthusiasm from my mother. I hadn't sought, nor needed, that since I was a boy. Might've been she was preoccupied. Or maybe she was weary of hearing me make promises she knew I wouldn't keep.

After the call, I wrote a few subcontractors' checks, then stood in the kitchen drinking coffee. Hearing Saturday morning stirrings from upstairs, I glanced at my watch and wrote a time on the notepad beside the kitchen telephone. At 8:02, Sara walked into the kitchen. I handed her a steaming cup and tapped my finger on the notepad: 8:03. She looked at it, glanced at me, and sat at the kitchen table.

"So you're clairvoyant now?" She didn't seem as impressed as I'd have figured.

I was undeterred. "I call it observant. I know it takes you between forty-one and forty-four minutes to shower, dress and all those other things you do. I was just off by a minute." I smiled at her, and once again she realized what a brilliant man she'd married.

Sara sipped her coffee, watching me over the rim. "Thanks for the java, Sherlock."

We woke the girls, and I fixed breakfast while they showered and dressed. They had a soccer game later that morning, and we'd all planned to spend the weekend together. I was going home Monday, for a week, to deal with Dad's legal issues, so I wanted to soak up as much of my family as possible. The girls had school and couldn't go with me. Summer would start soon, but the legal matters wouldn't keep.

Monday morning I left for home at five sharp, taking Lucy and Ethel with me. Mama was fond of them, and the dogs loved to run and explore all that open land. We couldn't let them off leash in our busy neighborhood, so Parker's Knoll was a special treat for them.

I-20 traffic was heavy, and I didn't arrive until ten o'clock. Mama sat on her back porch with a lapful of yarn and coffee close at hand. She waved as I stepped down from the truck followed by the dogs. They began to chase each other in the field between the house and barn.

I stepped up onto the porch and kissed Mama's cheek. Her porch was an extension of her house as well as her personality. The rocking chairs were strewn with hand-made quilts, and her ferns and English ivy overflowed terracotta pots covered in broken blue and white china mosaics, casualties from clumsy children or grands. Firewood was stacked in a rust-speckled iron frame, handy to the back door.

"Anymore coffee?" I asked.

"Course there is, son. I'll fix you a cup." She started to rise.

"Keep your seat, Mama. I'll get it." I walked through the mud room into the kitchen. More blue and white plates adorned one wall, a small sampling of her much larger collection. There were dirty everyday dishes stacked in the sink and the milk sat on the counter. Returning the milk to the refrigerator, I poured my coffee, stepped back onto the porch, and sat in Dad's rocker, next to her. "Good coffee, Mama."

"Thank you, Bill," she said.

"I'm Jack, Mama. The good-looking son." I smiled at her.

She shook her head. "I'm sorry. I guess I'm a bit addled today."

"That's understandable. It's been a rough few days. Maybe you should pay your doctor a visit. Let her give you the once-over."

"I'm feeling puny is all. I don't need a doctor or any medical advice from my children, thank you."

"Sorry, Mama. Just worried about you." I squeezed her hand and she smiled back at me.

Could be that grief had taken a toll on her. Could be she was weary and needed rest. But there'd been something there, some flicker of something troubling. It might've been that Dad's death had made her consider her own life, the thinning thread that kept her from following him. Behind her smile, deep, deep in her eyes, I'd seen fear.

Hearing the soft squeal of brakes in need of attention, I turned to see Miss Ida Mae Sanders climb carefully from her old car. I stepped off the porch and walked toward her. When she looked up at me, she nodded. "Morning, Jack. You look well." She took my arm and we walked to the porch.

"Miss Ida Mae, you are as pretty as a spring day. That a new hairdo you're sporting?"

"Don't you get familiar with me, Jackson Parker. I don't cotton to your flirtatious words, and besides, I like my men with a little more meat on their bones. You're too old for me anyway." I had heard she liked her men young. I tried and failed to get shed of that image.

While Mama had a visit with her friend, I checked around the Knoll for anything needing to be done. My meeting with Dad's attorney was at four o'clock in Columbia, so I had time to waste. I checked the fences around the horse pastures for weak spots, noting any that might've needed attention. The fences were in fair shape for the most part but could use a hammer lick here and there. My father had always been particular in both the business of cabinetry and the running of his farm, but he'd struggled to keep up the farm like he used to—too proud to ask Bill for help most likely. The barn was stocked with chicken scratch, hay, and sweet feed for the horses. He might've neglected fence repairs but not his animals.

The chicken yard was quiet and orderly. Dad's old one-eyed rooster, Hemingway, strutted among his hens. His eye had been lost in a fight. He'd beat the other rooster with such authority it wouldn't roost in the coop with the others and was killed by a hawk two weeks later. By all accounts, Hemingway had showed no remorse for his part in the tragedy.

I found myself back in Dad's workshop. Mama had mentioned he'd worked on the tree house plans for years. He hadn't been a trained architect, but he was skilled with a pencil and T-square. He'd never asked me for help with a sketch, but as far as I knew, he'd never tried a full set of plans for a building, even one so small. As I looked for the plans, I noticed a stack of lumber covered by an oilcloth.

The wood was in a corner, on a huge rolling cart, separate from the wood he'd used for cabinets and furniture. I pulled the tarp back and discovered pine and cedar, separated by species and dimension. I started to cover the wood, but something about it struck me as unusual. The boards were standard sizes for construction, but each one was straight and true. I checked them one after another. Not only were they straight, but not one of the boards had a single knot or split. After checking a third of the stack, I realized each board was as perfect as the last.

I knew the effort Dad had made to accumulate all that unblemished lumber. It would have required his constant searching of lumber yards for weeks or months. He'd been used to selecting fine birch, maple, and oak for his cabinets and furniture, but building-grade lumber was a different story. Normally, it might be hidden behind drywall or beneath flooring, so perfection was not commonly valued. I began to understand how he'd spent much of his time since his retirement. These must be the boards Mama had mentioned he'd collected for the tree house. It seemed he'd been intent upon perfection.

The plans were laid out flat on Dad's shop desk, covered by an unbleached domestic scrap. The desk was simple and purposeful. He'd made it to be beautiful and functional, even though few folks would ever see it. He knew beauty could be found in the most humble of objects. You just had to pay attention.

I glanced at the plans, then rolled and placed them into a leather tube. I took them and returned to the house to get ready for my meeting. Mama was still having tea on the porch. She sat smiling and listening to one of Miss Ida Mae's fanciful stories about an affair she'd had with a state senator back in her youth. Lucy and Ethel curled up together beside Mama's rocker. She reached down and scratched Lucy behind an ear. I sat on a porch rail and listened as Miss Ida Mae finished her tale.

She must've been close to ninety years old and, by her own admission, had never felt the matrimonial itch. Miss Ida Mae had retired from teaching grade school in her sixties and promptly taken up skydiving and long-distance hiking. She had enough jumps to qualify as a skydiving instructor, and she'd hiked the Appalachian Trail in sections, finishing on her seventy-fifth birthday. The wide age gap between her and Mama didn't hinder their attachment to one another. They'd been friends for decades. I was happy Mama had such a close friend, but I hoped to God she wouldn't start jumping out of planes.

I retreated to the kitchen to tackle the dishes in the sink before Mama realized she'd left them and got embarrassed. Then I cleaned myself up for the meeting in Columbia. Dad's letter had made it clear that it fell to me to handle any and all legal matters upon his passing. My mother and siblings had seemed more than happy to entrust these matters to me.

Damn cowards.

The law offices of Whitaker Blackstone and Lawrence Ramsey were located on Devine Street in Columbia. They were a few blocks from the bars and shopping found in Five Points and close to the genteel neighborhoods of Shandon and Heathwood. Whit Blackstone spent most of his time fishing or punishing a little white ball. But at sixty-eight years old, Larry Ramsey still put in seventy hours a week. Louise Tillman had been their receptionist for at least thirty-five years. She'd known me since I was a boy. I'd dated her granddaughter, Denise, in high school, and our brief but tumultuous relationship had ended with her hand across my face and a shitload of angry words. Still don't know what I said to provoke her.

I walked up to Mrs. Tillman's desk and smiled.

"Do you have an appointment, sir?" she asked.

"Mrs. Tillman, it's me. Jack Parker."

"Indeed you are. Do you have an appointment?"

"Well, yes, ma'am. I have an appointment with Larry at four." She frowned at my use of Ramsey's Christian name, the common version at that. But it seemed to me her frown passed displeasure and headed straight for animosity.

"Very good, sir. I'll let Mr. Ramsey know you are here. Please have a seat. May I serve you a coffee or water?"

"No, ma'am. Thank you." I decided to sit and wait. And keep my pie hole shut.

Lawrence Ramsey walked out with his hand extended. "Jack. I'm so sorry about your daddy. He was a true gentleman and a fine cabinet maker. He put in my kitchen cabinets twenty years ago."

"Thank you, Larry. I appreciate your kind words. Dad thought a lot of you too."

"Let's step into my office and chat a bit." Although slight, he walked with a big man's swagger. I followed him into his paneled office and sat in one of the leather chairs around a long mahogany table; it had to be a hundred years old. A sweat-beaded water pitcher sat plumb center of the table on a pretentious silver tray. Larry took two glasses from the small bar in the corner and poured both half full of water, placing each on a coaster.

He fetched a file from his desk and sat across from me, squaring the file's bottom with the table's edge. He opened the file, took a sip of water and said, "Tom was smart with his money and left you all in decent shape." He slid the open file to me.

"What's this?" I asked.

"The first page is a summary of the few assets your father accumulated and which now belong to Elizabeth in total," Larry responded. "Behind the summary are the investment account statements and the specifics of his life insurance policy, which is substantial. Of the life insurance, each child will receive twenty-five thousand dollars with the remainder going to your mama."

"Wait a minute, Larry. I don't understand. I reviewed Dad's will four or five years ago, and my mother is supposed to get everything. We don't inherit anything until they've both passed. She might need that money for herself; Mama's still right young."

"True, that was the language in the original will. However, Tom and Elizabeth came to see me six months ago and changed your father's will so that you each get the aforementioned sum. The farm is, as you know, debt free and in Elizabeth's name. Your daddy made sure that Lizzie wouldn't need for anything. He didn't make this decision lightly, Jack."

"Do you have any idea why he made such a drastic change? It seems like a lot of money, and he never said a word to me, or my brother or sisters, as far as I know. He must have given you a reason. It doesn't make sense."

Larry took a deep breath. "Jack, it's not that unusual for a will to provide something for the children while the remaining parent still lives. I do know why Tom wanted to change his will, but he asked that I keep silent about it. I must honor my client's last wishes, no matter my own personal feelings. Talk to your mama, Jack. Talk to Lizzie."

I left Larry's offices feeling unsettled and ambushed. I was having trouble reconciling that Dad had insisted on me as his executor and yet had failed to inform me that he was giving us the money. As usual, my mind had jumped to the what-the-hell-was-he-thinking side of the issue. I was racking up a sackful of questions and shit for answers so far.

Out on the sidewalk, I shaded my eyes against the setting sun. I stood by my truck, trying to get my bearings, and realized Paddy's Pub was three blocks down the street. And I realized something else of profound importance: I needed a strong drink.

CHAPTER THREE

After three and a half days of meetings with Larry and Dad's insurance agent, I was happy to be back with my wife and daughters on Friday evening. I took them out for Mexican at La Hacienda and a movie. The film was the newest in a series of vampire romances—might've been werewolves. I used the time to contemplate life's great mysteries. Then Sara was shaking me. The house lights were up and folks were leaving the theater. A few older patrons glanced at me as they passed and smiled in understanding.

"Good nap?" Sara asked.

"Resting my eyes," I told her.

At home, I was wide awake. With Sara and the girls in bed, I used the quiet time to look at the tree house plans more carefully. I hadn't had a chance to study them much while at Mama's house. Her forgetful spells had intensified, and I'd spent much of my time sitting with her and trying to gauge her fitness. And afraid it might upset her, I chose not to ask about the change in Dad's will. I'd decided to come back to Atlanta after Maggie had arranged to stay with Mama for a few days. As a nurse, my youngest sister was far better prepared than me to care for our mother.

I opened the plans on my drawing table, surprised at the thick sheaf of pages. Plans for every area of the tree house were drawn in my father's clean style. Notations filled the borders. There were exploded details for windows, the porch, the roof, the framing, and more. I'd reviewed my fair share of building plans with fewer details than this little tree house. The plans were well rendered and scaled accurately from what I could tell. But most remarkable was the quantity of wood carvings incorporated throughout. There were detailed drawings of those intended for the door and window frames, as well as posts, rails, lintels, and fascia. They depicted flowers, ivy, honeysuckle, bees, lizards, and other small woodland creatures, all to be created within the wood. Dad had always drawn freehand, but he'd usually opted for simple and elegant. Those drawings were anything but simple.

I fell asleep, sometime in the wee hours, still thinking about the living images my father had drawn.

I wasn't the first one up, but I woke when I heard movement downstairs. I showered and dressed quickly. Sara sat at the kitchen table, drinking coffee and working on a sketch. I poured myself a cup and stood behind her. She was drawing Dad in profile. In her picture, he was whittling a pine scrap. Although he'd worked with wood all day, he had still loved to carve little figures for the kids in the evenings. Wren and Lily each had quite a few of his carved critters on their shelves.

"Late night?" Sara asked.

"Yep. I was studying Dad's tree house plans."

"Oh? What do you think?"

When I hesitated, Sara looked up from her sketch, a question in her eyes.

"The plans are incredible. He must have spent hundreds of hours on them. There are detailed carving sketches which are, I don't know, magical. Want to have a look?"

"You bet I do. They must be special."

I wanted her perspective as both daughter-in-law and artist—maybe I had just been tired when I had looked at them before. She quietly studied each page. When she finished the last drawing, she looked up at me. "Oh, my God, Jack."

"I know," I said. "I'd have never thought he had it in him." I traced an ivy vine's graceful curve with my finger. "Not in a million years."

We made breakfast together, and then Sara and the girls went shopping for summer clothes. I reviewed a set of blueprints for a potential client and wrote up a bid for her. Satisfied with my work, I took the dogs for a long run. When I returned, my message light was blinking. I figured my client was checking on my progress, so I showered before listening.

But the message was from Bill. "Hey, bud. Mama's in the hospital. The doctors think she's had a stroke. Maggie found her sitting on the kitchen floor. She's conscious and seems aware of her surroundings but hasn't spoken a word. The docs are keeping her overnight to run their tests. Give me a shout when you get this." When I returned his call, Bill didn't know anything more than he'd said in his message. I told him I'd be there the next morning.

When Sara and the girls returned a short time later, they already knew about Mama. My sister Audrey had called Sara with the news. Lily buried her face in my chest when she saw me. I held her and stroked her long dark hair. Wren didn't cry, but the tears threatened. I kissed her head and touched her chin. The girls went upstairs to their rooms, and Sara hugged me for a long minute.

"Want to drive home tonight or wait until morning?" she asked.

"The girls have school. I can go by myself in the morning."

"There's only a week of school left. They don't do much the last week, and both girls have finished all their tests. We'll all go, Jack. The girls need to see their grandmother."

"Good plan, honey. What would I do without you?"

Sara smiled and touched my chest. "Let's not find out."

We left before sunup, and both girls fell asleep in the back seat.

Sara read for a while then closed her eyes. Her breathing became steady and I knew she was asleep too. Lucy and Ethel were with friends. I left the radio off in favor of the soft sounds of the three people I loved most in this world.

Bill was at Mama's house feeding the horses and chickens and making sure all was well. He raised a hand at the sound of tires on gravel. After setting our bags inside, we followed him to the Baptist Hospital in Columbia. When we arrived, the waiting room was filled with Parkers. We made a noisy bunch, and hospital staff kept walking by frowning in our direction.

We couldn't all visit Mama, so only my siblings and I remained at the hospital. Everyone else headed to Audrey's house, there in Columbia, before we all got kicked out. I watched Lily and Tara walk to the elevator with their arms around each other.

"How's Mama?" I asked, looking from sister to sister.

"She doesn't seem to have any paralysis in her limbs or any other physical problems," Maggie said. "But she still hasn't said a thing. According to her nurse, she hasn't even attempted to speak. She's asleep now, but Diana promised she would let us know when she wakes. Diana's a fantastic nurse, and Dr. Holliday is one of the best. Mama's in good hands."

The hospital staff had arranged the chairs and sofas for multiple families. Large potted plants and half walls between them afforded at least a measure of privacy. We sat close to the open hallway and prepared to wait, using the time to catch up on each other's news. Most of the conversation was about our children's exploits and accomplishments. I watched Maggie as Audrey talked about Izzy's latest academic achievement.

Maggie, divorced and childless, was quiet. She and her husband had tried to conceive for two years, then consulted a fertility specialist. Her husband left her when the specialist said it would be next to impossible for her to have children. Steve wouldn't consider adoption and implied our baby sister was not whole since she couldn't conceive. Bill was even angrier than me. It was all I could do to keep him from castrating the son of a bitch.

"Listen, Bill," Maggie had said. "Don't do anything stupid, all right? Steve did me a big favor by leaving. I'm so thankful I discovered what an asshole he is now rather than sometime later." She'd hugged Bill and smiled, holding her head up all the while. She'd been right. She was better off without him. In any case, she said she had all the kids she needed. She'd always heaped attention on her nieces and nephews, and they all thought she was the butter and blackberry preserves on their biscuits.

Soon, we were allowed to see Mama. She was sitting up and alert. Her hospital gown and blankets were arranged just so, and her hair was coifed as if she'd just left the beauty parlor. Bill and I stood back a bit as our sisters fussed about her bed, straightening her already neat bedclothes. I watched Mama for any signs of confusion or disorientation. Nothing. Her pulse was steady, and her blood pressure was normal. She sat quietly, watching us each in turn. Lastly, she fixed her eyes on me and there they stayed.

She surprised us all when she said, "Jack, I hope you didn't drive all the way from Atlanta for this. And you from Greenville as well, Lauren?" She clucked her displeasure. "Can't an old girl have a little spell every once in a while, without all this foolishness?"

I replied, "I don't know about Lauren, but I left a book at your house and came home to fetch it. Nobody said anything about a party here at the Baptist."

She gave me one of those looks reserved for the times when, as a boy, I'd forgotten to zip my britches or tracked horse shit on her freshly mopped kitchen floor.

The tests hadn't revealed anything to indicate Mama needed to stay at the hospital any longer, so I drove her home after one night's stay. With her settled back in her house, I sat on her porch and discussed how to proceed with Bill and our sisters.

"It makes sense for me to stay with her," Maggie said, meaning she was the only one without children. "I'll just need help while I'm working."

I nodded at my middle sister. "Lauren needs to get back to Greenville, I'd imagine." She nodded, her eyes downcast. I knew Lauren would rather be here with Mama—we all would—but she had to get home to take care of her own kids. "Sara and the girls are going to return to Atlanta for the last few days of school, but I'm staying. They can join me back here in a week or ten days. I have Dad's truck to use if I need it."

Bill scratched his chin and looked at me. "I'm five minutes away, so I'll be stopping by pretty often. I know Kathy would be happy to give you guys some relief too. Audrey, can you sit with Mama some?" We all looked at our oldest sister.

Audrey appeared to be somewhere other than the porch. She stared past the barn at something I suspected she alone could see, and then she looked back at my brother. "Sure, Bill. Whatever you guys need." Without another word, she walked to her car, and drove away, leaving us staring after her.

After a couple days of rest, Mama seemed to be back to her normal goings on. She was cleaning, cooking, and barely staying out of trouble with Miss Ida Mae. When not working, she was out and about, and all our planning who to stay with her was for shit. Her mind was as sharp as ever. The doctors said she'd had a small stroke, but I believed she'd held her emotions inside for too long and had needed to crack her release valve a quarter turn.

I considered asking her about the will change but thought it best to let her continue to recuperate for a while. But I did need to meet with Bill and the girls and tell them about Dad's will. All they knew was that he'd changed it. We agreed to meet for barbecue the following weekend, when Lauren would be home again. Audrey seemed more than a little interested in the will's details. I knew she and Brad had struggled with money a bit because of a bad real estate deal, but they were not, as far as I knew, broke. My oldest sister was not a greedy person, but she wore the worry around her eyes and mouth.

In the morning, I ate breakfast with my mama and sister. Maggie was staying home with Mama all day, learning to crochet. She had the ambitious notion to make blankets for all eight nieces and nephews for Christmas. I hoped she either learned fast or had quick fingers.

Pointing to a shoebox on the kitchen table, Mama said to me, "That box there has Tom's pocket clutter inside. It's everything he carried with him. Could you sort through it when you get the chance? I don't think I can right now. Anything you want, I'm sure your daddy would've wanted you to have. His credit cards are in there too."

"I'll cancel the cards and sort through the rest. You sure there's nothing you want, Mama?"

She'd avoided looking at the box all through breakfast. Of a sudden, she couldn't take her eyes off it. "No, son. What would I do with a pocket knife and a handful of coins?" She nodded at the box and sipped her coffee. "Do whatever you will with it."

Borrowing one of Dad's fishing rods, I grabbed his tackle box and headed for the woods. I walked a foot-worn trail, which curved to run alongside a neighbor's property line and then made a sharp turn to the north, past a grand old holly tree. Because of my recurring dream where I was running blindly, I always got an ill feeling walking that path, same as when I first started a run.

In my nightmare, I ran but no person or animal chased me. Still, I was terrified. I might go months without it or have it nights in a row. Since my father had passed, I'd had it almost every night, it seemed. I didn't wake or cry out, but I remembered it vividly come morning.

The trail forked to the right and ended at a long-abandoned kaolin mine. The mine was nothing but a great big pit, forty acres or so and maybe two hundred feet deep at the middle. There were gullies and hills and saddles all throughout. Close grown saplings and medicine vine formed a maze of trails and had been our playground when we were kids. Kaolin is buttery-soft clay used in the making of dishes like those on Mama's kitchen wall. We'd carried buckets full of the china clay home. Audrey and Lauren had made their own little plates and bowls, and little Maggie had squeezed it between her fingers and toes for the pure pleasure of it.

The mine and surrounding woods were on Doc Johnson's property. Doc had agreed we could use his land as long as we cared for it as our own and helped to keep poachers at bay. Bill still walked those woods, in sections, once a week. To him, a promise was an oath, and he would keep it or be damned. Although Doc lived up North, Bill patrolled those woods as if he might show up any day and demand an accounting. Over the years, my brother had chased off more than a few hunters, hikers and kids looking to take a buck, smoke a joint or screw.

Climbing down a bluff to the mine's floor, I found myself in a different world. The air was ten degrees cooler, and the thick tree growth crowning the mine's rim kept out most external sound. Trails twisted among the dozens of ponds. Tall pines showed this mine had been abandoned years before I'd been born.

All but the smallest ponds held fish, though I had never figured out how they came to be there in the first place. There were blue-gills, pumpkinseeds, bass, mollies, and shellcrackers throughout the ponds. The mine was home to turtles, deer, possums, otters, and both red and grey foxes. And there were snakes. At one time or another, Bill and I had discovered every poisonous snake native to South Carolina, as well as many of their nonpoisonous cousins. But all other snakes paled in comparison to the water moccasin. Moccasins have a hostile disposition and a quarrelsome attitude— and that's on their good days.

I found the clearing I was looking for beside one of the larger ponds. It had always been one of the best spots. Casting was easy, and there were big bass beneath that still, black water. That pond was the place I'd first wet my line as a kid, before my father lost interest in me.

Tying on a "blackberry fire" worm, I made a few casts to get a feel for Dad's rod and tinkered with the drag on the reel. My first serious cast landed the worm two inches behind a half-submerged log. Some skills didn't fade over time or from disuse. I began to reel, and the worm slid over the log and down the near side. I gave a couple quick, easy tugs and cranked a few more turns. I tugged twice more and felt a jolt through the rod as a fish grabbed the worm and dove for cover. I counted three one-thousands and pulled back on the rod hard, setting the hook in its mouth. The bass dove deep, bending the rod into a half-circle and then turned hard for the surface, leaving the water, sweeping its tail as if still swimming. Couple minutes after, I knelt at the pond's edge holding the four-pound bass by its lower lip. After admiring it for a quick minute, I released it to the dark water. I fished for another hour, catching and releasing a half-dozen bass. That first one had been the largest.

Scrabbling up the cliff, I left the mine behind. I couldn't begin to guess how often I'd made that climb or how many hundreds of fish I'd pulled from those ponds. But none would ever compare to the first I caught as a boy, when Dad had introduced me to that secret world. His laugh that day had been pure joy as he saw my wide eyes and wider grin. "You're a natural fisherman, son," he'd said. I'd grinned all the more, my six-year-old chest swelling with pride. Wasn't too long after that he stopped taking me fishing altogether.

CHAPTER FOUR

A couple days before Sara and the girls were to return, I was sitting at the kitchen table with Mama. She shelled beans while I worked on a cup of coffee. She was humming a tune I'd heard before but couldn't quite latch onto.

"What are you humming, Mama? I can't quite recall it."

"It's an old hymn, honey. I'm not sure which."

"I'm curious about something else. Your lawyer said Dad changed his will not long before he died. We each get a portion of the insurance money. Can you tell me about that?"

Her hands quieted for a time. "What else did Larry Ramsey tell you?" She continued her work without so much as a glance up at me.

"He didn't tell me much. I know the will was originally set up to pass everything to you, so I questioned Larry about the change. He admitted y'all had changed it recently but wouldn't give a reason. He said I should talk to you."

Mama frowned at her beans for so long I thought she'd not answer. Then she looked up at me. "Your father was dying, Jack. He was in the late stages of cancer; his brain was eat up with it. If he hadn't had that heart attack, he'd have been just as dead within a year. The cancer was too far along to even treat. He'd have suffered, son. My Tom would have suffered and become a stranger to me, to his children. He was scared but not of death. He was fearful of losing control of his mind, of not recognizing his own family." She was quiet for another spell, staring at her wall of blue and white plates, the bright gone from her eyes.

"Mama, why didn't Dad tell me about the cancer? Does Bill know or the girls?"

She looked up sharply at me. "Course not. Tom didn't want anybody to know yet, most of all his children. We figured he had time, son. And after his heart attack, well I didn't want to burden you all with it. What would have been the purpose?"

"But we could have at least made things easier around here for you both."

"That's why he didn't want to tell you, son. Your daddy knew you and your brother and sisters would have swooped in and taken over his life. Don't you see that he would have felt useless with you all over here making sure he didn't have to lift a finger? As for the will, he knew I would have enough money to last the rest of my life. And we both agreed you all could benefit from it sooner rather than later—especially Audrey."

"You know about Audrey's problems?"

"Honey, I'm neither blind nor stupid."

"Not by a long stretch, Mama."

I stood beneath a live oak tree which had been ancient when my father was a boy. Three grown men couldn't have circled it with joined hands. A few of the lower limbs were as large as full-grown pine trunks. Within the oak's limbs was the skeletal birth of Dad's tree house. The floor was solid and level. The walls were framed and plumb. The roof trusses spread over the structure, protecting the room beneath. But it was still just a frame. There was nothing to stop wind or rain or sleet. The frame sat within the tree in such a manner that no limbs had been removed or altered. The irregular angles and curves left me with the impression of something organic, a living extension of the oak. I'd studied Dad's drawings and knew he'd made a sound construction plan. Properly finished, it would withstand wind, weather, time, and generations of Parker children. It only needed finishing. It needed the breath of life.

Up in the framework, I surveyed Parker's Knoll. A faint breeze rippled the old oak's leaves. Horses grazed in the distance, beyond the barn. The chickens' soft clucks floated on the air as they hunted for insects or scratch. My father had chosen the location with care. I wondered if he'd climbed several oaks to survey the view before he'd settled on that tree, that particular spot, that precise angle among the boughs. I smiled at the thought of Dad sitting on a limb, looking out over the farm he'd loved and tended, nodding in satisfaction.

Earlier in the week, Sara and I had made a successful offer on a farm house and twenty acres, four miles down the road from Parker's Knoll. As soon as we closed escrow on the new house, we'd move. Our house in Atlanta was in a decent neighborhood and would sell easily. But the money Dad had left us would be a Godsend while we had two mortgages to pay. Sara loved the new house with its deep porches and wide pine flooring. "It has character," she'd said, meaning, "It's old as shit." But you couldn't deny its beauty. She looked forward to setting up her paint studio in one of the old storage sheds. My siblings hadn't been surprised by our decision. Everybody knew we'd been looking for a reason to move back home for years. And they knew that Dad's passing had cleared away my last excuse for putting it off.

As I climbed down from the oak and touched the rough tree bark, I realized I was going to finish what my father had started. I'd probably made that decision the day of Dad's funeral, standing in his workshop. And Sara most surely had thought the same. When I called to tell her, she wasn't surprised. I said, "You sound like you expected as much."

"You're your daddy's son," she'd said. "How could you not finish it?"

With the farm in no immediate need of repair and Sara and the girls not due until the next day, I had time to kill. I knew that once we closed on our house, my free time would be scarce. So I began planning how to continue with the tree house construction. Dad had included a cut list for each section. I knew I'd be able to make most of the cuts in the shop for later assembly. I wanted to tackle those intricate carvings too. I was nervous about them. They'd be tedious and difficult but fine-looking all the same.

Inside the workshop, I switched on the lights and spread Dad's plans on his shop desk. I spent a couple hours on the table saw, checking each piece off the list. Standing in his shop, bathed in fresh-sawn pine's heady scent, I could've been seventeen years old again. That shop was the one place I'd felt at ease with my father. There, our wall didn't feel so impossible to climb, and our silence didn't go quite so deep. What if I'd kept working there instead of striking out on my own? Would it have mattered?

The saw blade was sharp and true, and I cut board after board, each according to Dad's plans. I marked each board with a carpenter's pencil, bundling them together to be assembled later. I stopped after a couple hours to compare the lumber list to the stack he'd collected. I was satisfied there'd be enough wood to finish the project, as long as I didn't make too many screw-ups with the saw.

Dad's home office was as much a reflection of his personality as Mama's porch was of hers. Bookshelves and framed photographs lined the wall opposite his desk. Other walls were hung with several of Sara's landscape paintings, rolling woodlands or open vistas from the Sandhills. I sat at his desk with the shoebox, my father reduced to the contents of a small box, the items he'd carried with him each day. Someone from the hospital or the funeral home had packed up everything into a little box and handed it to my mother. Here's your parting gift. Thanks for playing.

Inside the box were items he'd either needed or wanted to have with him all the time. I held his wallet with his credit and identification cards and photos of his grandchildren. Nestled in the bottom were a pocket knife, a small penlight, an old silver dollar, loose change, and his keys. One last item seemed out of place: a small silver cross. It had been made for a necklace, but it had no chain. The cross was finely engraved but worn, as if somebody had passed a thumb over it many times. I made a list of credit card numbers then replaced each treasure back into the box. The cross I slipped into my pocket.

Sara and the girls arrived in the afternoon. While Wren and Lily spent time with their grandma, my wife and I exercised the horses. Both geldings were gentle and predictable. My father had raised and trained them, and he'd trusted those horses with his grandchildren. I saddled them and we trotted toward the woods. Sara hadn't been to the kaolin mines in years, and the horses would make the trip a lot quicker. We gave them slack reins and they found their own way to the mine.

"Could this be the path from your dream?" Sara asked. I'd shared the dream with her a few times over the years.

"You know, I think it is," I said. "This is the path we always used to go fishing or camping in the mine. I don't recall anything bad happening there—well, maybe the time Bill got that bass hook caught in my scalp." I'd hugged a pine and made him yank it out so I wouldn't have to tell Mama or go to the emergency room to have it cut out. That hook had left a nasty scar. "But that certainly wasn't terrifying."

She laughed. "No. I don't think you'd run from a hook-wielding little brother. Maybe it has to do with all those snakes you two caught. That's pretty scary."

"I don't think that's it either."

"It could be something as simple as a horror movie you watched as a boy," she said. "Are you still having the dream a lot? You haven't mentioned it lately."

"Every once and again. I think you're right. It's probably a monster movie I watched as a kid. It's stuck in my subconscious, and that dream seems to come back whenever I'm stressed." A little white lie. No need to concern Sara with the dream's increased occurrence.

"Excellent work, Dr. Freud."

The path down into the mine was too steep for the horses, so we tied them at the top and descended on foot, down the bluff. At the bottom, Sara looked back up where we left the horses. "I can't see the geldings up there. It's like they've vanished. Such a different world down here, Jack. I'm always surprised how much cooler and darker it is. Almost like it's always evening." She clutched her arms against a graveyard shiver.

"Bill and I would spend as much time here as we could to escape the summer heat. Whenever we'd finished our chores, we would grab our fishing poles and head down here. We'd stay as long as possible, catching fish or frogs. Cook a few whenever we got hungry. When I was six or seven, when Dad first showed me this place, I told him I wanted to build a cabin down here to sleep in on occasion."

"Why didn't you?" Sara picked up a flat stone and studied it.

"Well, I was too young for one thing. But he convinced me not to build it, even when I got older. He said he believed this was one of the last unspoiled kaolin mines around. He pointed out that after the miners had created this world by removing all the clay, natural law had reclaimed it and wiped out all signs of man, that nature had made something good from man's destruction. Of course, he was right. A cabin would have spoiled it. And at six years old, I thought he knew everything."

"Tom was such a gentle soul—kind and caring." Sara skipped her stone across the pond at our feet.

"He was gentle, kind, caring, and secretive." I squatted down, looking for a stone to skip. "Mama told me he had brain cancer. The doctors couldn't help him. If he'd not had the heart attack, he wouldn't have lived more than a year. And I suspect his mind would have started to fail one thought at a time. Dad wouldn't have wanted to go slowly, losing his mental capacity. Mama said he wasn't ready to tell anyone, but I wish he'd told me."

"Honey, I'm so sorry. But I think I understand why he might not want anyone to know."

"Why's that?"

"If Tom knew nothing could be done, he probably didn't want to burden you, Bill, and the girls with it. Maybe he just wanted to live a normal life as long as possible, without all the fussing about, without the sympathy."

"Maybe. That's what Mama said too." My stone skipped six times and landed in the grass on the far bank without a sound, leaving behind overlapping ripples.

We rode back toward the farm in silence, dismounting when we emerged from the woods, and walked the horses to the barn. After we unsaddled and rubbed down the horses, Sara wanted to see the tree house site. As we walked in that direction, she said, "Oh, I forgot. Your parents' lawyer called for you this morning. He asked that you call him when you have a chance."

"Did he say what about? I thought I'd taken care of everything."

"Something about Carolina House. Does that mean anything to you?" she asked.

"Not at all. Guess I'll find out when I talk to him."

When I got Larry on the phone, he asked me to meet him at his office on Monday.

He sounded agitated but I didn't question him. One last detail needing my attention.

Bill, our sisters, and I decided to have supper at Barbie Q, out on Sumter Highway, fifteen miles east of Columbia. Ray and Barbie Halfacre served the best pork barbeque in the Midlands. Open every day, except Sunday, for lunch and supper, they were always packed. Ray slow-cooked the pigs, drank beer, and told his jokes. Barbie took care of everything else.

Between bites of chopped pork and hash and rice, we sipped sweet tea and talked about Dad's will. "Here's how the will was set up," I said. Audrey watched me intently, her food forgotten. "We're each to receive twenty-five thousand dollars from his life insurance policy. Mama gets the rest and a few other assets. The Knoll, of course, she already owns free and clear." I looked at my siblings one at a time. "Mama has enough money to live comfortably and run the farm for the rest of her life. Dad wanted us to have this money. At first, I felt our getting anything wasn't right, but I guess I've changed my mind. And it's not up to me anyway. I wanted to see how y'all felt."

"Jack's right." Audrey spoke before my words had a chance to fade.

Bill looked at her and said, "I agree with Jack too. And if for some reason Mama develops a gambling problem and blows it all, we'll take care of her."

"Real nice, Bill," Lauren said. She rolled her eyes and laughed.

Audrey laughed as well, but the relief was there in her eyes. I knew what that money would mean for her family. Her eyes revealed something else: fear or worry. She caught my eye, and the worry hid itself behind her smile. But I'd seen something. As my other sisters teased Bill about his comment, I placed my hand on Audrey's arm. "Everything okay?"

"Everything's good, big brother. Everything's fine."

I squeezed her arm and nodded, not the least bit convinced she was anything approaching fine. Turning back to the table, I said, "One last thing." My face must've given the gravity of my news away.

"What is it, Jack?" Bill's laughter died like a switch had been thrown.

I cleared my throat. "Mama told me Dad had brain cancer and would have survived maybe another year at most. It's likely he would have been in agony toward the end, and his mind would've failed quickly. Neither he nor Mama wanted us fussing about, so they didn't say anything. I guess he felt he had time to put things in order, maybe live a normal life for a while. I thought y'all should know."

My siblings were quiet for a bit, but they seemed to handle the news well, with the exception of Maggie. She was pissed and said, "Daddy still should've told us. We're his kids. That's what families do. Families stick together and fight together. Such bullshit." She looked at me, shaking her head..

"I'm sorry, Maggie. I guess he and Mama were doing what they considered best." I covered her hand with my own. At the other end of the table, Bill watched me. And nodded.

As we finished our meal, Maggie seemed to have made a tentative peace with my revelations. She was quiet, and the fire seemed to have gone out of her. I gave my siblings Larry's office number, so they could schedule appointments to sign documents and whatnot. Having said all I needed to say, I concluded by asking, "Any other business? No? Meeting adjourned."

"Think I'll have the banana pudding, please. Double helping," Bill told a passing waiter. That got a little smile from my baby sister.

I was in Larry Ramsey's waiting room once again, on my best

behavior and watching Mrs. Tillman. When I'd walked in, she'd pointed to a chair for me to sit in and then ignored me with a focus I found impressive.

Larry walked into the waiting room, right arm on autopilot. "So sorry to have kept you waiting, Jack. Please come on in," he said. "This won't take long."

I looked at Mrs. Tillman as we walked past her desk and winked at her. "No problem, Larry," I replied. "Lou and I were having a nice chat." Louise Tillman narrowed her eyes but said nothing.

I sat at the same antique table, and Larry performed his water glass ritual again. He sat at the table and opened a file. Then he shut it. He seemed agitated or at least uncertain how to start. I didn't say a word—just watched his agitation show itself in his spilling water all over that expensive table.

Larry jumped up and pressed the intercom button. "Mrs. Tillman, please come in here at once," he said.

Mrs. Tillman walked in and, seeing the mess, looked at me without a word, her face a dark cloud of resentment. She mopped up the water with a couple hand towels from Larry's private bathroom then left without a word, her scowl intact.

"Will she ever retire, Larry?" I asked.

Larry pinched the bridge of his nose and shook his head. "Lord, I hope so."

"So, what is it you needed to tell me?"

"Jack, Carolina House is all in a tizzy. Since your father passed, they can't seem to agree on anything. Cassie Little calls me at all hours to ask advice. I don't want to seem insensitive, but her non-legal problems are not mine no matter how long she's known Tom. I can't continue to do it." Larry took a careful sip from his refilled water glass. "I know you're still grieving for your daddy, but you need to hurry up and step in to take the reins."

"Wait a damn minute, Larry," I said. "That's all fascinating as hell, but I don't have a clue what you're talking about. I don't know anything about a Carolina House or anyone called Cassie Little." I lifted my glass and then replaced it on the coaster without drinking.

Larry shook his head. "You truly don't know about Carolina House at all, do you?"

Another surprise from the grave. "I've never heard of it. My father chose not to trust me with certain knowledge, so why don't you just fill me in, Larry?" It came out harsher than I'd meant, but he didn't seem to notice or take offense.

He took a breath and another sip. "Carolina House is both a charitable organization and an actual house for battered and abused women and their children," he said. "Jack, this is your daddy's project. He started it and was chairman of the board. Tom bought and renovated the house years ago with private funds he raised. He furnished it with furniture and cabinets he made. And afterward, he continued to make and sell furniture to procure operating funds."

I sat there staring at him for what seemed like a week but was probably closer to half a minute. When I reclaimed my tongue, I asked, "So it's one of those safe houses, a place for women to escape abusive men? And my father, Tom Parker, started it?"

"Jack, it's so much more than that. Carolina House gives women a safe place to start over. They can begin or finish a degree or get technical training. They receive medical care or mental health counseling. They can get legal help as well. I do that myself, pro bono. Carolina House has helped dozens of women. And yes, Tom envisioned and brought to life this place, his dream for a long time."

I realized I was catching flies and closed my mouth. "And Cassie Little? Where does she fit in?"

Larry hesitated then said, "Cassie is house manager. She runs the day to day operations. She was, um, Tom's right hand at Carolina House."

His hesitation made me think that maybe Dad and this woman had been involved. But he'd loved my mama too much to cheat on her. And even he couldn't have faked that. "Well, I've never heard of it or her. He never said a damn word," I said, more frost in my voice than I'd intended.

"Well," Larry said, "it's kept as quiet as possible to protect the women from their abusers and the general public. Sometimes the media is a bit too curious. I don't know why your father never mentioned it to you. I suppose he didn't want to burden you. Your daddy was a private man, Jack, but he had a purpose for everything he did."

"Understatement of the year, Larry."

The will, the tree house, his cancer, and now this. I couldn't wait to see what came next.

CHAPTER FIVE

"Thank you all for meeting with me," I said to the small group gathered in Larry Ramsey's conference room. "I'm Jack Parker, Tom's son."

A woman, maybe a few years younger than Mama, stood up— the nodder from Dad's graveside. Her spiky gray hair, pierced nose, and large tattoo collection had me trying to imagine my own mother with the same. "I'm Cassandra Little—Cassie. I know who you are. Mr. Ramsey said you were handling your father's affairs. He also said you'd never heard of Carolina House." She hesitated. "Or me. I mean, us."

I saw what I took for pain on her face but could've been disappointment. "I'm afraid that's all true. I'm sorry, but my father and I didn't communicate all that well."

"I'm the manager for Carolina House. We all work there." She looked around at the others. "Jack, we're so sorry for your loss. We all loved Tom, but we are concerned about Carolina House's future. Those women have nowhere else to go. Tom was the driving force, and he handled all financial and legal matters. I run the operations, but your daddy paid the bills and organized the fundraising events. I don't know what we'll do without him."

She seemed earnest enough, and I felt bad for her. "But what is it you think I can do to help? I don't know anything about all this. I'd never heard of Carolina House before a couple days ago. I have power of attorney and will be happy to sign a few checks for you, but it sounds like you need to search for a permanent replacement for my father. I'm sure Larry can offer suggestions."

Cassie gazed at her shoes and then back up at me. "We'd hoped you might want to take over for your father now. It's his brain-child. He started it. I'm sure it wouldn't take up much time. Tom stopped by the house a few times a week to sign checks or have a meeting. He handled raising funds from home." She paused, as if she was unsure whether to continue. "Tom spoke about you so much, I feel as if I know you. I'm sorry if I misunderstood, but I thought he meant for you to take over someday. Must've got my signals crossed."

Dad told them I would be his successor? Now I was really confused. And wary. "I appreciate your situation and the vote of confidence, but I don't think I would have the time to dedicate to those women and you good folks."

A young woman with four gold hoops through her eyebrow and a stunning collection of inked birds up and down both arms said, "It's not confidence. It's desperation. See, Cassie, I told you he wouldn't do it. We're fucked." That earned her a frown.

"Hush up, Robin. You're not helping." Cassie turned from her scolding to watch me with eyes that had seen far too much and recognized when a situation was hopeless.

While I could sympathize with their concerns and needs, I left Larry's office content with my decision. I would help them in their search for a director and write whatever checks they needed in the meantime, but I couldn't take my father's place. I'd never had to raise funds or make decisions that affected people in such dire circumstances, and they'd be far better off without my interference. They needed a professional manager. Carolina House needed a leader.

When I finished telling Sara about Carolina House, about Cassie and the others, she was beaming. "That's amazing, Jack. Who knew Tom had this in him? How wonderful!"

"I hate to keep repeating myself, but I don't get it. It is wonderful, I guess, but what did Dad know about domestic abuse?"

"I don't care why he decided to start it. He did and that's all that matters. Of course, you're going to direct Carolina House, aren't you? You'll be wonderful."

Through Mama's kitchen window, I watched the light seep from the sky; the gathering darkness matched my mood. "Well, no. I don't have time for all that. We'll be closing on the house soon, and then I'll be busy with moving as well as trying to gin up work in Columbia. And there's the tree house, my other projects. I'm really busy, Sara."

Sara seemed not to have heard a word I'd said. She was quiet, watching me. "Jack, let's do it. If we both work on this, we can do a good job. I can handle the bookkeeping and fundraising. You'll be a fabulous director. We can't let those women lose Carolina House. They need it. They need us." That bull-headed woman was easy to adore. My wife had always been my compass. She had the ability to sort through my bullshit and keep me pointed in the right general direction, even when I resisted her with a zeal envied by street preachers.

And, of course, she was right.

For a couple of hours, I reviewed house plans for a bid I'd won since moving home. I found a couple concerns and made a note to call the architect. Since I was on schedule with the project, I went to the workshop and strapped on my tool belt. I grabbed a bundle of wood I'd sawn a few days before and hefted it onto my shoulder. Walking to the oak tree, I placed the bundle on some sawhorses I'd set up earlier.

Dad had already framed the tree house walls. The next step was to install bracing between the vertical studs. I used an extension ladder to move the bracing bundles up and stack them inside the tree house through the open walls. That was easier than hauling them up through the trap door, which would be the lone access to the house once the siding was in place.

As my head came level with the floor joists on my last trip up, I noticed something carved into a joist's corner—a small cross-shaped recess, no more than an inch high and skillfully done; its lines were crisp and tight. I reached into my pocket and took out the silver cross I'd found in Dad's effects. I stared at it, not quite understanding what I was seeing. Then I pressed the little silver cross into the carved recess on the floor joist. The fit was snug and perfect and permanent —I'd have needed a chisel to remove it, but I knew I never would. Dad had meant this cross to be embedded into the floor joist, but I didn't have a clue why. Maybe a good luck charm or religious dedication? Touching the cross once more, I climbed down shaking my head in wonder at a man so full of surprises.

Fastening the braces with blind screws, so nothing was visible, satisfied my deep need for order in a chaotic life. I'd done a neat and plumb job, and I thought Dad would've approved. As I followed his plans, everything fit just so, each new piece further strengthening the whole. He'd planned each cut, each screw placement, and each detail to perfection, almost as if he'd believed he wouldn't have time to finish. Standing below the tree house, I couldn't help but smile, thinking of my father detailing each step with instructions to complete the work he'd begun.

After cleaning up the job site, I carried the tools to the workshop. The next step in the process was sawing and carving trim. Selecting a few of the best boards, I placed them on a workbench to carve the next day. I'd need several chisels for the carvings: parting tools, gouges, flat blades, and whatnot. If I remembered correctly, Dad always kept most of his carving irons in a wooden storage box beneath the carving bench.

I opened a plain pine box, hoping to find chisels. Instead of carving tools, a collection of dusty plaques and recognition letters filled the box—all given to Dad or Carolina House. Looking at each item carefully, I realized the oldest award was over ten years old and the newest was dated just two weeks before his death. The awards and letters were given to my father or Carolina House for service on various charity boards or for specific contributions. Most of the letters were generic thank-you-kindlys from organizations I'd never heard of. These were the types of awards, handed out by the dozens, designed to stroke the contributor's ego, maybe in hopes of future financial support. But there were a hell of a lot. Dad had been busy.

I stood on Mama's porch watching Lucy and Ethel run in the field between the house and barn. Their pleasure was evident in their graceful, long-legged strides. Mama walked out onto the porch. She watched the dogs make a few laps, then noticed the pine box beside her chair. She sat in her rocker and opened the lid. After looking at one or two plaques, she shut the box.

"Where did you find these?"

"They were all in Dad's shop beneath a bench," I answered. "Why would he hide them? He should've been proud. I had no idea he was so involved in the community, was so… charitable. First Carolina House and now these. I don't understand, Mama."

She smiled at me. "Son, I knew about a few of these, but they were not something your father talked about much. He never went to a single ceremony and preferred to remain anonymous whenever possible. Most of the letters were mailed to him as a matter of course, I suppose. I didn't realize there were so many, but I know he didn't do anything for the sake of recognition. Tom just wanted to help out in any small way he could."

"And Carolina House? Why not involve his family or at least tell us?"

Mama sighed and looked at me. "Jack, Carolina House was just something he felt he needed to do. I suppose it satisfied his need to help others."

"I wish he would've told me about these things. It seems as if he went out of his way to hide what he was doing."

"Or maybe you were raising your kids and didn't notice. I don't think you can lay all the blame at your daddy's feet. You keep to yourself as much as he ever did. Sara sent me a copy of that article about you in Atlanta Architecture about a year ago. Did you mention that to him? Or to me for that matter?" Her eyes didn't waver from mine. She had me and we both knew it.

"Well, I didn't think y'all would be interested." My excuse sounded pitiful, even to me.

"Hmm." My mother's response about summed it up.

"But why a women's shelter? It all seems so peculiar. And all those awards were from organizations that are connected to domestic abuse awareness or prevention."

"Bad things happened in your father's family years ago. He didn't talk about them much. Sometimes old ghosts are best left in the graveyard." Mama rose from her chair and walked back inside, clearly finished with our discussion.

Sara and I arrived at Carolina House in the Heathwood neighborhood before noon. She wanted to look over the accounting books, and we both wanted to meet the residents and begin the process of getting everyone to trust us. The house sat back on a large lot, surrounded on all sides by a tall brick fence. No signs or plaques set the house apart from its neighbors. I pressed the code on the keypad. When the gate swung open, I parked on the house's sweeping front circular drive. All was quiet as we walked to the house save for the gravel crunching beneath our feet.

The huge brick house was nestled among the magnolias, oaks, and pines. Street noise was muffled by the fence, giving the grounds an intimate air of peaceful solitude. Homes like that, built in the early twentieth century, had generally stayed in families for generations. Heathwood was an old-money neighborhood where gossip stayed within the property lines. My father had been lucky to find the house.

To the left and behind the main house, Sara spied an ivy-covered carriage house. "That must be the office."

"I think we're supposed to meet Cassie there before we tour the house."

Cassie Little opened the office door as we approached and smiled. "Welcome to Carolina House." To my wife, she said, "Hi. I'm Cassie. You must be Sara."

"That's me. Thanks for offering to show us around. We're so excited to be a part of this wonderful place. The grounds are gorgeous."

Cassie looked at me with a little grin. "What changed your mind, Jack? I didn't think you were interested. Frankly, after our first meeting, I was surprised to hear from you."

I nodded at Sara. "She changed my mind. Sara has a way of helping me to see the possibility in everything."

Cassie hugged Sara and said, "Then I have you to thank."

My wife hugged her back but was too embarrassed to answer.

We walked into the office and sat on worn yet comfortable chairs. The office was in disarray, files and papers stacked everywhere. Cassie scanned the room and blushed. "I'm sorry about the mess. I wanted to organize everything before y'all got here, but I ran short on time."

Sara's eyes lit up; she loved to organize. She said, "Don't give it a thought, Cassie. That's why I'm here. You have more important matters to deal with."

After chatting for a few minutes, Cassie suggested we visit the house. "Afterward, Sara can examine the books as long as she likes. Follow me."

We entered the grand old house through a rear door. Two women were preparing lunch in the large kitchen. Cassie made introductions. One of the women, Chris, smiled and asked us to stay for lunch. "We're just having soup and sandwiches, but we'd love for y'all to join us. Wouldn't we, Mary?"

The other woman, Mary, was barely older than my own daughters and didn't look at us or speak. She nodded and resumed slicing tomatoes. According to the files Cassie had sent, she was pregnant, although she'd yet to show. I'd requested the files in order to familiarize myself with each resident's unique situation. The brutality these women had endured was heart wrenching.

Mary was the newest and youngest guest. Her pregnancy had been in jeopardy when she'd first arrived. Her boyfriend had beaten her daily for six months; the last beating had ended with her in the hospital and the boyfriend in lockup. A neighbor had called the law, saying, "He's going to beat that girl to death this time."

I'd called Cassie to talk about Mary. "He was out within three days, but Mary was in and out of the hospital by then. A social worker gave her the telephone number for Carolina House. When she called, your daddy picked her up and brought her here straightaway. Normally Tom didn't work shifts at the House, but in Mary's case, he stayed with her until she calmed and was convinced the boyfriend wouldn't be able to find her." Cassie had been quiet on her end of the phone for a long moment or two. "Tom was especially protective of Mary—and her baby. Poor girl didn't even know she was pregnant until the hospital told her that day. She nearly lost her child because of that thrashing. Your father was so relieved when he found out the baby was okay. We all were."

After lunch, we explored the house and Cassie gave us the tourguide spiel. There were seven bedrooms, all occupied, each with a private bath. The larger rooms were for the women with children. Some women were at work or school during the day. Those children of age were in school, and those too young were there with their mothers or the staff.

Sara spent about an hour looking over the books while Cassie and I walked the grounds. They had a small playground for the kids, a vegetable patch, and a cozy side garden with a bubbling fountain. The lawns were well maintained, weeded and mown. Cassie looked around the yard. "The residents tend the vegetable garden, keep the rest of the grounds in repair, and clean the house. The staff helps out and teaches any needed skills, but all residents, including the older kids, have chores and responsibilities. For most of these women, this is their first experience having a purpose other than trying to please their abusers."

As we drove home and listened to Billie Holiday's "All of Me," I began to think Sara and I had bitten off more than we could chew. I was sure Carolina House would take more time than we'd first allowed. I was trying to land contracts and work on the tree house, and Sara had a show soon and many other duties and responsibilities. Yet she hummed along with Billie and smiled like she'd grabbed the last biscuit off the plate.

"What's going on in that pretty head of yours, sweet girl?" I asked as I turned down the music.

"Oh, I was thinking about how low Carolina House's bank balance is," she replied.

"And that makes you happy?"

"Not at all. But that gives us an opportunity to jump right in and help out. We need to raise money. That makes me happy." Sara's fundraising skills for the girls' schools or teams were legendary in parts of Atlanta. She had a knack for getting folks to open their checkbooks and say, "How much?"

"I hope you're not suggesting I start making furniture to sell," I said.

"Of course not. I have a plan." She smiled. "But that is a great idea, Jack."

I wouldn't have said great idea.

CHAPTER SIX

We moved into our house on summer's hottest day. Stacked boxes filled every room, and I was irritable thinking about all the work ahead. But Sara had organized the move, the movers had done their part, so I figured it was time for me to shut my mouth and put my back into it. I tried to focus on good thoughts, like being back home and out of the damn city for good. We'd spent too much of our lives wedged between two other houses. At the new house, there were no neighbors within actual shouting distance. This was freedom. This was home. The girls ran off to explore with the dogs close behind, while I moved furniture and boxes every which way.

A deep porch encircled the house and offered views of woods and vistas from every vantage. When I'd first inspected this house, I knew a craftsman had built it, a master who'd married grace to practicality. It'd been built after the Civil War so wasn't drenched in all that sadness. Over the years, indoor plumbing had been added, but most everything else had been left original. That attention to detail was all but gone from modern homes. The previous owners had let the house go to seed, but the bones were still there, waiting for us to resurrect it. To save money, I'd planned to renovate while we lived in it. It was the only way we could've afforded that huge house and all that acreage.

The house sat back on the property, plumb center. The blacktop wasn't noticeable through the trees, and the sound of passing cars was but a faint whisper of rubber on asphalt. This was the piece of paradise I'd dreamt about but been unwilling to look for while my father was still alive. We were just a few miles from the Knoll, and that would've been intolerable then. I'd stayed away, trying to make the physical distance between us imitate the apathy we'd both nurtured. But I was home and should've been happy. So why wasn't I?

I drove over to Mama's house when Sara and the girls headed into Columbia to pick out paint colors. They didn't even ask me to help, and I think I was more relieved than offended. I would've just been in the way. I was told I had no fashion sense, which I suppose was true enough. The girls inherited their tastefulness from their mama. From me, they got raven hair, green eyes, and a stubborn streak wide as a four-lane blacktop.

I carved a few flowers and vines on the tree house door to help my fingers remember which end of the chisel to hold. The door and deck faced east to capture the morning warmth, and those carvings would light up something beautiful when the sun topped the pines. The door was the tree house's centerpiece, connecting not only the tree house to its deck but connecting all the carvings throughout. I tried my best to do justice to the design Dad had imagined and set down on paper.

As I carved, I began to recognize the flowers beneath the chisel blade. I'd thought they were just generic blossoms when I'd first studied the plans. But Carolina jessamine, honeysuckle, and dogwood blooms all came to life in three dimensions as the chips flew. Throughout the design, ivy twisted and curled back on itself. Each carving flowed into the next, creating a planned randomness, a wild Eden, a sanctuary among the boughs. It would be a place for

Tom Parker's grandchildren to gather, to dream, and to always be safe and welcome. The longer I worked on it, the more I knew that his project was far more than some half-assed notion he'd had; the tree house was a gift and a legacy for the entire Parker clan. How could I have never noticed that my father had such a gift? Even in death, he was thinking about and providing for this own. I was just a means, and at that moment, I was determined to do whatever I needed to reach his ends.

Sara knew how to throw a party. After our visit to Carolina House, she'd gone to work planning a pig picking, with live music and a silent auction. The fundraiser was at Parker's Knoll and featured a band from Charleston. Sara had sent out invitations by the bucketful. On the day of the event, there were over three hundred folks from across the state in the south pasture, each having paid a C-note to be there, enough to keep Carolina House in the black for a few months more. Of course, the promise of bottomless barbecue was like pouring honey to draw flies. But I was surprised so many people were there with so little detail. To protect Carolina House, the invitations had asked for support for a "good cause" and help to fight "the blight of domestic abuse." Said a lot about those folks, it did. Sara walked around talking to everybody and thanking them for their support. I knew the auction would be a big success too; generous Columbia business owners had donated troughs of merchandise, vacations, and hunts.

Bill and I were in charge of the pigs. We kept the pork coming until folks were full as ticks. I was never much use in the kitchen, but I could cook anything in a hole in the ground. I'd placed the stage near the cook pits, so that we would have a front row seat as we tended our cooking. The band was far too good to play at a barbecue, but they'd accepted unlimited food as their wages. The lead singer, Clive, was one of Bill's best friends, and that had a lot to do with it.

The last taillights disappeared down the driveway well after midnight. Mama and the kids were all in the house asleep. And since the hour was so late, Lauren and Andy would sleep at the Knoll and drive back to Greenville the next morning. As we sat around a fire pit winding down, Clive walked over and handed Maggie a beer. He was sleeping at Bill's house and so hanging out with us, even though his bandmates had long since gone. I'd known Clive for a long time, and he'd always been a decent man. Seemed like he and Maggie had found some common music. I remembered her having a crush on him when we were teenagers, though she was a good deal younger. The thought of her having a good man in her life made me hopeful but wary. After her experience with marriage, I'd say she was due for a normal relationship. But normal never came easy to a Parker.

I looked over to where Sara sat in a lawn chair chatting with my other sisters. I walked over to her and held out my hand. She took it and I helped her to her feet. We danced slow like she always wanted, not beholden to time or toil or any set schedule. I was grateful for my wife. She'd saved me when I was hell-bent on self-destruction. She'd redeemed me as much as I was redeemable. And for just that minute, nothing in the world mattered but us. "Thank you," I whispered to her. We left the girls sleeping at Mama's house and drove home as the sky hinted at a brand new day.

Bill had offered to help me shingle the tree house roof. We screwed down plywood and then covered it with tar paper. The shingles were mossy-green and would last until our kids' children were ready to play there. He whistled as we snapped a chalk line for the next shingle course.

He looked up at me. "So, Lauren says that Maggie and Clive have been sparking hot and heavy." He paused to measure and mark for the next chalk line. "He's a good guy."

"But?" I'd heard the question hanging there.

"But it's Maggie. After what happened before, I'm just worried.

And Clive is my friend. It could get sticky if things don't work out between them."

"I don't reckon there's anything we could do if we wanted. Maggie's not a kid. She'd likely tell us to mind our own damn business. I want to protect her too, but we can't always do that. Best we can do is to be there for her if she needs us."

"Yeah. I reckon you're right."

"Course I am." Except when I'm not.

With the roof finished, Bill and I fed the horses and chickens and then visited with Mama on the porch. She was wrapped in an afghan against a nip in the air she alone felt. I sat in Dad's rocker, and Bill sat on the porch railing facing Mama and me.

"You boys want coffee?" Mama asked.

"No, ma'am. I'm fine," I said.

"No thanks, Mama," Bill said.

"Pound cake?" She asked.

"Not for me," I answered.

"Jack's trying to watch his figure." Bill laughed at his own joke. "But I'll have some. Keep your seat, Mama. I'll get it. Would you like a piece?"

"No, honey. I had some earlier."

Bill walked inside to get his sugar fix. He returned with a quarter of the cake, a banana, and a big coffee mug. Somehow he balanced his feast on the railing and didn't spill a drop or crumb.

"How's everything over at your new house?" Mama looked up at me from her crocheting.

I didn't want to burden her with my misgivings and second thoughts, so I said, "Besides a lot of work to do, it's fine."

She must've noticed a hesitation or something in my answer. "What's wrong, son? You have that troubled look about your eyes."

Bill shook his head. "Jack's beginning to wonder why he felt such an urgency to move home. He thinks we can't take care of ourselves, but ain't quite so sure he can do any better." He looked at me full in the face, as if daring me to dispute him.

I hated being pushed into a corner, but, "Asshole," was all I could think to say.

Mama shook her head, but whether at my language or the tension between her sons, I didn't know. I resented the hell out of Bill for his two cents' worth. But truth was, he'd hit the nail squarely on the head. And I didn't know what to do about it.

The sun was just peeking over the pines, as if too shy to show itself fully. At that time each day, the time in between, everything always seemed clean and good to me, untainted by our fucked up lives. Standing on the tree house deck, I heard and then saw a pileated woodpecker high up in a sweetgum near Mama's house. His drumming on the tree sounded like a distant hammer. The hollow sound told me I'd have to take that tree down soon, before it had a chance to fall on Mama's house. Lucy and Ethel were asleep in a strip of feeble sunlight. Crunching gravel caused them to raise their heads. They looked toward the driveway then at me. "I hear it," I said.

Maggie pulled up next to my truck. As she walked toward the tree house, I could tell something was wrong and climbed down to meet her. My first thought was that Clive had done something stupid. She walked over and hugged me. I'd always been closer to her than to Lauren or Audrey—maybe because we were so similar in our ways. She kept her thoughts to herself, unless she was struggling with something fierce.

"What's going on, little squirrel?" She'd earned her nickname as a toddler, collecting acorns and hiding them in our boots, but I was the only one who still used it.

"Don't call me that," she said. Her attempt at a smile didn't work as she leaned against a sawhorse. "Jack, I found a lump yesterday. I have an appointment with an oncologist tomorrow. They want to do a biopsy. I'm so scared." Fresh tears spilled down her cheeks.

"Oh, Maggie. I'm so sorry. But don't get ahead of yourself. Let them do their tests. It could be nothing. It is nothing." I wanted to cry as well. "I'll go with you, all right?"

"That's not necessary. They won't have the results for a couple days anyway. Sorry to drop by so early, but I had to tell you. I figured you'd be here." She glanced at the house, still dark. "I haven't told Mama or Bill or the girls yet."

"I'm glad you told me, and I am going with you."

Maggie leaned against my shoulder. "Love you, big brother."

"Me too, little squirrel."

CHAPTER SEVEN

Cassie Little was Carolina House's soul and champion. Far as I could tell, she didn't have anything like a life outside those walls. When I'd first met her, and she'd expressed concern for the future of Carolina House, I'd believed she was worried for her own job. Not even close. She was truly dedicated to those women.

Sara and I sat in the office with her. She wanted to tell us her story.

"Tom knew about my past, but I think it's important you both should know as well," she said. "I was the first resident here at Carolina House. Somehow Tom found me and brought me to this house even before the ink was dry on the purchase contract." She took a deep breath and closed her eyes as if in prayer. "You may know all this already, but I need to say it."

At sixteen, she was married and pregnant. "When my father saw the first bruises he flew into a rage and had my marriage annulled. He was still angry about my eloping and told me that the child would be put up for adoption. I was so scared and confused." She looked at us as if wanting forgiveness or, at least, understanding. "Somehow I found enough pluck to leave home and had an abortion in a filthy room by a man that was no more a doctor than I was. He botched it and left me with an infection and massive scarring. I'd never be able to have a baby.

"I couldn't go home, so I traveled around and ended up living on the street and then with a much older man. He forced me to do things I couldn't even comprehend at the time."

Cassie began a journey of abuse and humiliation. She would find the nerve to leave one man and end up with another who was often worse. On countless occasions, she was traded to a filthy drug dealer if cash was short. At forty-nine years of age, Cassie was beyond all hope, barely holding on. "I tried to leave and would be dragged back by my hair, locked in a closet for days. I was convinced that was my lot in life, and I could only think of one way out. I went to the closest church and prayed God would either deliver me or give me the courage to swallow the pills in my purse.

"Tom walked into the church at that moment. I don't know how he found me, but he sat down and began to talk to me. He told me about a place where women could stay and not be afraid. Given what had happened with other men, I was skeptical, but oddly felt I could trust him." Cassie lived at Carolina House for a year as a resident. With Dad's encouragement, she'd received her high school equivalency and began a bachelor's degree in social work. She had felt so strongly that he'd saved her life, she accepted when he asked her to manage the house. The day after her graduation from Columbia College, Cassie Little became Carolina House's resident manager and strongest advocate.

She was quiet for a time when she finished her story. Looking up, she said, "You know, I believed in my heart I was worthless, broken beyond repair." Cassie drew in a deep breath. "Your daddy helped me when I had no hope. My life made a full circle." She smiled to herself.

Sara hugged Cassie and whispered something to her. They were becoming friends, and I felt as if I was intruding on something by being there. "Honey, Tom and this place gave you the opportunity. But you did the hard part," Sara said.

We were at Carolina House for another reason too. Chris, who we'd met on our first visit, was leaving the house. With her first apartment and a good job lined up, she and her two children were excited to be on their own soon. Chris had made great strides, and both her confidence and her smile were infectious. The House's tradition was to throw a party for the women who left to begin the next steps in their lives.

All the staff and residents were there, as well as a few of the foundation's benefactors. Even as we celebrated her new life, we had to be security minded, and all who entered the grounds had been vetted. At the gate, our people checked the benefactors' and the catering staff's identification. The caterer had performed background checks on all their staff and provided us a list. On the gate we had a private security guard we'd contracted for the evening. We'd left the gate open for ease of guests driving through. We felt secure with the guard there, and as opening the gate from inside required a remote or a button on the control panel in the house, our setup was born of convenience.

I watched Sara as she smiled and spoke to each person. She kept an eye on the buffet table, ready to alert the caterer should the food need replenishment. Carl, a staff member, approached Sara and whispered something to her. She pointed and he walked across the room to me. "The security guard has disappeared," he said. "I walked outside to take him food and couldn't find him anywhere."

Taking Carl's arm, I began to lead him outside. As we turned to leave, I heard a heavy thump and shouts from upstairs. I sprinted to the stairs and climbed them three at a time with Carl a step behind. The racket was coming from Mary's room. Her locked door gave way to my shoulder on the second try.

Mary was in a corner on the floor, sobbing, with her arms

wrapped around her knees, peering out from under her hair. Her eye had begun to swell shut, and her lip was a bloody mess. The guard was shoving her clothes into a backpack as I burst through the door. The anger rose up from my belly, tightening my chest, quickening my heart and settling behind my eyes, white and hot. Next thing I knew, I was sitting atop him pounding his face again and again. I was completely out of my head, out of control.

Carl pulled me off, and the guard scrabbled backward, against the wall. He looked at me with wild, wounded eyes, as if I was the monster. I realized then he was Mary's ex-boyfriend, and on his face now was the same look he'd likely seen on hers time and again. Fear. He was bleeding from his nose and mouth. Blood painted his shirtfront like some gruesome Rorschach. I looked up and saw Sara at the doorway, worried faces looking over her shoulder. I recognized something in her eyes—a scrap of uncertainty, a reluctant memory. Her expression chilled my heart.

The law arrived and took the ex-boyfriend away in handcuffs. If not for Carl swearing I was defending Mary, I would've been headed for lockup myself. I was uneasy with my reaction to the situation. This was an old feeling, and an unwelcome one. And I was upset that so many had witnessed it. I wasn't sorry I'd punished the bastard, but it wasn't meant for Mary—or Sara—to see. Mary had seen her share of viciousness from him. And my wife? Well, she'd seen enough violence from me to last her lifetime. I knew I'd messed up but couldn't figure how to make it right.

Sara either let me off the hook or enabled me, depending on your way of figuring. She said, "Jack, this has nothing to do with the past. Don't confuse anger at another man's cruelty with brutality for its own sake. There's a difference between beating a weaker person and giving a bully a lesson." She paused and placed a hand on my chest. "You would've stopped before you caused any permanent damage. I know it." Sounded like she was trying to convince herself more than me.

I wanted to believe her, but I couldn't brush aside my reaction as easily as my wife had. I'd always been hot tempered, but I hadn't lost control so mindlessly since before Wren was born. But the worst part, the part that made me question what the hell I was doing running a women's shelter, was I'd fucking enjoyed thumping that son of a bitch.

Sara squinted up at me. "What did you mean by, 'They'll be fine, they'll be fine'?"

"What?" I didn't remember saying anything.

"When you were, you know, hitting him, you kept repeating that."

"I don't know. I truly don't." I didn't know, and yet something about those words made me want to hide—to hide away and block out the world.

The waiting room at the oncologist's office was a fake-sunny-bright place with abstract paintings on the walls. Soft music seeped from hidden speakers like water from a cut bank, and the latest fashion magazines sat in heaps atop the useless little tables scattered about. I appreciated the attempt to provide a comforting distraction, but to me doctors' waiting rooms were fearful places. Cancer hung about that place like a drunk at last call. Most of those folks were probably focused on the handful of words their doctor would say—words that might determine whether they put more money away for retirement or said the hell with it all and moved to someplace warm and sunny to wait it out.

Maggie was nervous but in better spirits than the day before. I squeezed her hand. "I had an interesting evening last night," I said.

Maggie grinned. "I'm sure you did, Jack. Tell me about it."

I told her about the party and the fight. As I got to the part where I'd seen Mary's bruised and bleeding face and then attacked her ex, Maggie's eyes lost focus. I guessed I'd prompted an unpleasant memory, probably about her own ex-asshole, and I regretted telling her. But just as quickly she refocused on me and tried to smile.

"I'm sorry, honey. That was bone-headed of me. I shouldn't have burdened you with all my bullshit. Not today."

She tried again to smile. "It's okay. It just made me think about my marriage. I still sometimes wonder what is so wrong with me that he couldn't stick it out." Cruelty could find a body in more than just the physical.

"You know there is not one single thing wrong with you. His leaving was simple cowardice. Nothing to do with you. You do know that, don't you?"

She nodded and looked up at me. "I know. Sorry you had to witness the pity party."

"Little squirrel, you know I never miss a party."

When her name was called, Maggie gave me a quick hug and walked away with the nurse. She glanced back over her shoulder once and was gone. I felt more helpless than ever before in my life.

She emerged a short time later and told me it would be a few days until she got the results. I took Maggie to Palmetto's, her favorite little café in Columbia. We ate in silence, as if speaking our fears would give them life. Then I drove her back to my house where she'd left her car.

She hugged me and got in her car to leave, but not before promising to call as soon as she heard from the oncologist's office. "I'll let you know the minute I know anything." I watched her brake lights flash about halfway down the drive and thought she had something else to say. But she kept going forward—to what I didn't know.

My three girls were taking a pottery class in town, so I had the rest of the day to myself. The dogs and I were home alone and I was restless. "You two want to go for a ride?" Lucy and Ethel danced around with tongues lolling. "Don't get that slobber on my seats, hear?"

Mama wasn't home, so I headed straight for the workshop, then the tree house. With the outside sheathed and the trim coming along, the project was beginning to look more like a real house. The trim pieces, carved with the same flowers, leaves, and vines as the door, deepened the sense that it was a magical dwelling, as if some storybook giant had plucked a cottage from its foundations and placed it among that oak's boughs.

For most of the afternoon, I worked on the tree house while the dogs chased their own stubby tails or slept beneath the low-hanging limbs. Twilight fell, and the oak's leaves and branches appeared as black lace against the dusty blue sky. Deep in the woods an owl asked his question. Goosebumps covered my arms, and I told myself the evening chill was to blame. I didn't answer the damn bird, but I knew the question—who? Who would keep our family together with so much misery and black luck being heaped upon us? If it were up to me, we were screwed.

After returning the tools to the workshop, I walked to Mama's house. She was home so I stepped inside to say hello. Reading at her kitchen table with her hand to her mouth, she closed the book and smiled when I walked into her kitchen.

I laughed. "Why are you reading at the kitchen table? Wouldn't you be more comfortable in your living room?"

"Well, I was so caught up in the story I didn't want to stop and move." She patted the book. "It's a good one. I'm getting a good scare from it. Have you been working on that tree house all day?"

"Since about ten o'clock, I reckon. Starting to make some headway."

"My babies are going to love it, Jack. I'm looking forward to sitting on my porch watching and listening to them." Mama had a peaceful look about her. "It's good what you're doing, son. I wasn't so sure at first, but I'm so happy you decided to finish it. Your daddy would be so proud."

I hesitated and then said, "Mama, I'm proud of him too. He was trying to do some good, to make a difference. I wish I would have known when he was alive so I could have told him."

"Well, he didn't want praise or recognition. He just wanted to help folks. I'm sure he knew how you felt about him. Of course, there was no reason you couldn't have let him know you were proud of him just for being your daddy." She smiled that infuriating smile at me.

Her comment stung, but she was right. I could have made an effort to tell Dad or show him how I felt. I was proud of him—maybe even before I found out about Carolina House. He was a good father and husband, always working to provide for his family. Maybe he wasn't the warmest person to me, but he never scolded me, even when I'd done something foolish. I think he was proud of me in his own way, though I surely didn't give him much cause to puff his chest out. He must have realized I'd become a decent husband and father. Still, I'd never voiced anything to him, or he to me. So much was unsaid, left stranded in the branches like a child's kite. I guess we were alike in more ways than I'd ever credited.

Sara and I drove through the gate at Carolina House before nine o'clock. We had a meeting with Cassie to discuss the night of the party. She was on the telephone when we walked into the office but finished her call quickly, rubbing her right temple.

"Way too early for headaches, Cassie. What's wrong?" I asked.

Cassie looked from Sara to me. "That was the sheriff's department. They're releasing Mary's ex-boyfriend today. His name is Mark Dunbar, and he has a record—a long record. Apparently he's a not-so-small-time drug dealer. And he was arrested for possession of a gun while committing a violent crime six months back. He's a bad man, and they keep letting him go. How could he have found her here? I don't understand." She took an aspirin bottle from her desk and swallowed a couple.

"How's Mary?" Sara asked.

"That poor girl was just starting to settle and feel safe. Now, I don't know."

"Cassie, I'm sorry for what happened in Mary's room. What I

did was intolerable. I let my emotions control me." I inhaled. "If you think it would be best for the women, I'll stay away for a while. The last thing I want is to cause fretfulness or insecurity. I know most of these ladies are walking a fine line."

"Jack, you did what we all wish we could do. After what that man has put Mary through, I think he got off easy." Cassie narrowed her eyes. "Our so-called security company, on the other hand, has a heap of trouble coming their way. Apparently, Dunbar paid someone there to bypass the normal checks and place him with us on the night of the party. He doesn't even work for that company."

"Let's hope the sheriff's department takes that a little more seriously than they do his repeated abusive behavior," Sara said.

"From what I understand, the DEA and state law enforcement are involved as well. I'm not sure why the state is interested in Mr. Dunbar. I'd think the Feds would try to shut down any state investigation. I suppose they'll figure it out." Cassie shook her head. "This is all my fault. I contracted the security firm. I hired them on the basis of a verbal recommendation from our driver, Danny. Said his daddy had used them before. That's how he got onto the grounds. I was too trusting, too lax."

Sara covered Cassie's folded hands with her own. "Don't dwell on it, honey. We've all learned a valuable lesson. We need to be extra careful with outside vendors. I don't think we'll make that mistake again. But our real problem is Mark Dunbar and how to protect Mary from him."

Sara was right. I would've bet cash money we hadn't heard the last of that son of a bitch.

With the day fading into shadows, Sara and I sat on the porch steps watching our daughters play with the dogs. I got up and snagged a couple beers from the refrigerator.

"Thanks." She sipped her beer and after a minute said, "Everything okay?"

"I'm good." I hesitated, unsure how to ask the question. "Are you worried that I could hurt you or the girls?"

"God no, Jack. Why would you ask such a question?" She placed her hand on my arm.

"When you walked in on me wailing on Dunbar, the look on your face —you were terrified—like you thought it might all be starting again. I never want to see that look again. I felt like I was hurting you instead of that little shit I was hitting."

"I was terrified my husband might be hurt, terrified something might happen to my girls' daddy." She glanced at the girls to make sure they were far enough away and lowered her voice anyway. "I know it's not happening again, Jack. I know it."

"But do you ever wonder if I could snap and hurt you or the girls?"

Sara concentrated on peeling the label from her bottle, looked up at me. "Yes. I'm sorry, Jack, but that did flicker through my mind for a second."

"Shit."

She squeezed my arm. "But it came and went, and I haven't thought about it since. I know you're not like that anymore. I believe you think of Mary as your own daughter and got caught up in it all. Listen to me, if it had been one of our girls, I'd have been the one jumping on the bastard."

I kissed her fingers resting on my arm. "Yeah, I reckon you're right. I just got caught up in it."

What I didn't and couldn't say was that I'd enjoyed the hell out of hurting that boy. And I'd thought I was beyond all that.

CHAPTER EIGHT

Watching the second hand tick-tick-tick on my desk clock, I sat listening to a prospective client talk on the speaker phone about her dream home. I tried to take notes as she outlined her vision for the finished building, an oceanfront home on Folly Beach. Glancing at my notes, I realized I'd filled the pad's margins with sketches of ivy and honeysuckle and all manner of greenery. I found it hard to focus on her voice and wondered if I should reschedule the call to a time when I could offer my complete attention. My cellphone vibrated beside the pad. Maggie's name flashed, and I made my apologies to the client. Clicking off the landline with one hand, I answered Maggie's call with the other.

Maggie's voice was small, a whisper, a plea. "Jack." That one word, the word I loved to hear my wife say late at night, made the world go still when my sister said it.

In Columbia, I pulled up to Maggie's townhouse a bit after noon. She was sitting on her front steps, her arms wrapped around her knees. She was a little girl again, scared and lonely, and my heart howled. As I walked up to her, she tried to smile but began to cry.

I sat down and gathered her into my arms, wanting to take that hateful disease from her into my own body.

"Tell me everything the doctor said. I'll call Sally Phillips. She can get you into the best cancer treatment facility in the country." My mind was planning and organizing and jumping round like a snake-bit hound. "We'll beat this thing, Maggie. We'll take it by the throat and squeeze the fucking life from it."

Maggie pulled me back to her reality with a finger to my lips. "Jack, thank you for being here, but please listen to me. I need your support, and I need the rest of the family too. I will fight this, but I need to do it my way. Just be there for me when I need you, okay?"

Realizing how desperate I must have sounded, I tried to slam on my brakes. I said, "I'm sorry, little squirrel. I'll do whatever you want me to do. Whatever you need. But you should tell the family. Mama and Bill and the girls need to know."

"Can you get everyone together? Maybe we can do it the next time Lauren is down. I can't make all those calls right now."

"Of course, honey. But I think we should get Lauren to come down this weekend. She's just a couple hours away, and she'd be upset if we waited for her next visit. Does that sound all right?"

"Sure does. Thank you," she said. "You're a wonderful big brother—no matter what Bill says." The suggestion of a hint of a twinkle found her eye. If anyone could beat cancer, Maggie would.

I was roused by the dream of running through the woods. Glancing at my sleeping wife, I was relieved I hadn't disturbed her sleep. Slipping out of bed, I made my way downstairs to the kitchen. I couldn't move about the house but that Lucy and Ethel heard, and they sat side by side waiting for me. Opening the refrigerator, we inspected the possibilities. I pulled out leftover fried chicken. Two long tongues told me I'd made a good choice.

Since I was up, I drove to the Knoll to work on the tree house at dawn. Seemed like starting my day there was becoming a habit.

Walking out onto her porch, coffee in hand, Mama waved a good morning to me. Lucy and Ethel looked to me and I nodded. They raced off to say their good mornings to her. I couldn't hear what she said to them, but they followed her into the house, where left-over bacon probably sat cooling beside her cooktop.

I was installing the big double window on the south wall. The job would have gone easier with two, but Bill was working a double and couldn't help. Restless to have it done, I devised a series of tempo-rary braces to hold the heavy window while I plumbed, shimmed, and screwed it in place. Raising the window up to its opening was awkward as hell, but with the help of a block and tackle I managed. Once the window was in place, and I was sure it wouldn't fall out, I removed the temporary bracing and checked the window from the ground. I was proud to see it looked fine and true.

The two smaller windows on either side of the deck door were a breeze compared to the big picture window. I'd questioned Dad's choice of window placement, but I realized then that the big south window would provide warmth in the winter, and the windows on the east wall would provide plentiful morning light. The west and north walls wouldn't have windows. Bookshelves, padded bench seats, and cupboards would line those walls, providing ample stor-age and sitting space for the kids. I finished all the window work around midday, ate the sandwich Mama had left for me below, then fell asleep in the warm sun.

I heard a car door open and close. My siblings had begun to arrive. Maggie would tell Mama, Bill, and our sisters she had breast cancer. The knot in my stomach seemed at odds with the confidence I felt that she would beat the disease. But my young sis-ter should have been celebrating her life, not fighting for it. I took a breath, climbed down, and walked over to the house.

As I stepped up onto the porch, Lauren slid her phone into her purse and said, "Audrey's on her way."

Mama suggested we go inside and use the dining room. "I'll make coffee while we're waiting." She couldn't seem to keep still; she must've known something bad was coming.

When Audrey arrived, Maggie laid it all out for them. She was dry-eyed and determined. "I need you all, your love and support. There are lots of treatment options, and the survival rate is good when it's caught this early." She smiled, even as tears trailed to the upturned corners of her mouth.

My siåblings were silent, their eyes downcast. Mama stood and went to Maggie, smiling. She wrapped her arms around her youngest child and whispered to her. Maggie's face was buried in Mama's neck, and she nodded her head. Finally, Mama separated a bit and looked at Maggie's face. "My baby girl," she said.

We all crowded round Maggie and fell into the easy, teasing banter, which is common among close siblings uncomfortable with too much emotional bullshit. Laughter and wit were our medicines, and we dosed her well. Maggie's sweet smile and gentle laugh were at odds with her illness. Her courage and resolve shined like a glimpse of sunlight through a cloud-darkened sky. Among the five of us, I'd have given her the best chance to beat the cancer. Tough and determined, she'd never give up, not by a long damn stretch.

Bill asked, "Have you told Clive?"

Maggie glanced at Mama and said, "Not yet. We're meeting for supper tomorrow night. Maybe I'll tell him then. I reckon he needs to know so he can high-tail it. I want to be fair to him."

Bill looked as if she'd kicked his favorite hound. "Honey, I've known Clive all my life. He's not like that. Give him a chance, all right?"

"Oh, I know. I'm just preparing myself. I don't want to expect too much." She smiled. "Not all men are as wonderful as you two boys."

Bill grinned. "She must want something, Jack."

Of course, she wanted something. She wanted to be healthy in both her body and her relationship. Maggie wanted what most folks wanted: a normal life, a quiet existence. She wanted a chance.

Bill and I walked behind Lucy and Ethel as they traipsed through the brush searching for quail. Their focus was akin to that of a musician whose every note sought perfection. My girls were attentive to nothing aside from my signals and working the birds. A good brace of Vizslas covers twice the ground, never trespassing on the other's space. Still, my pups were deeply attuned to one another. Lucy made soft chuffing sounds to her sister. Ethel responded in kind, her throaty voice a half octave lower. Of a sudden, Ethel trotted over to Lucy, slowing to a delicate prance as she neared. Both dogs lifted a front paw and pointed their muzzles toward some low-lying brush. Their bodies were rigid, aligned like fence rails with each other. Ethel was half a muzzle behind out of respect for her sister's capture.

I clicked my tongue and the dogs rushed forward. The birds flew, and Bill dropped two with scary quickness. Lucy and Ethel ran to fetch and returned a couple minutes later each with a mouthful. They knew who'd killed the birds and sat in front of Bill. He took the quail and placed them in his game pocket.

Their job done, the dogs looked to me. I nodded and they ran off to search for more quail. Bill reloaded his over and under and pocketed the spent shell casings.

"I do enjoy hunting with your dogs, Jack. They're damn smart. You train dogs like Dad trained horses. Next ones are yours."

"You can have the next birds too," I said. "I'm here to work the dogs." What I didn't say was that I wanted to watch the dogs work and take no life that day. Bill was right; watching Dad had taught me how to train bird dogs. He'd used compassion and patience, but he'd always been in command. I remembered him spending countless hours working with his horses. He'd mildly corrected any mistakes, but he had corrected when needed. I suppose that's the way he'd raised Bill and my sisters, gently but firmly. Me, he'd left to fend for myself.

After supper, Sara looked at me and nodded slightly.

"Girls, your mama and I wanted to talk to you about your Aunt Maggie."

They looked at me and knew something was wrong. "Is Maggie okay? Is it about her boyfriend Clive?" Lily asked.

"It's not about Clive, baby. Maggie is sick. She found a lump in her breast, and the doctors have checked it. They say it's malignant."

Wren raised her pretty green eyes to mine and asked, "Is that like cancer, Daddy?"

"That's right, baby, she has cancer. It's serious, but she's strong and her doctors are doing everything possible to help her. We all believe she'll be fine." I looked at Sara, and she was watching the girls. "We thought you two were old enough to know the truth, and I need to ask you both for a favor."

"What favor, Daddy?" Lily asked.

Wren looked at her sister. "We love Maggie. We'll do anything to help her."

"That's what I want you both to do. Love on Maggie even more than you already do. She needs us all right now. She needs our support more than ever. You girls understand?"

Both girls had handled the news far better than I'd believed they would. In hushed tones, they talked about outings with their aunt and little gifts they could make for her. I was watching them as Sara got up and carried her plate over to the kitchen sink. She stood looking out the window at the dark, seeing her own reflection. She didn't make a sound, but her shoulders shook ever so faintly.

Bill called and suggested we have a fish fry to take Maggie's mind off her troubles. I didn't believe catfish and hushpuppies would begin to make her feel less fearful, but his heart was in the right place. So we found ourselves launching Bill's flat bottom before sunrise. We raced down the river without spotlights or running lights—the latter being on the wrong side of the regulations. How the hell Bill could see on that tar-black river, I couldn't have said.

The Wateree River has its share of deep holes, and Bill knew where just about all were located. It was those holes where we found his nets, and within a half hour, we had the bottom of the boat filled with catfish, gray and squirming. We poured ice over the fish and headed back to Bill's house to skin and fillet the cats.

Dad had taught Bill to build fishnets. I wasn't included in that part of their lives. But he'd showed only me how to build cabinets. I asked my brother, "Dad ever try to get you interested in furniture building?"

He tossed a catfish head into a barrel and took a swallow of beer. "Can't recall as he did. Why?" He wiped sweat on his forearm and went back to skinning.

"I was wondering why he taught you about nets and fishing and me about cabinets and furniture. I might've been interested in catfish and you in woodworking." I put a couple bags of fish in the icebox and tossed Bill another Budweiser.

"Were you?"

"Was I what?"

He cracked the beer, took a long pull, then wiped his mouth with the back of the hand holding his knife. "Were you interested in getting up before daylight, fishing nets, and skinning fish half the day?" He gestured at the table piled high with fish and fish guts.

"Not particularly, no."

"And I didn't give a rat's ass about breathing sawdust and picking splinters."

I drained my own beer and stared at my brother. "Your point?"

"Point is, maybe he knew us better than you credit him."

"Still could've asked us."

He shook his head and sighed. "What's the point, Jack? He's dead and that was years ago. Why stir up shit now? If you're so all-fired curious, why didn't you ask him when you had the chance?"

I didn't know how to answer, so I let it drop. Same as I always did.

As usually happened, our get-together grew to forty or fifty hungry mouths—family, friends, and friends of friends. What was supposed to be a simple meal of fried catfish, hushpuppies, and coleslaw had grown to a feast with crawfish, Lowcountry boil, and enough desserts to feed a college football team. Plywood and saw-horse tables sagged under the weight. Everybody filled plates and found a chair or soft piece of ground to sit and eat and talk. A fish fry is first and foremost a social event.

Bill had split logs stacked here and there to feed the four fire pits spaced around the field. Folks gathered around the fires to chat with friends old and new. The kids had already found the graham crackers, chocolate, marshmallows, and sticks. Groups of boys and groups of girls roasted marshmallows and peered at each other, giggling behind their hands. Most of the kids were at that age where they weren't quite sure whether they were attracted to or repulsed by the opposite sex. Their discomfort was funny as hell.

We had everything we needed except for our guest of honor. Maggie was nowhere to be seen. She'd called me earlier and said she was going to talk to Clive about her cancer before coming over. I'd thought she meant to speak to him a couple days before, and I wasn't sure the night of the fish fry was the best time to have that conversation. I'd held my tongue.

And then she was there. Alone. Maggie walked toward the party from Mama's house. I hadn't noticed her car parked among so many others and didn't know how long she'd been inside the house. I looked over at Bill, still cooking fish. He'd spotted her too. Bill's eyes found mine, and we both walked over to meet our sister. The daylight was gone, but as we approached her, firelight bounced off her wet cheeks.

"Can we take a walk?" Maggie asked. We fell in on either side of her and she hooked her arms through ours.

"What happened?" Bill asked when we were well away from everybody. His jaw was working like he was chewing a mouthful of briars.

Maggie sighed and said, "Clive wants to slow things down. He feels we're going too fast. He needs space. 'It's not you, it's me.' Pick your own cliché." She laughed, but the bitterness in her voice was an open wound with no remedy. "I guess I'm just proud he didn't break up with me by text or email."

Bill stared off into the night. He turned back to Maggie and said, "I'm so sorry, honey. If I'd thought for one second Clive could do something so shameful, I'd never have encouraged you to go out with him." He looked down at his boots. "Wouldn't have defended his sorry ass neither."

Maggie turned to Bill and placed her hands on his folded arms. "For God's sake, Bill. I'm a grown woman, and I make my own decisions. I don't need guilt or sympathy or anger from my brothers." She glanced over at me. "But I do need you guys. All right?"

Bill hugged her and whispered, "All right."

"Jack?"

"Course, little squirrel." I looked from my sister over to the party and found Mama. She was watching us with Audrey and Lauren on either side. At least this was some shitty news I didn't have to give her—she could read the signs. She caught my eye and nodded. Whether she was nodding to me or herself, I couldn't tell.

We drove home, the girls asleep in the back seat. Sara turned toward me, her legs tucked under her. "Maggie looked so sad tonight," she said. "Something happen with Clive?"

"He broke up with her." Saying it out loud left a bitter taste on my tongue.

"He broke up with her because she has cancer?"

"He said he needs space or whatever. But his timing is pretty damn convenient. I imagine he doesn't want to deal with a sick girlfriend. He hurt Maggie, but she'll be all right. She's had experience with assholes before. But Bill might not get over this so easily. Clive was his friend. He feels responsible and angry. He wants to protect Maggie and crack Clive's head." My brother and I both seemed to be full to overflowing with rage lately.

"You don't think he would actually injure Clive, do you?"

"No. Bill wouldn't hurt somebody over a break up. He trusted Clive with our sister, and he thinks he pushed them together. Maggie is still a little pigtailed girl to him, and he thinks she needs his protection. Honestly, I feel that way myself. Same as I'd feel if it were Wren or Lily."

"Unfortunately, Clive has every right to be a jackass." My wife knew how to clear away the meat and gristle and get down to the bone of the issue. "But if that bastard actually broke up with Maggie because she has breast cancer, there is a special hell waiting for his sorry ass." And Sara could gnaw hell out of that bone too, once she had her teeth round it.

CHAPTER NINE

When I crawled out from under the house, Mary was reading beneath a clematis-covered arbor. Cassie had called me about a leak, and I'd decided to fix it myself instead of calling a plumber. Carolina House didn't have money to spare, so I fixed what I could. I walked over to the arbor.

"Mind if I sit for a spell?" I asked. Mary glanced up at me and shook her head. "Thanks. What're you reading?"

She held the book up so I could read the cover. She was reading Shakespeare. I wouldn't say I understood everything Mr. William Shakespeare wrote, but I sure thought his words sounded like poetry. I said, "Romeo and Juliet is a good one. But it gives me the shivers."

"I love it. I could read Shakespeare all day." She spoke just above a whisper and blushed a deep crimson.

"What is it?" I asked, hoping I'd not made her to feel ill at ease by poking my nose into her business.

She looked into my eyes for the first time since I'd sat down. "He never let me read."

"He never let you read Shakespeare?"

"He never let me read anything. I asked him for a book a couple times, and he said I was too stupid to understand it." She dropped her eyes again, and I felt a familiar heat behind my own.

"You know he was only trying to control and shame you, right?"

"Oh, I know. A therapist told me that when I first came to stay here, but I think I already knew it my own self." She looked up at me once more. "That's why I called here that first time—because I figured out what he was doing. When I was in the hospital, because of what Mark done to me, a lady gave me the number here. Your daddy answered the phone. He came and got me, saved my life, you know?" Mary looked at me again, and her eyes sparkled with intelligence and defiance, as if she was daring me to challenge her words. I didn't.

I had an image of Dad driving her from the hospital, speaking to her in his low voice, encouraging her with words I'd heard him say to my sisters years past. "You're strong," he'd told them. "You set your own course." I thought Mary would have a chance at a future with her baby because of my father. Split my heart to think he'd never see her make it.

Mary said, "I do love Romeo and Juliet, but it makes me shiver too." She smiled, but there was a sadness there in her eyes I had no way of understanding.

It was unclear whether the girls were chasing the dogs or the dogs were chasing the girls. The four of them seemed to be having a big time. Sara and I watched from the porch steps. The evening was soft and sweet, with just enough darkness to cast everything a bit out of focus. The first stars appeared over the pine tops, and I felt a crispness to the air which hadn't been noticeable the week before.

Sara sat with her legs drawn up, her chin resting on her knees. She seemed to be looking past the girls and dogs, through the distant trees, to a place of her own imaginings. I reached into my pocket and held out a penny to her, a tired but precious gesture between us.

She looked at my outstretched hand and smiled. "I was thinking about Maggie. Remember when she was a teenager and the girls were little? She loved taking care of them whenever she came to visit us. Pretended they were her own." Sara took the penny and rubbed her thumb across its edge. "She was like that with all the kids. She's been to more recitals, soccer games, and birthday parties than most parents. She's driven to Atlanta and Greenville countless times. More than anyone I've ever known, Maggie gives love without any expectations."

"She is special. That's a fact. God gave Maggie an extra big heart." I knew Sara had something weighing on her mind, but I also knew she'd talk to me in her own time and her own way. I'd learned that she preferred to sort and organize her thoughts first. Only then would she communicate her mind and heart to me. She wouldn't be hurried.

"First, she can't have children. Jack, if any woman was born to be a mother, it's Maggie. And now, this hideous cancer could take her from us. It's just not fair. On top of all that, she's rejected by a husband and now a boyfriend, both for reasons beyond her control. She's better off without either, but why are people so cruel to each other?"

I thought her emotions were likely born of feeling helpless and maybe the loss of some of her faith in humanity. Yet I had no answers for her, at least none she would've wanted to hear, none that would satisfy her need for fairness in the world. My idea of justice was Old Testament, and hers was strictly New. I did believe a reason existed for all the pain—fate, karma, God's divine plan, whatever you want to call it. But that would have sounded canned and been little comfort to Sara or even Maggie. So I kept my thoughts to myself, while the weight of it settled over me like the dirt I'd shoveled into my father's grave.

Sara had always been close to my sisters. Having none of her own, she'd embraced joining our large family. Audrey, Lauren, and Maggie considered Sara and Kathy as their own sisters. Those five women were loyal to one another. There was nothing any one wouldn't have done for the others. I knew the other four were frustrated that they couldn't do anything to save Maggie. Still, they encouraged her and seemed to form a protective force around her. One or another of them made a point to stop by Maggie's house every day to check on her, pretending some contrived reason or another. Their excuses, however thin, were acts of love and were taken as such.

Lauren was spending more time than usual in the Midlands. She checked in on Mama and Maggie and the rest of us. She was a year younger than Audrey, but had always acted the part of the eldest sister. I think she was missing the family as much as I had before moving home from Atlanta. No matter how much we all fussed and fought, I believed that my brother and sisters, like me, only felt completely safe and whole when we were all together.

Another reason for Lauren to drive down was the get-togethers the five "sisters" had without fail. No matter what was happening, Lauren would drive to Columbia the second Friday each month to meet up with the others for drinking and fun. Sara had done the same before we'd moved home. She once told me they talked about books, movies, kids, family—and men. She rarely gave any specifics, and for that I was grateful. But when something truly bothered her about one of my sisters, she'd confide in me.

"I'm worried about Audrey," Sara said, brushing her hair before bed. "She stares off into space, and she's not taking care of herself. She's struggling with something, Jack. Lauren agrees with me, and we think you should speak to her."

"Me? Why me?"

"Well, if we talk to her, she might think we're ganging up on her and become defensive. If you talk to her, it's just her big brother showing concern."

I realized I was being worked, but I didn't see any way around it. "Don't you think she'll know you and Lauren put me up to it?"

"She won't know if you're smart about it. You can be clever when you put your mind to it, Jack. I have faith in you." Her reflection smiled at me, and she didn't miss a stroke with her hair brush.

Most times I didn't think I was clever at all.

Audrey and I sat on the restaurant's deck, overlooking the Congaree River. Across the river was Columbia, the Capitol's tarnished copper dome visible at the top of the Vista. Below, people walked dogs, jogged, or biked along the Riverwalk. My sister picked at her salad and had little to say. She answered my questions in short, clipped phrases. Audrey's face was drawn and her eyes wouldn't hold mine. Her hair looked like she hadn't washed it in a week and her nails were chewed down to nothing. Sara had been right to worry about her. My wife had confirmed what I'd suspected since that night at Barbie Q. Something more than a real estate deal gone bad was troubling my sister, and I needed to have a conversation with her.

"Honey, what's going on? Whatever it is, your family loves you. You're not alone."

Audrey began to cry, her face in her hands. I let her cry without interruption. After a time, she collected herself and looked up at me. "I guess I need to visit the powder room. I'll be right back. Sorry."

I stood as she retreated to compose herself, hoping she wouldn't keep right on walking past the ladies room to her car.

Ten minutes later she returned and sat across from me. "I'm sorry about that. I've wanted to talk to you about this, but with everything going on with Maggie, it didn't seem important."

"Audrey, I know you're worried about Maggie, as we all are, but you can always talk to Lauren or Bill or me about anything. Well, maybe not Bill." That earned me a smile. "Tell me whatever you feel comfortable saying, and if you want, I'll tell you what I think.

I'll do whatever I can to help you. I hope you know that."

"I do know." We watched a kayaker on the river below. Just when I thought she wasn't going to continue, she said, "I miss Daddy. I used to have a talk with him every so often. I felt I could tell him anything and he would always listen. He wasn't impatient or condescending. So it means a lot to me for you to say that."

I was surprised Audrey had talked to our father about her problems rather than Mama. I guess I was imposing my own screwed-up relationship with Dad on hers. He'd always been close to his daughters. Maybe Audrey was one of the reasons he'd left some money to us instead of everything to Mama. Maybe she'd told him about her financial difficulties. But I thought she and Brad had paid their debts, and I wondered what had her so worried still.

"Brad is addicted to prescription painkillers." She looked at me and shook her head. "He owed his dealer a lot of money. We tapped out Brad's 401(k) and Izzy's college fund, then we borrowed against the property his grandmother left him to pay the dealer off. After six months, the bank called the loan. The money from Dad saved us. After paying the bank, we even had a little left over. We were going to put some back in Izzy's college fund and pay back part of the 401(k). Brad said he'd stopped taking the pills and promised to go to rehab." She looked down at the river, as if it could carry her problems along its current, all the way to the Atlantic.

"But he didn't go to rehab, did he? And he didn't stop using?"

She shook her head. "I don't think he was ever serious about rehab, and he never stopped buying and using pills. He spent the money we had left and then some. No college fund. No investment. Brad owes this guy a hell of a lot. We get calls in the middle of the night demanding money. This dealer is dangerous, and there is no way the banks will let us borrow against that property again. I don't know where we'll find the money. I'm so scared, Jack. What will happen to us if we can't pay him?"

"I know you're scared, honey. We'll figure something out. How much does Brad owe this guy?"

Audrey closed her eyes for a minute, shaking her head. "Eight thousand."

"All right, honey. Let me worry about that, and you concentrate on your family. Are you going to stay with Brad if he gets himself right?"

"Maybe. Oh, Jack, I don't know. It's not just that he's endangering himself by taking drugs and dealing with this person. Izzy and I are in danger too. I'm a wreck worrying someone might show up at our house or Izzy's school. I can't eat or sleep." I hadn't noticed until that moment, but Audrey had lost weight. Her skin was pressed against more bone than flesh, and she couldn't seem to keep her hands still.

"Audrey, I'm going to ask you something. I need you to stay calm and look me in the eye when you answer. This might piss you off." I truly hated what I knew I had to ask.

"What is it, Jack? What's wrong?" She couldn't look me in the eyes.

"Honey, are you taking pills too?"

"Kiss my ass, you bastard. I open up to you, and you think I've done something wrong. You never change. Or did little miss perfect put you up to that accusation?"

I knew her jealousy of Lauren had prompted that last bit, and I ignored it. But she'd said all that without ever looking at me. Not sure she'd have been able to protest her innocence so hotly had she been looking in my eyes.

I sat watching her.

Waiting.

Audrey studied her hands and seemed to realize for the first time that they were shaking. She raised her eyes to mine and said in a low but decisive voice, "Yes. I need help."

CHAPTER TEN

Audrey's confession had surprised me. I hadn't expected her to admit taking pills right off. Figured I'd have to work on her a spell. She'd never had a comfortable relationship with the truth—apparently we had that in common. But when we'd played truth or dare as kids, which we'd called truth or trouble, she'd always chosen trouble without blink or complaint. Her admission meant she'd reached a low point and wanted help. I took encouragement from that.

I'd suggested we get together with Bill and our sisters and talk about her problem. She'd flatly refused. Audrey would only allow me to tell our brother. I suspected she was too embarrassed for her sisters to know the full measure of her situation. She'd promised to let the girls know soon, and with some reservation, I took her at her word.

A couple days later, she and I sat on my back porch watching the day fade and my dogs chase squirrels, real and imagined.

Bill walked up the steps and hugged Audrey. He said, "Hey, darlin'."

We sat around a small wooden table and stared at each other as if trying not to be the first to flinch. Finally Audrey said, "I'm so sorry. Our family has enough going on without my bullshit. But I don't know what to do. I feel like I'm trying to hold an armful of sand." She wasn't near as weepy as she'd been two days before and I was encouraged. But her hands were restless still, twitching and squeezing, as if they weren't connected to her body.

Bill covered her hands with his own and asked, "Does Brad know you're here?"

"He does. I told him I was asking you guys for help and if he tried to stop me or didn't follow your advice, I would take Izzy and leave. He didn't put up a fight. Actually, he seemed relieved to have it put to him plainly." Audrey shook her head and looked down at Bill's rough hands covering her own.

Watching her face for a reaction, I said, "Are you both willing to go into rehab for a while? It won't be easy, but I think it might be the best way for you both to get a grip on this. Might be the only way. We'll take care of Izzy and look after your house, so you don't have to do anything but work on getting better. And I'd suggest you tell Izzy the truth." Her eyes flared and she started to say something, but I held up a hand. "Audrey, Izzy is damn sharp and may already know or at least suspect what's going on. You want to get out in front of this."

She nodded. "We'll tell her. I'll let her know what a mess we've made—I've made. My poor baby girl deserves better parents, a better life." Audrey dropped her head into her hands.

"How did this happen, Audrey?" Bill asked. "I've never even seen you drink more than one beer."

She watched the dogs tree a bushy-tail, and then run off in search of other distractions. "You remember a couple years ago when Brad was in that wreck and hurt his back? He was in dreadful pain. His doctor gave him a couple prescriptions—powerful medications. The pills made him so relaxed and happy that I decided to try them too. They took the stress right away. Brad kept getting refills long after the physical pain was gone, but finally his doctor realized he was being played and cut him off. We were able to get more pills from other doctors, but eventually that dried up too. By then, we were both hooked and needing more and more pills for the same feeling. Someone at Brad's job gave him a guy's name, called him 'a pharmaceutical rep.'" Her laugh was sour, wretched. "This man said he could get us anything we wanted and in any amount. We bought more and more pills then and other stuff." She covered her eyes with a hand. "And when our money ran out, he let us run a tab, like we were buying shots at a bar."

"What's his name, this guy?" I asked. I was afraid Audrey wouldn't give me his name without a fight, but I needed it to put the brakes on their drive over the cliff.

She blew out a long breath. "His name is Mark Dunbar."

"Fuck me sideways."

Bill looked at me. "You know him, Jack?"

"We've met."

Maggie's oncologist paced like a cornered wildcat. You could tell that he, like everyone who met her, adored my sister. I felt for him and couldn't imagine having to give patients such hard news. Pulling his chair around to our side of the desk, he took her hands and looked at her. I'd known what was coming since we walked in, but I willed myself to remain still. Hell, maybe I was wrong. But that was doubtful. I had an unfortunate instinct about trouble.

"Maggie, this cancer is aggressive and has metastasized. We've not been able to slow it at all. At this point our best—our only— recourse is to remove your right breast. And we need to do it soon. There are some excellent reconstructive surgeons here in Columbia or down in Charleston. I'm so sorry." He'd spit it out all in one breath, like he was ripping a bandage off. Dr. Dupree squeezed Maggie's hands and swallowed.

She'd maintained eye contact with him, while he was speaking, but looked at me soon as he'd said his piece. Her face showed nothing. I knew she was waiting for my reaction. She wanted to see if her big brother would show defeat with a shift of the eyes or a quiver of the mouth. I stared into my sister's eyes and tried to convey a confidence I didn't know how to feel. I told her, "Honey, I can't begin to imagine myself in your place, but you are not your body. You are a beautiful, intelligent, amazing woman. Let's get you well, then we'll deal with the after." Even to my own ears, I sounded like a poor substitute for confidence. I sounded empty.

Maggie took a deep breath, looked at her doctor, and nodded.

When I parked my truck, Mama was returning from the chicken yard with her egg basket. She waved and I walked out to meet her. I took the basket, and she took my arm as we headed toward her house. We walked without talking, but she kept looking up to my face every few steps, as if she was waiting for me to speak. I hated having to give her troublesome news about her children. Nevertheless, by an arbitrary function of birth order, it fell to me to talk to my mother about her daughters.

As I put the eggs away in the refrigerator, Mama sat at her kitchen table, her hands folded around a teacup. She took a sip, watching me. Her eyes followed me as I put away the basket and washed my hands at the big farm sink, then dried them on a dish towel. Her patience crumpled like a beer can under a boot.

"You going to fidget about all morning or are you going to tell me?" It had always been difficult for me to keep anything from my mother. As a boy, whenever I'd done something wrong or had something to hide, I'd avoid her for as long as possible. I figured if I could duck her for a day or two, I had a chance to get away with my secret. But if she saw me soon after, it was like I had a sign spelling out whatever I'd been up to. And my goose was as good as cooked. Now, she knew something was wrong.

"I need to talk to you about Maggie and Audrey, Mama."

I told her about Maggie's upcoming mastectomy and Audrey's addiction and resulting problems. As I spoke, Mama was quiet, studying my face as if she'd never truly seen it before. She was still capable of surprising me. Instead of weeping or losing her calm, she smiled at me and reached for my hand, as if to transfer her strength to me. "You're so much like your daddy," she said.

I wasn't altogether sure how I felt about that. "Mama, why are you smiling? Didn't you hear what I told you?"

"Son, I know you're taking care of your sisters as well as anybody could. Maggie will come through this because she's a fighter, but she draws courage from you. Don't forget that. She's always looked up to you, always been so proud of you. And I'm proud of you too, the way you take care of our family." Her echoing Dad's words sent a painful jolt through my insides.

"And Audrey?" I asked. "Do you think she'll be all right?"

"I think that depends on Audrey. If she makes up her mind to focus on Izzy instead of her own selfishness, she'll beat that addiction. She's a Parker and she has the tools within her. All we can do is pray for her and be there if she needs us. But honestly, I don't know what to do about that drug dealer person. Is your sister in any danger? How much do they owe him?" She looked up at me. "Is Izzy in danger, son?"

"You help support Audrey, Mama. Don't worry about the dealer or the money. It's not much, I'm sure. Maybe a few hundred. That's the easy part. And don't fret over Audrey or Izzy. Everything is under control. Bill and I will take care of this guy." But as I held Mama's hand, trying to give her encouragement, I wondered why I'd just lied to her.

Picking up her teacup, she brought it close to her lips and then set it back in the saucer without drinking. "You boys be careful. You hear me, Jack? Take care of this but don't do anything that might reap harm for you or this family. I've lost a husband, but I won't lose any of my children or grandchildren. I won't have that. I won't."

"Yes, ma'am. I'll handle it."

The morning was crisp and cold. A weak sun failed to breach the hazy cloud cover. I stood below the tree house, trying to rid my mind of the problems that had plagued my family lately. I needed a few hours' relief, so I walked to the workshop and began to carve the last trim pieces needed for the corners, fascia, and windows. Soon I was engrossed in my task, whistling a half-remembered tune as my fingers caressed a trumpet-shaped honeysuckle blossom so real I could smell its syrupy nectar. I understood why my father had loved working with wood. Each board held a singular beauty, as unique as a fingerprint. The grain, which gave the wood its visual appeal, also provided its great strength and flexibility. The wood Dad had hand-picked was warm to the touch, unlike stone or tile or metal. It pulsed with life.

As a boy, I'd always enjoyed watching my father whittle a pine scrap on the porch after supper, a habit he'd maintained until his death. The floor around his rocker would be littered with fragrant shavings, big bold curls, and delicate little slivers. I'd sit with my back against the railing, watching and wishing I could become one of the magical figures he carved. I wished I could be someone other than myself, someone who could tell his father what lay upon his heart. Instead, I asked him questions about whittling—safe questions.

When I would ask how he knew what to carve, he would say the wood became what it needed to be. Wood has a soul, a remnant of the living creature it once was, he would tell me. He said if the wood wanted to be a dog or fish or little bearded man, then that's what it would be and couldn't be changed. I don't think he believed half of the bullshit he told me, but I believed anything he said to me when I was a boy.

A born storyteller, his manner was quiet and sincere, and we kids listened with spellbound attention. Dad would take my sisters, or even Bill, onto his lap and let them hold the pine stock. He would ask them what they reckoned the wood wanted to become, listening to their reasonings, his head tilted, nodding. He'd never permitted me that small privilege after I reached eight or nine—maybe because I was the first-born, too old for such foolish games. But it only served to deepen the feeling that he was building a wall between us, almost as if he was afraid of me, fearful of the physical contact. Soon after, I stopped believing or even listening to his stories.

I'd tried to fill the tree house carvings with the same life my father had breathed into his little whittled figures. I skimmed my thumb over the flowers and vines, checking for rough patches in need of a stroke with a chisel or gentle pass with fine sandpaper. Satisfied and somewhat more tranquil, I put away the tools and straightened the workshop. My peaceful feeling lasted just long enough for me to step out into the morning's cool. I heard a loud ruckus coming from the chicken yard.

Jogging round the barn, I saw a gray fox trotting off toward the woods, glancing back over his shoulder at me as he disappeared into the shadows. I didn't believe he'd grabbed a hen, but I counted them to be sure. Most of the hens, and all of the chicks, were not out in the yard, having chosen the coop's safety instead. One hen had remained outside with Hemingway. He strutted and looked about, confident and alert. He appeared to have bested the fox, but I was troubled such a shy creature as a gray would've approached in daylight. He'd been either crazed with hunger or rabid. Living so close to the woods, rabies was a constant concern when there were kids or dogs about.

I walked round the chicken yard and found where the fox had tried to dig under and nose through the fence. Squatting down, I noticed several small drops on the dirt inside the fence, a dark red, almost black. Looked like old fox had his nose thumped by Hemingway. He'd not soon forget that lesson. The birds had calmed considerably, and satisfied they were safe, I left Hemingway in charge. God's truth, he hadn't needed any help from me to protect his family.

After supper that evening, the girls went off to their rooms. Sara and I sat in the family room watching the news. I was beginning to nod off when she said something to me.

"Sorry. What's that?"

"I asked about your talk with Lizzie. How did it go?"

"Better than I expected. She was optimistic about Maggie and practical about Audrey. She knows it's up to Audrey to fight her addiction. But I think she's anxious about that dealer. Kind of hard to believe he's Mary's ex-boyfriend too."

Sara worried her bottom lip with a finger, a nervous habit she'd had as long as I'd known her, both sweet and troubling. Not much made my wife nervous. "What if this guy won't leave Audrey and Brad alone? He might try to hurt Izzy to get to them. People get crazy about money and drugs. And don't forget—you're not his favorite person either."

"I wouldn't fret about the money; it's not all that much. Izzy will be with us while Audrey and Brad are in rehab, and we won't let anything happen to her." I took a deep breath. "Bill and I are going to put an end to this. We're going to speak to this guy. Straighten it all out. He won't bother us again. All right?"

"What are you guys up to? Please don't do something that could come back to hurt you, Jack." She was likely thinking of the night I'd attacked Mary's ex-boyfriend—and my past. Hell, I didn't blame her for being uneasy about what I might do.

"We're just going to have a conversation with the man. I want to make sure he understands the situation. I'm cutting off their line of credit with him."

Sara looked uncertain but didn't ask any further questions. That was good because I'd already lied about the money to both her and Mama and I didn't know why. She was concerned I might hurt that man beyond a bloody nose, or he might hurt me. So not telling her my plan was just an extension to the original lie. That's how I convinced myself I was doing the right thing.

According to Brad, Mark Dunbar conducted his business out of a shit-stained bar a few miles south of Columbia. Mark had never met my brother, so Bill had arranged a face-to-face with him. He'd said he might want to become a regular customer if they could come to terms. Apparently, my brother had a need for prescription pills bordering on lust.

Dunbar sat in a booth, facing away from the door. He must've felt at ease, because he was more interested in his phone than who might walk into the bar behind him. I'd arrived long before him and sat at the bar, behind Dunbar and to his right. I'd nursed a longneck for three quarters of an hour and ordered another as Dunbar had arrived. The bartender gave me a belligerent stare. I slid him a twenty as an apology for taking up a stool. "Don't need any change." Without acknowledging me, he slid the money into his pocket.

Bill walked in at ten o'clock. He came within a few feet of me and asked the bartender if Mark Dunbar was around. Mr. Friendly nodded toward Dunbar's booth. Bill walked over and sat across the table from him. They made small talk for a minute or two, and then I walked over and slid in beside Bill before they were done with their how-are-yous. Dunbar was pissed off at being disturbed while conducting business, and then he recognized me. He looked from me to Bill and then back to me.

"What the fuck is this?" Dunbar was as indignant as a drug-pushing piece of shit could manage. "You're the guy that jumped me. Who is this asshole?" he asked, indicating Bill. "Look, I haven't been near Mary. Ask her if you don't believe me. Not that it's any of your business."

"This is my brother, Bill. We're not here about Mary. You've been selling drugs to our sister and her husband, Brad. A lot of shit. We're here to tell you to stop."

He grinned and started to laugh—a loud braying—drawing curious stares from the barflies. "So you two are the cavalry here to save Sis? You think you can come in here and scare me? Just because you sucker punched me before doesn't mean you're a big shit. There's two of you. Big fucking deal. I'm surrounded by friends right now." He looked around the bar and back at me. His smirk was more than Bill could take.

"If you sell drugs to my sister again, I'll wire your feet to a couple of cinder blocks and drop you in a hole in Otter Flats," Bill said. "Your head will be right below the surface, and you'll drown inches away from air. I'll sit in my boat and watch you die, you piece of shit. You might not be found in that maze for weeks or months. Reckon which will get him first, Jack? Turtles or gators?"

Dunbar still smiled but had stopped braying. "How terrifying. Normally I'd just ignore you, but I like Brad. So I'll tell you boys what I'm willing to do. If he doesn't come to me again, I won't sell anything to him. If he does want my product and comes to me, well I don't want to discriminate against anyone. And clients have to assume any risk themselves. Caveat emptor, right boys? Oh, and there is the matter of a small sum owed to me by your brother-in-law and sister." He laughed. "I guess I'll need to contact Brad or her after all for collection purposes. Of course, if he's short on cash, maybe I can work out a trade with Audrey." His smile widened and I could feel Bill rising from his seat to put the fear of God into Dunbar—in front of forty witnesses.

I placed a hand on his arm. "Let's go, Bill. We're not going to get anything done here." We'd gain little by trading insults with Dunbar. We needed to approach the problem from another angle. I stood to go and Bill followed.

"You fellows have a nice evening, now. Give my love to Mary and your sister. She's got a real sweet tooth for my product. Looking forward to seeing her real soon." Dunbar's laugh bounced round my head until the closing barroom door sucked the foul sound from the air.

In the truck, I said to my brother, "'Wire your feet to a couple of cinder blocks?' Are we the mafia now?" I grinned at Bill and he chuckled. We could either laugh about it or go back in there and start a fight we couldn't possibly win. I'd done that far too often when I was younger.

"I thought it sounded good at the time. Too much?"

"Naw. Actually, it sounded pretty good. Let's hope he was only crowing for his friends and this is the end of it all." I wanted it to be over so we could concentrate on helping Audrey, but I wondered if we'd just put a target on her back instead. Dunbar reeked of evil, and I could see why Mary had wanted so desperately to get away. Dad must've heard the despair in her voice that day she'd called Carolina House. Why else would he have driven out to pick her up and stayed with her until she felt safe? My gut told me Dunbar was far more dangerous than I'd first believed and that he was capable of anything. No way in hell was that going to be our last encounter.

"What about the money, Jack?"

"Don't worry about it. I'm sure they paid him most of it with the money Dad left. I don't think they owed much more." I didn't look in Bill's eyes as I told the familiar lie again. But I figured it better to keep him in the dark to the plan I'd begun to form.

"Beer?" Bill asked. His thoughts had clearly taken a better path than mine. He had the enviable ability to go from fists and threats to mellow and beer in the twitch of a doe's tail. He didn't fret and ruminate over every detail of everything like me. He'd always been able to forgive and forget, to take life as it came.

I'd never acquired that certain virtue.

"We just left a bar. Why didn't you have a beer in there?"

"I didn't especially care for the company."

"Well, maybe one."

CHAPTER ELEVEN

My mother, much like my father since his passing, had the ability to surprise me time and again. She wasn't in her house or on her porch when I stopped by for a visit. I found her in the tree house, sitting on the deck with her back against the east wall. Her eyes were closed and she was smiling. She looked so peaceful. With all we'd been through lately, I was tempted to leave her to her stillness. As I started to turn away, she opened her eyes and looked down at me.

"Jack, what a nice surprise. I'm enjoying the sunshine. Come join me."

I climbed up wondering why my sixty-year-old mother was sitting in a tree. I walked out onto the deck and sat against the wall beside her. "Everything all right, Mama? I didn't expect to find you up here."

"I wanted to see all this fine work you've done that my grand-children keep going on about." She looked over at me. "Son, it's beautiful. You're doing such a remarkable job."

"Thank you. But you should've waited until I could help you climb up here. What if you'd fallen?"

"Nonsense. I'm not helpless." Mama drew in a deep breath

and said, "I wanted to be alone up here for a bit. I feel so close to Tom here. I know it sounds maudlin, but I don't care. I miss him. Just wanted to think about him working on something he felt was important."

"It's not maudlin. I know you miss him. We all do—in our own ways."

She ignored my comment and smiled to herself, her gaze on Dad's workshop in the distance. "I think you've built it just as your daddy would have. You two were always so much alike. You certainly inherited his talent with tools and wood." She turned toward me and brushed her fingers across the door frame carvings.

I'd never thought of myself as anything like my father. "Mama, I think Dad and I were about as opposite as a father and son could be."

Something flickered across her face. I figured maybe I'd made her sad, but then her smile returned, and she said, "You're as stubborn as he ever was. There's no denying that."

"I thought I got my stubbornness from you, Mama." And I smiled back.

With Audrey and Brad in rehab and Izzy at my house, I was able to focus on Maggie. Daylight was still tucked away when I picked her up from Mama's house, where she'd slept the night before. But I'd have been surprised if she'd slept at all. As we drove to the hospital in Columbia, she was quiet, staring out at the dark. "Want to listen to some music?" I asked, thinking something soft might soothe her nerves and mine.

"No thanks. I like the quiet." She turned to look at me. "Thank you for doing this, Jack." Bill, Lauren, and Mama had wanted to be with Maggie too, but she'd insisted she would be too frazzled with everyone about. She'd asked me to accompany her and I was grateful. As we approached the hospital, I reached for her hand and gave it a squeeze. Glancing at her face, I saw both the strong woman she'd become and the little girl with the scraped knee, stone faced and brave as her brother bandaged her wound. I'd been proud of the girl. I was in awe of the woman.

As we waited for her to be called back and prepared for surgery, Maggie smiled at me, but her smile was sad and her words tore me to pieces. "Jack, you and Daddy and Bill are the only men who have never let me down. Who's going to want me now?"

I was angry we lived in such a world where she would think that. "Maggie, I know you aren't that cynical. There are good men out there. Some lucky man will find you and treat you like a queen. This surgery doesn't change a damn thing." My own words sounded hollow to me, lacking conviction. I had no possible way of understanding what she was feeling. How then could I say anything that would help her?

"I don't want to be treated like a queen. I just want to be treated like a human."

"Honey, I didn't mean to suggest you needed a man to take care of you. I'm sorry if I sounded patronizing." My talent for fucking up a conversation once again left me needing a pardon.

"I know what you meant, and I appreciate the respect you have for women. I just needed to be selfish for a moment." She touched my hand. "It's enough that you're here, Jack." She smiled again, and that time, it found her eyes.

While Maggie was in recovery, her doctor told me the surgery had gone well and he believed they'd removed all the malignant tissue. He would have to monitor her and test and biopsy her and what-not, but she should be able to begin reconstructive surgery soon. She had, at first, not wanted to have the restorative surgery. Over the previous week she changed her mind at least a half dozen times. I'd offered her my support but no advice, one side or the other.

I was given instructions for Maggie's home care and follow-up office visits. She'd need to stay in the hospital a couple nights. Once she was released, I'd drive her to her checkups until she got sick of me, which at some point she was likely to do. Although filled with self-doubt and uncertainty at times, Maggie had always been independent. Maybe, like me, she figured she had to be self-reliant. At least she'd agreed to stay with Mama while she recovered. She'd only conceded that to us after Lauren and I had begged and badgered her. I think she was relieved to be under Mama's care for a while, and our mother was thrilled to look after her baby girl.

Bill and I took turns stopping by Mama's to check on Maggie. We were there each morning and evening. After a few days, she told us to please not come by so often. "Once every day or two is fine, Jack. I appreciate you both, but I need time alone, and you guys need to be with your families."

"You are my family, little squirrel," I said.

She gave me a look reserved for stray dogs and brothers of dubious intelligence. I'd seen her give Bill the look often enough. "You know what I mean, Jack. Go take your girls out to a nice supper and movie. Be a husband and dad for a while. It's all right to take a break from being a big brother every now and again."

I understood what Maggie was telling me but couldn't shake the need to watch over her. I thought if I took my eyes off her for more than a heartbeat, she'd disappear. It didn't make sense, but a lot didn't make sense to me anymore. I was getting used to the confusion, and that scared me worse than anything.

Sara and our girls had supper plans with Izzy, Kathy, and Tara. Afterward they'd all catch a late movie and wouldn't be home until well after midnight. That left me with time to kill and a bad idea niggling away at the edge of my brain.

I'd always believed a reminder could help to reinforce a desired behavior. That's why I was sitting in my truck, parked in the last row of the gravel lot outside Mark Dunbar's favorite bar—one more pickup in a sea of trucks. With my family occupied, I had the time to wait him out. But my patience wasn't tested; Dunbar drove up to the bar towing a flat-bottom boat at five after ten. He circled the building and parked on the side, his truck facing the main lot. All I could see inside his truck's cab was shadow and dark. I didn't even know for sure it was him until he stepped out into the light. He strutted into the bar, and I waited ten minutes.

Just as I was getting ready to head in after him, he swaggered right back out. He jumped in his truck and sprayed dust and gravel as he left the lot and screeched onto the blacktop. I followed as he weaved and swerved his way to I-26 and headed toward Charleston. Dunbar reached speeds in excess of a hundred a half dozen times, his boat and trailer swaying back and forth like a pine tree in a spring storm. I considered leaving off the chase as an alternative to getting locked up for breaking the sound barrier.

As we approached Highway 601, I'd about decided to take a left and drive straight through St. Matthews to home. I could be there in forty-five minutes, sitting on my porch with a beer. But Dunbar took the same exit and turned right onto 601, heading toward Orangeburg. I continued to follow him as he took back roads, driving deep into Orangeburg's rural outskirts, until the distance between driveways was measured in miles and even 911 would need directions. Trailing him undetected, with but the two of us on the road, presented obvious difficulties, so I drove with my lights off. The moon threw enough shine for me to keep left of the white line, and I was far enough behind Dunbar so he'd not notice.

After a quarter hour, he slowed and turned right onto a dirt and gravel road. His rig was immediately swallowed by the woods. As I rolled by, I could see he'd parked his truck in a clearing about a hundred yards through the trees. I drove another sixty yards up the blacktop and parked out of sight on a fire break. Stepping from my truck and not knowing if there were houses about, I listened for voices or other human clamorings, a radio, drunken laughter. All was quiet aside from the breeze in the treetops.

Another pair of headlights turned down the way Dunbar had

come. I slow-trotted back to the dirt road and made my way toward the clearing, keeping to the edge of the woods and careful to avoid the gravel's crunch or the moonlight's reach. Night blinded by their own headlights, they weren't likely to see me anyway.

I'd stumbled onto a drug deal. From twenty yards away, I saw Dunbar speaking to a couple of rich, young assholes in button-downs, jeans, and boots that'd never seen a stirrup or a plowed field. After talking briefly, they exchanged what I assumed was trust fund money for pills, pot, or something of a more volatile nature. Made little difference to me. I wasn't there to save those knot-heads from that snake. It was their own damn fault if they were too fucking stupid to mind its tail rattling. I'd done plenty of dumb shit at that age and had to learn my own hard lessons. Meeting a prick like Dunbar out there in the middle of nowhere told me those boys were either big on balls or shy on smarts.

I was concerned Dunbar might leave the clearing first, but the boys got in their daddy's Escalade and hauled ass. Dunbar was talking on his phone before their tires hit the blacktop, so he didn't hear me walk up behind him. As he ended the call and slid the phone into his pocket, I said, "Beautiful night for a drug deal."

He whirled round to face me. The surprise and fear were clear on his face, but to his credit, they were gone just as fast. "You. What the fuck is this? Why you following me? You a faggot?" He tried to take control with his insulting, rapid-fire questions. And he was stalling for time, thinking about reaching for the pistol tucked away at the small of his back, the grip pointed the wrong way—gangster bullshit. The gun was easy to spot there but hard to draw with any speed.

I landed a right jab below his left eye. Off balance, he spun to the ground, catching himself with his outstretched arms. I grabbed the pistol from his belt. He looked around at me and rose to his feet. Eyes on the gun pointed in his direction, he said, "That's the second time you've sucker punched me. That one is going to cost you some blood." That struck me as a funny thing to say to a man pointing a gun at you, but I gave him points for the boldness of it.

SCOTT SHARPE

I threw the pistol ten feet away and popped him again before it hit the ground. "I hope I have your undivided attention now, Mark. I don't think you understood the message my brother and I tried to deliver to you before."

He grinned at me like the devil was tickling his funny bone and said, "Don't say I didn't warn you, dickhead." He took a step back, and I heard a twig snap behind me before pain and blackness swallowed me whole.

I came to in the bottom of what I figured was Dunbar's boat, still trailered and headed down the blacktop to God knew where. I had no clue how long I'd been out. Something was lodged against my ribs, sending me a jab of pain every time the son of a bitch hit a pothole. Between his taillights and the moon, I could see I was tied at the wrists with anchor rope or something of the kind. My ankles were bound to each other and to a couple eight-by-sixteen cinder blocks. Didn't take a genius to figure out what these boys had planned for me.

As the fog lifted from my brain, I realized two things: I had a bastard of a headache from where I'd been clocked, and if I didn't find a way to get loose before we got to wherever we were headed, I'd be swimming with my boots on.

In the dim light, I saw nothing useful directly in front of me, and I could only roll partway onto my back due to the cinder block situation. When I tried to roll, whatever had been sticking in my ribs came free. I looked down and found a rusty wooden-handled brush saw, likely used to trim overhanging limbs and whatnot. I managed to wedge it against a welded seam and started sawing at my ropes. My hands came loose as we turned off blacktop onto dirt. I grabbed the saw and went to work on the rope binding my feet.

Before I cut through, we slid to a stop, and I heard two truck doors open and slam shut. Footsteps crunched gravel on their way back to the boat. I straightened up and crossed my wrists like I was

106

still bound. When Dunbar walked up to the port side and looked in on me, I tried to look like I was out-of-my-mind scared.

Dunbar's face was taillight-stained red. Meanness seeped from his pores like sweat, foul and slick. He said, "I hope you're comfortable. We're going to take us a short ride up to Otter Flats. You've got yourself a date with the turtles and gators, Mr. Jack Parker." He looked up and said to the man leaning on the starboard gunnel, "Unclip the winch cable and grab the rods and gear from the truck. We might as well get in a little fishing tonight."

I reached above my head, grabbed the bench seat for leverage, and swung my legs up and forward with everything I could muster. Fifty pounds of concrete caught him square in the face. He went down, and the blocks' momentum and weight carried me right on over the side, smacking my head first on the gunnel then the ground. The ropes broke free from my ankles, and I rolled over onto my back, trying to get my bearings and trying to see whereabout asshole number two was.

He stepped over the trailer tongue while raising a four-foot gaff. He took two steps and brought it down hard toward my head. I deflected it with my arm enough so it missed my eye but grazed my left cheek. A pain that was both sharp and dull at the same time told me the gaff's sharp hook was imbedded in my shoulder at least a couple inches. Grabbing the gaff near the hook, I kicked asshole two in the knee cap and felt it give. He let go of the gaff and went down with a scream. And I plucked the damn hook from my shoulder without passing out, which was when I started to think I might just leave there alive.

Struggling to my knees and then my feet, I looked about for asshole one. Dunbar was lying on his back, with blood pouring from his nose where the concrete had hit him square. He was moaning and cussing. Asshole two was curled up holding his knee, and unless I missed my guess, he'd never walk proper again. I stepped over to him and said, "If you have a need to blame anybody for that knee—besides your own self—blame your buddy over there." I hit him with the gaff's less dangerous end, like I was swinging for the fence, and watched his eyes roll back in his ugly head.

Fresh pain exploded where the gaff had stuck me. I turned to my left, which was exactly the wrong way to turn, as a boat paddle caught my jaw. The paddle broke and Dunbar was left holding a foot of useless wood. I dropped the gaff and lit into him with every damn ounce of strength I had left. When I was done, he was sitting in the dirt with his back against an oversized truck tire, sucking air. I said, "You weren't listening, Mark. My brother said wire, not rope. You should've paid attention." I picked up the gaff and hit another homer.

For the second time that night, I took Dunbar's pistol, a cheap, throwaway chrome .45. It had fallen under the boat when the cinder blocks had hit him in the face. I ejected the magazine and thumbed out a cartridge: +P hollow points, nasty bullets designed for maximum flesh ruination. I'd been lucky he'd lost it, or I'd have taken a bullet to the head instead of a paddle blade. I thought to toss the gun in the river, but reloaded it instead and tossed it onto the truck seat.

Then I turned to deal with the men who'd meant to drown me. Less than gentle, I hossed them both into the boat and tossed a fat wad of cash onto the floor next to Dunbar. I cut the fuel line, removed the straps, and unclipped the winch hook. Backing the boat down the ramp until the skids were wet, I braked hard, sliding the boat off the trailer. The current tugged the flat bottom from the shore and sent assholes one and two floating down the river. Hell, I didn't even know which river it was at the time. Dunbar's comment about Otter Flats made me think it was the Santee, below the confluence. I wondered how far they'd float before they got stuck in a brush pile. Sparkleberry Swamp? The lower end of Lake Marion? The only certainty was that they'd be in at least as much pain as me when they woke. No doubt they'd be pissed, but maybe old Mark would retire from dealing poison for a time—at least to my sister.

I sat in Dunbar's truck at the dry end of the ramp waiting for my breathing to settle. My head throbbed where it had bounced around like a pinball in the boat's bilge, and my left arm had gone numb below the spot where the gaff's hook had skewered it. That ragged hole was still percolating blood, so I wrapped my T-shirt around it to stem the flow as best I could.

I dropped the trailer and followed the dirt road until I found blacktop. Guessing that right was north—and home—I drove until a South Carolina 267 sign winked headlights back at me. Regaining my bearings, I hit 601 and turned southwest, away from home, to collect my truck. I left Dunbar's in a ditch, lights still on, so it would be sure to be dead when he found it.

When I got home around three, Sara was sitting in the kitchen drinking coffee. She stood and came to me. Examining my head, my shoulder, and my impressive collection of scrapes and bruises, she asked, "Is all this blood yours?"

Truth was I couldn't tell where my blood ended and theirs began. "Most, I reckon." I tried to gauge her disposition. "But not all of it."

She was quiet as she patched me up. I watched her in the mirror, but she was concentrating on her work. She wouldn't look up at me. My shoulder was the only place that needed stitching. The scratch on my face was shallow and already scabbing. She tied the last knot and traced her finger along an old scar on my back. Finally meeting my eyes, she said, "I'm not going through this again, Jack. Tell me now if this is going to keep happening. We talked about this when Wren was born. I don't want my girls raised around this." She shook her head as she packed away her needle and thread. "You promised me."

"I didn't mean for this to happen. I wanted to talk to him again and threaten him into staying away from Audrey and Mary."

She put the first aid kit beneath the vanity sink, slammed the door shut, and turned with eyes blazing. "And what's next? Dunbar sits waiting for you at a job site and puts a bullet in you? Or what if he comes here or to the girls' school? Are we going to have to look over our shoulders from now on?"

"And you think by letting him run roughshod over Audrey and Brad that he'll be content killing them slowly? This man is dangerous, and the law won't do shit. So I'm trying to protect this family the best way I know."

She stepped up and put her hands on my chest. "You better know what you're doing, Jack. You think about those two little girls sleeping down the hall." She dropped her hands to her sides as if she was exhausted, as if she'd given up. "I'm going to bed."

I watched her walk away. She was rightfully angry, but I'd known she would be. Before our girls came along, she'd patched me up when she could, driven me to the hospital when she couldn't. She'd tolerated my self-destruction, knowing I was just blowing off steam. But she'd never understood my tendencies. Sara thought the world could be tamed with kindness and love—one of the reasons I'd fallen for her. But she'd not seen the evil I'd seen. She'd not looked into his eyes nor smelled the vile, sadistic bastard up close like I had. I knew I'd done what needed doing.

Izzy was the first downstairs the next morning. I was cooking bacon and mixing up pancake batter. She yawned and smiled at me. Sitting at the kitchen table, she put her head down on her arms.

"Still sleepy, honey?" I asked. "We're pretty relaxed around here. Wren and Lily usually sleep late on Saturdays, unless they have plans."

"I couldn't sleep, so I thought I'd come downstairs," she said. "I was afraid I might wake somebody." She cocked her head, looking up at me. "What happened to your face?"

"Oh, I had a little accident. I'm fine. And you'd have to blow a bugle to wake those three. You hungry? I'm fixing chocolate chip pancakes."

"Not right now." She hugged herself, as if she was chilled.

"You worried about your mama and daddy?

"Yes, sir." She looked as if she might cry. "What's going to happen to them? Are they in trouble?"

"They're not in trouble. They're doing a good thing. You remember when your mama talked to you about the problem she and your daddy have with those pain medications? Well, they're in a place sort of like a hospital. The people there are helping them." Setting the bacon pan on a trivet, I walked over to sit beside my niece. "When they finish there, your mama and daddy will be so much happier. You'll be surprised how they've changed." I hoped I was telling her the truth.

"It's kind of scary." She tried a little smile.

"I know, honey. It's okay to be afraid. Everyone, even adults, get scared sometimes."

"Do you ever get scared?"

"I sure do."

"I think my mama has been scared for a long time."

"I think you're right." I stood and kissed the top of her head and returned to the bacon. "If there's anything we can do to make you feel more at home, you tell us. This is your home, Izzy. Even when your mama and daddy are better and you're back in your own room, this is still your home too. It always will be."

She stood and hugged me. "I'm hungry now." Always a good sign.

CHAPTER TWELVE

Audrey was scheduled for release from rehab. Brad would need to stay on another week or two, minimum. Lauren, Maggie, Bill, and I waited for our sister in the small lounge used for such private purposes. She walked in and began to cry as she ran toward Maggie. They hugged and whispered to one another as the rest of us stood back. Our two wounded sisters communicated in a language I wasn't sure I had the emotional means to understand. Lauren did and joined them. Glancing at my brother, I knew he was humbled by the compassion and respect our sisters shared for one another. Only when Audrey looked over at us and smiled, did we join them.

Audrey's first concern was Izzy. "How's my baby girl, Jack?" Her gaze was steady and her hands were quiet.

"Izzy is fine. And she sure misses you and her daddy." I hugged her and caught her up on family news. She knew Maggie had been scheduled for surgery, but until seeing her little sister, she'd had no idea of the outcome. We had an understanding: should anything happen to Izzy or Maggie, she'd have been notified. Still, the look of relief on her face, upon seeing a smiling, healthy sister, put a lot of my own shit into perspective.

Audrey was anxious to see her girl, so I drove her straight to my house, and my siblings followed. Mama was there and hugged her first daughter for a long minute then held her face in both hands. "Let me get a good look. Oh, just wonderful, honey. I'm so proud of you."

When Izzy walked into the room, the tears began to rain in earnest. To watch those crying, laughing, hugging women, a body would need to be thick as mud not to recognize their unbreakable bond. I turned away from them to find my brother standing in the kitchen doorway, arms folded.

"I hope to hell we ain't expected to slobber and cry all over Brad when he gets sprung," Bill said.

"Don't believe we're obliged to, no."

"That's a relief. Got anything to eat?"

I sighed and pointed to the refrigerator.

Sara and I spent the morning at Carolina House. She and Cassie had budgeting to accomplish, and I was there to make a few repairs to the house. I also had a few books for Mary. I found her in the library, a hand on her rounding belly, reading aloud a children's book about a family of bears. "Morning, Mary. How are you?"

She looked up from her book and blushed, but her smile could've lit the world. "Good morning, Jack. I'm fine, thanks." The change in Mary over the last few weeks was remarkable. She seemed to have made the decision to put her troubles out of her mind or at least hide them from sight. "I was reading to the baby. Can't sing a lick, but my doctor said it's good to sing or read out loud or play music for babies, even before they're born." That was more than I'd ever heard her say in a single breath.

"It's true. Sara read to our girls every day before and after they were born. Now, they both love to read." I sat down on the sofa beside her. "I brought a few books for you." Setting the books down on the coffee table, I grabbed the first one. "There are a couple books of poetry, a few classics and this one here." I handed her an old, well-thumbed copy of Romeo and Juliet. "I've had this one forever, and I've read it at least a half-dozen times."

Mary held the book and traced the leather cover with a gentle finger. She lifted the book to her nose and breathed in the sweet mustiness. "Thank you, Jack, but I can't take this. You might want one of your girls to have it someday. It's far too valuable to give away."

"Nonsense," I said. "You would do me a great favor by accepting it; Sara says our bookshelves will collapse if we don't start culling. I have others for my girls. This one's for you." I rose to leave.

"Thank you again, Jack. Thank you for the books and all of this." She gestured around and blushed again, but not quite so deeply.

"You have my father to thank for all this, Mary. But you are welcome for the books. Don't be afraid to open and read that one. It won't fall apart." I touched her hand and left to attend my chores. I knew only she could steer her own course, and my job was to nudge her where and when I had the chance.

Brad was released two days before Thanksgiving. The Parkers were cautiously excited the whole family would be together for our first Thanksgiving since my father's death. We gathered at Mama's with muted thankfulness, as if afraid that true joy might bring our old friend trouble out to play.

A Parker tradition was for each family to invite at least one non-family member to join our dinner. There were so many people with no place to go on Thanksgiving. Dad had started it years before when he'd brought old Asa Gibson. Asa was newly widowed and his kids were grown and gone, too busy with their own lives to visit their daddy. He cried through the turkey and stuffing, but by the time the pie was cut, he was smiling. What I remember most was how Mama looked at my father. He'd not told her he was bringing a guest, and by all rights, she could've been mad as hell. But she'd gazed at my father throughout the meal with nothing less than unfiltered love and respect. I didn't truly understand it all until years later.

Everybody was finishing last-minute dishes, setting tables, or sitting around loafing and talking. Maggie, normally an early bird, was absent. I asked my siblings if they'd heard from her. Nobody had spoken to her all day. She hadn't answered her phone or responded to my texts. As I was about to grab Bill and head out to look for her, she walked in through the mud room.

Her Thanksgiving guest was a man close to her age. He was handsome and fit in a way that made other men stand a little straighter and puff out their chests. He stood close to Maggie, smiling, while she introduced him to family and friends. As the Parker clan wondered about the relationship status of this man and our little sister, Lauren's five-year-old, John, asked, "Is he your boyfriend, Maggie?" The resulting silence was broken by Maggie's laughter, rich and sweet.

She looked at her friend, Mike, and then back at John. "Yes, John, Mike is my boyfriend." Poor man was then engulfed by Parkers, all talking at once.

I heard Wren say to Lily, "He's a hottie." Her wide smile was undiminished by my stern disapproving frown.

As my mother and siblings surrounded Mike and peppered him with their questions, Maggie caught my eye and walked over to me. She gave me a little hug, and I put my arm over her shoulder and kissed the top of her head. She'd wanted to surprise the family, but I'd known her secret for a few days. My concern at her absence was that she might've been in an accident, nothing more.

Maggie had gone back and forth on breast reconstruction since her mastectomy. But she'd made a final decision a couple weeks before. "I'm not having the surgery," she'd said. "I think I wanted to have it, in the first place, for someone else, to fit some unknown person's idea of how I should look. It doesn't matter to me. I'm going to let this unfold and see what happens. Make sense?"

"It does, little squirrel."

Two days later she'd met Mike at the hospital, where they both worked, and liked him right away. He was the new administrator—kind, funny, and smart. Mike must have felt the same toward her because he'd asked her out the next day. She'd turned him down, and he'd asked her a couple more times. She'd said no to each invite.

"Why won't you go out with me?" he'd asked.

Maggie had told Mike everything and then prepared herself for another rejection. She'd been wrong.

Mike had said, "We all have scars, Maggie. My attraction to you has nothing to do with any scars you may or may not have, physical or otherwise." He'd then told her if she could accept him, he would be honored.

"But there's nothing wrong with you."

"And there's nothing wrong with you either, Maggie," he'd responded.

In Mama's kitchen, with my sister smiling, I wanted to hug Mike.

"Everything going all right, little squirrel?"

Maggie put her face against my shoulder. "Right as rain, big brother."

"Then I have a question for you," I said.

"Fire away."

"Can the boy cook?"

"Just wait till you taste his sweet potato pie." She laughed again, and it filled my emptiness for a time.

The day after Thanksgiving was a balmy seventy-five degrees. You had to love South Carolina for the variation in weather, if nothing else. Zell Branham had agreed to meet me at Mama's to tighten one of the geldings' shoes. I'd promised Sara we could ride that weekend but had noticed the loose shoe a few days before. In answer to my plea for help, Zell arrived at noon, pulled his big wooden toolbox from his pickup, and joined me in the paddock. "I sure do appreciate you coming out on the day after Thanksgiving, Zell. It's the chestnut there. The shoe on his left foreleg has worked itself loose."

"Ain't no trouble at all. I been taking care of these horses ever since Mr. Tom brought them home. This here horse is seven, eight years old, and nobody has worked on his hooves 'cept me. Where are my manners? I sure am sorry about your daddy, Jack. I hope you'll give my commiserations to Ms. Lizzie." He patted the horse's neck and clipped a lead rope to his halter. "I'll make my apologies for not speaking to y'all at the graveside, but I was sort of broke up."

I suspected his colorful arrival had something to do with it, but I appreciated the sentiment. "Thank you for your kindness, Zell. I'll be sure to tell Mama you asked after her."

"Mr. Tom was a wonderful man. I sure do owe him a lot. And my wife—good Lord but she reckoned him a saint. Sue always baked a pie for me to bring your daddy, when she knew I was coming by to work on his horses. Near about broke her heart when she heard about his passing. Couldn't even brace herself up for to go to the funeral." Zell removed his hat and then replaced it. He handed the lead rope to me. "Hold him for me, if you would."

"Thank you again for your kind words." Truthfully, I didn't realize Dad knew him other than as the farrier who worked on his horses.

He lifted the gelding's leg and held it between his knees. "Oh, your daddy saved my marriage for certain," he said around a mouthful of hoof nails. "Few years back, Sue was working with me one morning. Mr. Tom saw that she had a shiner, which I'm sorry to say I'd give to her. He took me aside and talked to me and helped me to see the wrongness of what I done. Then he talked to Sue and told her if I ever hit her again, he'd help her find a safe place to stay and that she didn't have to put up with such foolishness from me or any other. I tell you, it put the fear of God in me, the thought of losing her. I ain't never raised a hand to her since that day, and I've truly tried to be a better man in every way. I thank the good Lord your daddy talked sense into me and my wife give me another chance." He dropped the chestnut's leg and led him in a circle, watching his gait. "Keep an eye on that shoe. If it gives you anymore trouble, holler at me."

"Thank you. I will." It was quite a story he'd told and might have surprised me before Dad had passed. But I found it in keeping with the Tom Parker I was learning to understand. "Zell, I'm glad he was able to help you and Sue. Seems like he tried to help a good share of folks, more than I'd ever credited. But I appreciate you telling me. What's the damage today?" I pulled out my wallet.

"No, sir. I ain't charged your daddy a penny since that day, and I never will charge for Tom Parker's horses."

"Kind of you, Zell, but I can't let you do that."

He looked at me through squinted eyes. "Course you can. You got no choice." Then that old boy smiled, touched his hat, and left me standing there holding the gelding.

I got home at dusk. Wren and Lily were spending the night with Mama, and Sara and I were going out for pizza and a movie. The first floor was dark. I could hear Sara moving around upstairs, so I grabbed a longneck from the refrigerator and headed up to shower and change. Our bedroom light was off, and Sara was in the bathroom, the door open. I heard the familiar sounds of my wife getting herself ready. I sat on the bed to relax and await my turn.

She paused in the open doorway. Her silhouette in profile made my sap rise. Time evaporated and we were back in high school, fumbling through the first attempt at love for us both. I remembered kissing Sara for the very first time. Ever since then, I'd always thought of her kisses like the last notes of a favorite song. You didn't ever want them to end.

"Did you hear me, Jack?" Sara asked.

"Sorry, sweet girl. What did you say?"

"I said if you'll hop in the shower, I'll scrub your back."

And just like that, our plans changed.

Supper was leftovers from the refrigerator and a bottle of wine we'd picked up at the Biltmore House Winery the year before. The movie was a DVD in the living room, which we didn't watch.

In the morning I fixed bacon, eggs, toast, and grits while Sara showered. She asked, "Did you cook enough?"

"Figured you might be hungry. I sure am." She laughed and picked up a piece of toast.

After breakfast, we drove over to the Knoll to exercise the horses. Sara rode the chestnut gelding with the mended shoe, and I saddled the palomino for myself. After watching the chestnut's gait for a few turns, I was satisfied the shoe was proper mended. We took several laps around the farm, mostly walking the horses and chatting. Occasionally, we picked up the pace to a canter or even a gallop.

Having grown up around them, I'd always loved horses. I could remember but one scary experience. When I was five, I'd been helping my father with barn chores one morning. A couple mares were eating together inside a double stall. I was riding on Dad's shoulders, and he sat me on one of the horses while he'd poured feed into their buckets, in adjacent corners. The horses had evidently been in the midst of a feud, because, as I lay with my legs and arms straddling one's withers and my head in her mane, the other one took a nip at mine. Her teeth caught me a quarter inch above my eye, and I'd bled like a stuck pig.

Dad had swept me off the mare's back and carried me to the house. By the time he'd walked that short distance, he was covered in my blood as well. He'd said, "That little cut sure made a lot of blood. But you were brave, Jack. I'm mighty proud of you." I don't remember much from that age. Fact is, that's one of the few clear memories I had before my eighth birthday. But I remembered that morning as if it had just happened. The stitches and tetanus shot were nothing; my father had been proud of me.

As Sara and I rubbed the horses down, I tried and failed to recall another time when Dad had said he was proud of me. Somehow he had difficulty saying anything substantial to me. He'd spoken less about matters of the heart and more of things practical, as I grew from his brave little boy into his rebellious teenager. I reckon my bullshit antics disappointed him and he'd held it in his heart, unable to get past it. Or maybe he had other trials and tribulations of which I wasn't privy. I imagined I'd never know, but still, I liked to think that, in his own way, he was at least a little bit proud of his oldest son.

CHAPTER THIRTEEN

I'd formed a friendship with Mary over the weeks since we'd met. She was blossoming before my eyes, full of curiosity and awe. Her shyness was fading, and her wit seemed to sharpen more each time I saw her. Our common love of books was an excuse for me to spend time with her. And I felt obliged to watch over her, as Dad had before his death.

I did have another reason for spending time with Mary. I was concerned Mark Dunbar might still attempt some spitefulness on her. I didn't have any real evidence of any intended actions on his part, only a niggling, itchy gut feeling. He'd not release his control over her without making more trouble. Of that I was sure. I believed he'd take her away if he had the chance. Of course, he might try to hurt her just to take revenge on me for setting his ass adrift on the Santee. He'd intended to drown me in Otter Flats, so good sense said I should be heedful in protecting Mary and her unborn baby.

Though her pregnancy wasn't considered high risk, we were careful to have a staff member near Mary at all times. Sara, Cassie, and I took turns escorting her to her prenatal checkups. I figured Mary was worried about what would happen after the baby was born. The thought of raising a child alone and having to provide for all that child's needs must've scared her something fierce. I also believed she was terrified Dunbar would find out about the baby and try to take it from her. I had a strong paternal urge to make sure she had a better than fair chance at a decent life. Her happiness required, in part, that she be protected, until that son of a bitch could no longer harm her. The police had been unable to find him, but I was sure they were too overworked to put much effort into pursuing a man they considered a low priority. So her safety fell to me.

I knew Mary would be a wonderful, dedicated mother. She'd been our guest at Thanksgiving, and I'd watched her with my daughters, nieces, and nephews. They'd led her to the unfinished tree house and told her the story of their grandfather's years of planning and design, which was taking on legend status in the Parker clan. When Lily told her I had taken Dad's plans and was building it as I thought her Papa would have, Mary had looked over at me and smiled. She'd asked the kids questions, and her interest in their answers had been genuine. But she was little more than a child herself.

Mary and I sat in the side garden at Carolina House. She stared into the trees as her forgotten tea cooled. I was relieved when she asked the question I figured she'd held in her heart since she'd found out she was pregnant. "Jack, what am I going to do when the baby is born? I've never supported myself or held a job. I try to make plans, but I always end up frustrated and hopeless. My baby deserves everything I never had, but for the life of me I can't figure out what to do."

"I know you've been worried about that for a while. I started to talk to you about it a few times but figured it best if you brought it up. I don't want to offer unwanted advice or overstep any boundaries."

Mary smiled. "You could never do that. Thanks to you and Tom, I realize all men are not horrible and violent. I know now there are

kind and gentle men out there. Thank you for showing me that."
Her saying that sent a shiver clear to my bones.

"What about the night I found Mark in your room? I wasn't
either kind or gentle then." I had trouble maintaining eye contact
with her. I'd dreaded that bit of conversation since that night.

"I know you were defending me, Jack. I appreciate that you cared
about me so much. That's not the kind of violence I mean. Mark's
violence was directed at me and was his way of controlling every
piece of my life. All he ever wanted was to hurt and humiliate me."
She lowered her eyes. "I had to ask permission to use the bathroom
if he was there. If he was in a particularly bad mood, he'd make me
wait a long time. Twice I peed myself. I think that was worse than
all the cuts and bruises—much worse." Her voice was a whisper as
she raised her eyes once more. "Then I found Carolina House and
Tom, and then the whole Parker family."

"Thank you for trusting me with that. I know it's hard to talk
about your life with him, and I'm glad you shared with me. As for
the Parkers, well, you were a blessing to Dad and you're a blessing
to Carolina House and to my family. Mama and the kids ask about
you all the time. And I have a few ideas about after the baby is born
if you're interested."

"I am interested. Tell me what you're thinking." She leaned forward, watching me.

As I told Mary my ideas, she began to smile and nod. She seemed
receptive, and that would go a long way toward the start of a new
life for her and the baby. I'd no doubt that with her intelligence and
persistence, Mary would do well at whatever she put her mind to.

Work on the tree house was moving along faster than I'd have
figured, thanks to Dad's detailed plans and copious notes. They
were specific down to the number of paint coats and the colors and
sizes of the bench cushions. I painted one whole wall with chalk-
board paint so the kids could draw, write, or pretend school. In the

shop, I was making a low table—my first furniture piece since high school—where they could paint, sculpt, or play games. Benches lined two walls, providing both seating and storage for art supplies and whatnot.

The tree house would be the palette for Tom Parker's grandchildren to express their creativity. Dad understood the basic human desire to create. He sure had a bucketful of it himself. But his cabinets and furniture had only hinted at the clever originality he'd possessed but never fully used. Since his death, I'd taken the opportunity to study the portfolio of furniture Dad had made throughout his life. At first glance the pieces seemed plain, even simple. But when I traced a curve's arc or a bit of detail carving, I understood why his work had been in such demand. He knew beauty, knew what was pleasing to the eye and how to capture it in wood. Folks had traveled from as far west as Texas and as far north as New York to have Tom Parker craft one of his elegant, understated pieces. As far as I knew, he'd never advertised, relying on word of mouth alone.

I'd always wondered why he never expanded. True, his work had been in demand and he charged appropriately, but that would have been all the more reason to add workers and increase his client base. His waiting list had been six months but could easily have been three years. More heart breaking, his oldest son hadn't recognized his gift while he was alive. It took building that tree house for me to begin to appreciate the extent of his talent and vision. I'd had to carve his designs to understand anything about his passion. Whether from laziness or negligence or selfishness, I'd failed my father as I'd always thought he'd failed me.

I stopped by Bill's house on the way home. His mare, Brandy, had a new foal, and Bill was out at his barn with the horses when I drove up. I took a couple carrots I'd brought from home and walked over. Mother and filly were in a dry, comfortable stall, and my brother leaned on the top rail watching the little girl take laps around her mama. Brandy watched her daughter's antics with maternal patience. When I stepped up beside Bill, the mare blew a greeting and walked over. I rubbed her nose and fed her a carrot.

Bill nodded and said, "Better give Brandy that other carrot you have in your pocket too. Little sister over there is on a strict diet of her mama's milk."

I laughed and gave Brandy the other carrot. When she was sure there were no more, she turned and watched the filly again. Soon the foal tired and looked to her mother for a supper teat.

"She's beautiful," I said. "Congratulations."

"Well, I'm not the father."

"That's because Brandy has good taste."

"Fair point." Bill grinned at me.

"Have you talked to Audrey or Brad in the last day or two?" I asked.

"No. I've been pretty busy at work the last few days. I picked up a couple extra shifts." He frowned. "Something wrong?"

"I don't think so, but I've tried to call Audrey a couple times. She doesn't pick up and hasn't called back."

"You know Audrey, Jack. She can get a bit overwhelmed sometimes. Might've turned her phone off till she can get her feet back under her." He hung a coiled lead rope on a nail beside the stall door and turned to me. "Might be she just ain't had the time."

"Maybe."

"You want to ride into town and check on her?"

"I'd feel better if we did. Brad won't answer either."

"All right. Let me tell Kathy what I'm doing."

We drove into Columbia and got to Audrey's around half past eight. The house was dark and still. We walked round the property but saw no sign of life. A couple newspapers were on the porch, where they'd been thrown, and the mailbox held at least a few days' worth of mail. My brother looked at me and shook his head. "This don't feel right."

"Not a bit right." I called both Maggie and Mama. No luck. Finally, I called Lauren.

"Hey, Jack. How's my big brother?"

"Hey, honey. I'm a little worried about Audrey. Bill and I are standing in front of her house. Looks like nobody's been home in a day or two. She won't answer her phone either. Have you heard from her?"

"Jack, I'm so glad you called. They showed up two days ago with Izzy, but Audrey and Brad were acting strange. She woke me early the next morning and asked if Izzy could stay for a day or two while they went off. Of course, I said Izzy could stay as long as needed. That was yesterday."

"Any idea what that's all about?"

"Not a clue. I'm used to Audrey's drama, and I know she and Brad have been through a lot lately. I figured they needed time alone together to talk."

"I'm sure that's all it is, honey. Likely everything is fine."

"You're probably right. But they've been gone since yesterday morning, and Audrey hasn't called Izzy once."

"That's strange."

Lauren sighed. "It sure is. Audrey might have a lot of faults but neglecting Izzy is not one of them."

When I got home, there was a voice message from Lauren saying Audrey had returned but Brad was not with her. I tried to call Audrey, but she didn't pick up and I left a message for her to call. I was tempted to spy on her activity, so I could determine if she was using again. But after tailing Dunbar to the ends of the earth and winding up with the mean end of a fish gaff in my shoulder, the cloak and dagger shit had worn thin. I decided to ask her straight out. She'd been honest before, and I hoped she would be again.

While I waited for Audrey to return my call and Sara and the girls to return home, I began supper preparations. With the charcoal laid and ready for the match and the steaks warming to room temperature, I chopped vegetables to marinate and grill for Wren, who was a fresh-new vegan. I wasn't sure she understood what that was, but I admired her conviction, however short lived it might turn out to be. The salad was tossed and the table was set.

When I heard the crunch of Sara's tires in the driveway, I placed the steaks and vegetable kabobs on the hot grill. "Right on time," I said, as Sara walked over and kissed my cheek. "You three relax. The table is set and the food will be ready soon."

"Thanks, honey. Smells good already. I'll go wash up and open a couple beers."

At the table, Wren said, "Thank you for the veggies, Daddy. I don't see how y'all can eat meat." She wrinkled her nose.

"It's delicious. That's how we can eat it," Lily said around a mouthful of ribeye.

Sara held a napkin to her mouth to hide a smile. Wren rolled her eyes, and Lily laughed at her sister. At times like that I felt blessed beyond anything I knew I would ever deserve.

CHAPTER FOURTEEN

Audrey returned my call as we were clearing the supper table. I asked Sara to leave the dishes for me, then answered the phone. "Just wanted to say hello and check on you and Izzy."

"We're fine, thanks. Just got back from visiting Lauren." We chewed the fat for a time, and she didn't mention anything about Brad. Audrey sounded exhausted. Instead of questioning her, I asked her to meet me for breakfast at the little café on top of Horrell Hill the next morning. She loved the place, and it sat about halfway between our houses. After she'd agreed and we'd ended the call, I realized I might need reinforcement.

Sara looked up from her magazine when I walked into the family room. "How's Audrey?"

"She's all right, a little distracted maybe. We're having breakfast tomorrow at Hilltop. Care to join us?"

"Sounds good. Everything all right? You seem a bit distracted yourself."

"It's probably nothing. I'll tell you about it on the way to breakfast in the morning." I turned to my daughters. "So what are we watching tonight? Football? News?" Eye rolls were my answer. When I turned back to Sara, she was watching me but didn't say a word.

The girls chose The Princess Bride for our movie. About fifteen minutes into the movie, I fell asleep. I woke to find myself stretched out on the sofa, covered in a heavy quilt, my own pillow beneath my head. The house was quiet and pitch black, the fire long dead. My pulse was hammering, and all I could manage were quick, shallow breaths. The nightmarish race through the woods had again waylaid my sleeping. I sat up, the commotion waking the dogs. Curiosity brought them to investigate. "Come on, girls." I coaxed them up beside me and burrowed myself beneath the quilt and two warm dogs. I knew I wouldn't sleep again that night, so I settled in to wait for morning.

On the short drive to the café, I told Sara about Audrey showing up at Lauren's doorstep and then disappearing with Brad for a couple days. She remarked on the oddity of Audrey's leaving Izzy like that, especially after being away from her daughter while in rehab.

"I had the same thought. That's not like her at all. I don't know what's going on with Audrey, but I hope she'll confide in us so we can help her."

Sara hesitated, and then said, "Jack, it's wonderful that you always try to be there for Bill and your sisters, but you can't solve all their problems. At some point, you have to let them grow up and run their own lives. Maybe you should give Audrey a little space. Remember, you called her. She hasn't asked for any help."

"I'm worried Audrey and Brad may be buying drugs again, from Dunbar or somebody else. I'll be damned if I'll stand by and let that piece-of-shit drug dealer destroy my family." My outburst left me breathless. I felt the anger behind my eyes like a fever and struggled to contain it.

Sara watched me. I glanced at her then back to the road, but not before I saw the hurt in her eyes. She said, "I'm sorry, honey. I shouldn't have said anything." Her apology silenced me, left me wretched and regretful for having been such an asshole. Reaching across, I squeezed her leg. I was sorry as well, but the words wouldn't come. So, we drove to the café in uneasy silence.

Audrey looked as if she'd not slept in a night or two. She walked over to our table, and we stood to hug her. We ordered breakfast and talked about children until our food arrived. She pushed her food around on her plate and looked on the verge of tears. My sister seemed smaller, less substantial than when I'd seen her last.

Sara said, "Honey, you don't look well. Is everything okay?" She rubbed Audrey's arm and left her hand there.

"I'm fine." She seemed confused by her own automatic, obvious bullshit. "Not really. I'm not fine at all. It's Brad. I think—no—I know he's at the drugs again. He says he isn't, but I know the signs." Audrey took a sip of water. "We went to Greenville and left Izzy with Lauren for a bit. I tried to get Brad to talk about it. I tried to encourage him to let me help. He denied it again and again and finally walked out. He was so angry. I haven't heard from him since. I searched Greenville for most of a day, but I didn't know where to look. So I picked up Izzy and came home."

"Have you heard from Brad at all?" Sara asked.

"Not a word. He won't answer a call or text. I don't know what to think."

"Do you know whereabout he's getting the drugs?" I asked. "Is it that same son of a bitch, Mark Dunbar?"

Audrey's face showed nothing but despair. "I think so, yes."

"What makes you think it's him?"

"When Izzy and I got home, I was unpacking and putting away our clothes. I found this on the floor beside our chifferobe." She pulled a small plastic bag from her purse and handed it to me. A label with a grinning skull adorned one corner. The bag was empty. "I'd swept around that armoire two days before we left for Greenville, and I'm sure it wasn't there then. It's the same as we got from him before. That label is supposed to be Dunbar's trademark—sort of his signature. At least that's what Brad said when he first started buying from him."

"I'm sorry I have to ask, but have you taken any drugs since rehab?"

"You don't have to be sorry, Jack. I know I've made a mess of everything. No, I haven't touched any drugs since then, not even aspirin. It's a struggle every single day, but my Izzy deserves so much better than what she's had to suffer. I think about her when I'm tempted. I'm trying so hard." She looked at Sara and began to cry.

"We know you are, honey," Sara said. "We're all so proud of you."

"Brad's been gone for four days, Audrey," I said. "Why haven't you said anything? Have you called the police? It doesn't make sense to me." I'd never been able to understand my sister's reasonings or her wait-and-see attitude about every damn thing.

"It's not that unusual for Brad to be gone for a long time. We've been having problems for years, even before any of this drug business started. I am beginning to worry though. No matter how mad at me he was, he would always text me to let me know he's all right." And we didn't know if he was in Greenville or Columbia—he could've been anywhere.

Audrey placed her napkin on the table and said, "I told Brad if he didn't stop with the drugs I'd leave him. I will, Jack." She chewed her lip for a minute. "Maybe he's made the choice for us both."

Driving home, Sara was quiet at first, staring at the trees and fields. While Audrey hadn't touched her food, my wife's appetite had declined throughout breakfast. She began to say something, then hesitated, trying to find the right words, I supposed. After a couple false starts, she said, "Jack, I'm truly sorry about what I said earlier. I know you love your family. I love them too. We need to do whatever we can to help Audrey. I know she doesn't have the strength to deal with this. She's so lost."

It seemed as if all five of Tom and Lizzie Parker's children were always in various stages of trouble. Bill and Lauren had problems, like everyone else, but seemed to handle whatever was thrown at them. Maggie attracted immature men like a winning lottery ticket draws long-lost cousins. Although she might've had trouble choosing appropriate mates, she had no control over the cancer that had assaulted her body. But she was strong and dealt with her problems head on.

Our Audrey though seemed to be a magnet for trouble and strife. Misery found her no matter how hard she tried to avoid it. Becoming addicted to pills wasn't her choice but taking them in the first place was. Audrey wasn't a victim of circumstance, just poor judgment. Brad hadn't followed his doctor's instructions for controlling his pain with the pills. But Audrey had had no medical reason for using them in the first place. She'd only done what she always had, pretend and deny. At least she seemed to have taken a cautious control of her own addiction. But how long could she hold out, watching Brad sink into the swamp of oblivion, before she followed? I hoped she was serious about leaving him but it seemed doubtful. She'd likely forgive him, and then it would happen again and again, dragging them both ever deeper, past the point of redemption.

And, me? I was caught up in it all, stumbling blind and drunk through a china shop, knowing I'd have to pay for any damage I caused. Maybe I was the most screwed up of the entire brood, intent on running my siblings' lives. I was involved with their darkest and most disturbing sides. Sure, I checked on their health and families, but the sordid parts drew me in, the sad and tragic portions, which kept me awake figuring how to help. Maybe Sara was right. Maybe I should've let my family, especially Audrey, work out their own problems. I figured my father had dealt with Audrey's difficulties before his death. I was just continuing the dysfunction, enabling her to slide further into the murk. But enabling was surely the least of my sins.

Although I didn't think we had much of a chance locating Brad, we tried. Bill and Maggie called law jurisdictions and hospitals for

Columbia and the Midlands. Lauren and I did the same for the Greenville area. We began the slow, painstaking process of calling, connecting to the correct department, and pleading for any scrap of information once the right person was reached. Everything was confidential. Are you related? Are you the spouse? A tangle of apathy, regulations, and cover-your-ass met us at every turn. I was discouraged and irritable after an hour. Then Audrey called.

She could barely speak. Her words were clipped, breathless. "The Spartanburg police called. Brad's in the hospital, in intensive care. Overdosed. Found him. Cheap motel room. He was unconscious. A prostitute in his room." Audrey sounded as if she were in shock. "Oh God, Jack, she's dead."

Anger and despair snuck up on me slowly, like a swollen, cresting river. Had I caused this? Was it retribution for the humiliation and violence Dunbar had suffered at my hands? I'd given him a clear ultimatum, and now Brad was in intensive care, found with a dead woman. All this because of my private war with the devil.

Lauren, who was much closer to Spartanburg, was waiting for us at the Medical Center. "They won't let me see him," she said. "They won't even tell me if he's still alive."

"I got hold of a nurse as we drove into town," Audrey said. "He's been stabilized and isn't in immediate danger." She'd regained most of her composure on the long ride upstate but had said little to Bill or me, preferring to sit staring out at the night. I hadn't pressed her to speak, thinking the calm and quiet might do her good.

I walked over to the volunteer at the reception table. "We're the family of Brad Matthews. His wife is here now. Could you please ask the charge nurse to come out?"

"Yes, sir. I surely will." She picked up the telephone and spoke in a hush. "He will be right out. There's coffee and cookies if you folks are in need of nourishment." She pointed to a small table in the corner. "And I'll be praying for your family." I carried four coffee cups over to my siblings. Bill stood to help me and handed cups to our sisters.

"Where's Maggie?" Lauren asked.

Bill said, "She's with Izzy. We promised to keep her updated."

"Does Mama know?"

"Not yet," I said, thinking of yet another conversation I would have with our mother about her flagging family. Of course, it was irrational, but deep down I blamed my father for the slide, as if his death had started a chain reaction of ruinous events. God's truth, we'd been headed that way for years. We were only picking up speed since he'd passed.

Audrey hadn't said anything to Izzy about her father yet. She'd told her Maggie was hoping her niece would spend time with her. Izzy had been more than happy to oblige. But after being shuffled from me to Lauren and then to Maggie, my niece must've been confused why her mama kept disappearing. My poor sister was struggling to hold her shit together. And she was losing.

The charge nurse walked out and looked at the volunteer. She pointed in our direction, and he came over to our little alcove. Bill and I stood as he stepped closer. He was the tallest man I'd ever seen, closer to seven feet than six.

"Mrs. Matthews?" He looked from Lauren to Audrey and back.

"That's me," Audrey said. Her voice was small, almost no sound at all.

"I'm Rodney. Mrs. McBride told me you were out here." He indicated the volunteer. "I wanted to let you know everything we know so far. Would you prefer to talk in private?"

"No. These are my brothers and my sister—my family. They can hear whatever you have to say."

"All right. Well, Mr. Matthews was brought in by ambulance just after eleven this morning. He was in cardiac arrest as they arrived and has had two additional episodes. He was revived each time and is in critical but stable condition now."

"Thank God," Audrey said. Her face seemed drained of blood and her eyes had lost focus. Concerned she might pass out, I guided her to a chair. But she seemed to regain a bit of color and said, "Thank you."

Something about the nurse's face made me ask, "What else?"

He knew what I was asking. He turned to Audrey and asked, "Ma'am?"

Audrey looked up at him blankly.

The tall nurse took a breath and said, "His heart was stopped for a bit longer the last time. Whatever oxygen he had was what we forced into his lungs. He's on a ventilator now and sedated. We won't know the extent of any damage to his heart or his brain until he's awake and we're able to run a battery of tests."

She nodded and said, "Thank you for telling me the truth. Do you think there's brain damage?"

"Too early to tell. Like I said, we'll need to run those tests. Let's worry about keeping him stable overnight first." He watched her until she raised her eyes once more. "One last thing," he said. "Have you spoken to the Spartanburg police?"

"Yes. They're who called me first. I spoke to an investigator briefly. I'm supposed to call her tonight." Audrey looked toward the double doors leading to the ICU. "When can I see my husband?"

"You can't see him until morning, but I'll let you know if there are any changes in his condition. I'm here all night, and I'll check out here first, but we have your number if you're gone." This man had delivered bad news many times and looked Audrey in the eye as he spoke to her. He dealt with pain daily, and not just the physical kind. If he was any indication of the care Brad would receive there, then my brother-in-law was in the best of hands.

Audrey said, "I'll be out here. I'm not leaving." As the nurse returned to the ICU, my sister called the investigator. When she ended the call, she said, "Investigator Olsen is coming over to talk to us—I mean to me." She shook her head.

"We'll be right here if you want us, honey," Lauren said.

"Yes, please. You all need to hear everything." Audrey sat down and closed her eyes.

Lauren looked at Bill and me and shrugged. Neither she nor Bill knew about the woman found with Brad.

"How much do you all know about what happened to Brad tonight?" Audrey asked.

"They don't know, honey," I said. "I haven't said anything to anyone other than that Brad was found and he'd overdosed."

Audrey looked at me, her eyes pleading. Make this go away, Jack. You're my big brother. Make this disappear. She nodded at me and said, "Please tell them, Jack."

Bill and Lauren looked from Audrey to me. Confusion was etched on their faces and they were worried. "Jack," Lauren said.

"Brad was found in a motel room by the cleaning staff. He hadn't been seen in a couple of days, and they figured maybe he'd left without paying. The housekeeping supervisor used her key and found him unconscious and the room wrecked. A prostitute was in his room too. She was dead." My mouth had gone dry, and I crossed the room to retrieve a water bottle from the refreshment table.

Bill's eyes were closed, his head shaking in unconscious denial. He looked at me as if waiting for the punchline. "Dead? How could she—I don't understand—how did she die? Are they saying Brad killed her?"

"They haven't said anything yet. I don't know. But there doesn't seem to be any urgency." I had no idea what the law thought, but we'd find out soon enough.

"There's something else," Audrey said. I knew what she was going to say and closed my eyes to wait. Wasn't a damn thing I could do to slow it down. "This wasn't the first time Brad has been with a prostitute. I know of at least three other times. I'm sure there were more, maybe many more."

I'd known about one of Brad's encounters for a long time but didn't know Audrey knew until then. On a hunting trip six years before, Brad had killed a six pack in the time it took most of us to drink a single beer. He'd told the group about a recent business trip where he'd been with a whore. I'd grabbed him by his collar, wanting to hurt him. I hadn't hit him but came damn close. I'd threatened to tell Audrey and beat him to a pulp if he ever did it again. On the way home, I drove him to a clinic and made him get tested for every known venereal disease. He'd promised that his indiscretion was the first and last time, and I'd wanted to believe him. So I had. I had been naive and should've told Audrey and encouraged her to leave his sorry ass then. So much pain might have been avoided. But if she'd known anyway, and chose to stay with him, would I have made a difference? Still, I'd failed my sister, and the would-haves felt a lot like cowardice.

We sat without further conversation, awkward and fretful, until the investigator arrived. Angela Olsen was a veteran Spartanburg cop. With handshakes all around, she dispensed with the pleasantries and got down to business. She wanted to give my sister the full story and tell her how the case stood.

"The girl found in your husband's room was a known prostitute and addict. I've arrested her myself. She'd overdosed before, been in a program. She just didn't make it this time. However tragic, her death has been ruled accidental, and Mr. Matthews will not be charged concerning her passing." Investigator Olsen paused, and then said, "Your husband will be charged for possession and solicitation of a minor. The girl was sixteen." The investigator closed her notepad and stood tapping her pen on the pad like she was weighing choices. "You may want to contact a lawyer."

"I deserve this," Audrey said in a voice so small I thought I might've imagined it.

If Olsen heard her, she ignored the comment. "Your husband had a lot of drugs with him. We'll be interested to know where he got them. We didn't find any cash in the room, so it's likely he paid the girl in drugs. The district attorney is considering charging Mr. Matthews for dealing and distribution, but I'll recommend against it. At this point, I don't think that was his intent."

Audrey sat stunned, staring at the floor. I asked, "Will he be locked up if—when—he recovers?"

Olsen glanced at my sister then turned to me. "There is an officer stationed outside his door for now. Judge Richardson will hold a hearing three days from now, but if you have a lawyer, Mr. Matthews doesn't need to be there. If the judge sets bail and you all can cover it, then we'll remove the officer, and Mr. Matthews will be free until the trial."

The investigator left and we were quiet. Nobody seemed to know what to say or do.

Lauren sat on the arm of Audrey's chair with her arm around her sister. Their heads were close as they seemed to watch the same piece of floor. Bill looked at me and shook his head, letting go of the breath he'd been holding. I couldn't believe it either. I'd have guessed for certain Brad would be charged with manslaughter, at the least. But the charges were serious enough, and we had some grim shit to deal with.

And we didn't know how quickly Brad might recover, if at all. That must've weighed on Audrey's mind as much as the legal troubles. I read it in her eyes. She was tired of the emotional bullshit and the drama that had plagued her marriage for so many years. I hadn't realized all she'd known about her husband's screwing around. I hoped she'd have the strength to leave him, for Izzy's sake if nothing more. I was of the opinion that she should wash her hands of the whole damn mess. She had other ideas.

"Where am I going to find the money for bail, for a lawyer?" Audrey couldn't look at us.

I was surprised to hear myself say, "Don't worry, honey. We'll figure it out. I'll call Larry Ramsey." Audrey nodded, as the tears traced down her cheeks.

I didn't know why I said that. I'd been willing to cut and run, leave Brad to plow his own field. But the desperation in Audrey's eyes had brought me up short. I couldn't let myself be a part of more heartache for my sister. Maybe I remembered all the bad shit I'd done early on and tempered my judgment on Brad. Or maybe I was just getting too soft.

Compassion for someone not blood-kin was a new feeling for me.

I wasn't so sure I liked it.

CHAPTER FIFTEEN

I parked my truck beside Mama's car and walked over to the grove of oaks. Standing before the tree house Dad had designed and started to frame, I wondered, for the first time, why I'd thought it so important to finish. My reasonings were no longer clear in my mind. Maybe I was just tired from the little sleep I'd stolen in the waiting room the night before. But instead of going home to rest, I'd headed straight to Parker's Knoll where the family had always gathered to laugh together and cry together. Except me—I'd been gone for long stretches, months, and years at a time. I'd come home, and all the trouble that had followed me my whole life had come with me. I'd wanted to blame my father, but the truth was the bad shit had started when I'd come home.

Mama needed to know what had happened with Brad, and it fell to me to tell her. Seemed I was forever giving her news of some misfortune or other that had ensnared one of her children. She must've hated to see me coming. I wondered if she blamed me for all we'd been through, not consciously, but deep down where she had no control over her thoughts and feelings. Was that why she'd been uninterested in my moving home? I didn't doubt she loved me, but sometimes it's better to love someone from a safe distance—even your own child.

The morning cold cut through my shirt, and I shivered as I studied the unfinished tree house. The oak seemed naked and exposed against the curdled sky. Squirrels raced each other from limb to limb and tree to tree, running along paths only they could recognize. Otherwise the Knoll was quiet as a gravedigger's patron.

"You need a jacket, son." Mama put her arm around my waist and hugged me gently. I hadn't heard her approach. "You'll catch your death out here."

"Yes'm." I didn't move.

"What's happened? I know that look. You had that same look when you left the Knoll after high school."

I pushed aside the sting of her words and said, "Can we go inside? I could use coffee." I couldn't stop shivering, and the temperature was just a small measure of the reason.

I sat at Mama's kitchen table as she poured coffee. The warmth began to spread through me as I searched for a way to tell her about Brad and Audrey. I'd thought not to mention the prostitute, but a lie by omission was still a lie, no matter my intentions. I was sick to death of my lies and secrets, and she deserved to know everything. Audrey was her first daughter, and she loved her every bit as much as she loved her other four children. She needed to know.

So I told her everything, and she sat sipping her coffee until I ran short on words. Mama didn't comment on Audrey's situation or ask any questions. She said, "Thank you for telling me, for telling me everything. I know it wasn't easy." She was composed and smiling. "More coffee?"

"Mama, I'm glad you're not upset, but you seem to be taking all of this better than I'd expected. Do you know something I don't?"

"Not a thing. I'm just proud of my children today."

"Even Bill?" I asked. That brightened Mama's smile all the more.

"I'm proud of you all for taking such fine care of one another. My friend, Alice, tells me all her kids do is squabble and fuss and blame." Her finger traced the swirling pattern on the threadbare tablecloth. "I know you five have your issues with one another, but you always come together in the end. I'm especially proud of you, son."

"Thank you. That means the world to me. I'm sorry to bring you awful news all the time. We seem to be having one long streak of bad luck since Dad passed."

"Nonsense. Luck hasn't a thing to do with it. God gives us free will, and sometimes, well, sometimes we make terrible mistakes. We can only hope that in the end, the balance tips in our favor. That's the truest way to measure a life."

"What balance is that?"

"The balance of our good deeds measured against our bad ones."

"And how do you think I'm doing?"

She studied my face, her eyes unreadable. "You're my first born, and I think I understand you pretty well. But nobody truly knows what's in another's heart. You keep your thoughts close, and I know you've done things you're not proud of. You're more like your daddy than any of my kids, Jack." She held up a hand to halt any argument. "But like your father, I know you more than make up for the mistakes, even the terrible ones. When your life is done, when you've been weighed and measured, I've no doubt you'll come down on the right side of the scales."

I rose and kissed the top of her head. "Thank you, Mama. If you'll excuse me, I have a powerful need to see my wife and daughters." As I stepped outside onto her porch, I glanced back and saw my mother smiling. Her eyes were closed tightly, yet still the tears found a path to her cheeks.

I arrived home at seven, with the house still sleeping. I checked on my girls, then slipped into bed beside my wife. Seemed I'd just fallen asleep when I heard a commotion downstairs. I pulled on clothes, glancing at the clock beside the bed: 9:30. Downstairs, I found Lily on her knees, sweeping up large, jagged pieces of glass from a broken tea pitcher.

She looked up as I walked into the kitchen. "Stop, Daddy. There's glass everywhere. I'm sorry I woke you." She smiled sheepishly. "I was making iced tea and it slipped." She gasped and placed a finger in her mouth.

"Don't move, honey. Give me one second." I grabbed a first aid kit from the bathroom. In the kitchen, I lifted her onto the counter. "Let's have a look at that finger."

"It won't need stitches, will it?" Her eyes pleaded.

I studied her finger and began to clean the small cut. "I don't believe it will, baby girl. We'll clean it and put a bandage on it. You'll be fine as rain."

Lily smiled and said, "Thank you, Daddy. I'm sorry about waking you up. Mama said you had a long night. Are Audrey and Brad all right?"

"Audrey is fine, honey, but Brad is sick. We won't know much until the doctors run some tests on him." I finished wrapping her finger and began to put the first aid kit back together.

"What happened to him?" Even though they didn't know them as well as they might've, both girls were fond of their uncles. But I didn't know how much to tell her just yet. She noticed my hesitation and asked, "Did something bad happen?"

"Honey, I need to talk to your mama first, and then I'll tell you about Brad and Audrey. Sound good?"

She looked doubtful, but said, "Sure. I guess I better finish cleaning up this mess before Mama gets home."

"Where is Mama, honey?"

"She and Wren drove to town for groceries. I wanted to stay here and surprise you with the tea." She wrinkled her nose. "Surprise."

I laughed at her sweet joke. "I'll take care of the glass, baby. Would you mind taking Lucy and Ethel out to play? I don't want them in here until I can get all this glass up." I lifted her off the counter, to a clear spot on the floor.

"Okay. I'll throw a ball for them." She tiptoed between the shards and left the kitchen.

After clearing the glass from the floor, I showered and retreated to my office to work on a project, which was due in a week. My client was demanding and needy, requiring constant reassurance. He called at any hour of the day or night, so I tried to stay a step ahead. He was a difficult customer, but I needed the work; since moving home, business had been much slower than I'd hoped.

Before I realized it, three hours had passed. I stepped from my office to find Sara and my girls sitting in the living room with Maggie and Izzy.

I hugged Maggie. "Well, well. My third-favorite sister is here." I touched Izzy's nose. "Hey, sweet pea."

Maggie stuck her tongue out at me, and the girls all giggled. "I came to see my third-favorite brother," she said.

"You only have two brothers, Maggie," Lily said.

"Exactly." Maggie winked at her and smiled at me.

"Can you three play outside for a bit?" Sara asked. "We need to talk to Maggie."

"Is it about my daddy?" Izzy asked. Audrey had a lot to explain to her daughter.

"That's part of it," Sara said. "There are other things as well—grownup stuff. You all would be bored."

"We're not little kids, Mama," Wren said. She left the room with a pout on her lips.

Sara ignored Wren's attitude and comment. When the girls were outside, she asked, "Is Brad going to be okay?"

"Bill and I left Spartanburg around four this morning, and he wasn't conscious," I said. "I'm assuming his condition hasn't changed. I asked Audrey or Lauren to call us if anything happens." I held up my phone. "Nothing yet."

When I'd finished telling them everything we'd learned the night before, Maggie shook her head like she couldn't believe it. It did seem surreal.

"Audrey should leave his sorry ass," I said. "He's shown a pattern of screwing around and lying over the course of their marriage. The drugs could be a life-long problem, and he's not likely to change. Hell, he might do a stretch in prison for his latest stunt. I hope to God she won't pine for him if that's the case."

Sara said, "Audrey's in a difficult position. If she stays with Brad, she's the object of pity and rumors. If she doesn't, she's hard hearted, leaving her husband in his time of need. I know she shouldn't care what others think."

"But Audrey does care," Maggie said, finishing Sara's thought. "She doesn't want to let anyone down. If Brad begs her forgiveness, she'll probably fold." She closed her eyes and sighed.

"I don't know," I said. "Maybe Audrey will find something inside herself—some strength. I have to believe she'll do what's right for herself and Izzy."

"I hope you're right, Jack." Maggie looked from Sara to me. "What do we tell Izzy?"

"Nothing for now other than her dad is sick and in a hospital upstate. We'll need to talk to Audrey about what she wants Izzy to know and when. Anything about Brad's sleazy habits should come from her, preferably before Izzy sees it on the news or hears it from a friend." What a mess. I prayed I wouldn't be drafted into telling Izzy about her father's illicit behavior. I didn't want to break her heart. That would be too much. But I knew if my sister asked, I'd do it.

"What is Audrey going to do for now, while Brad is in the hospital?" Sara asked. "If she's staying up there with him, even for a few days, she'll need things—clothes, toiletries."

"Lauren will take care of all that," I said. "She's much closer than we are. All we can do is wait on Audrey to call." We'd all become good at waiting.

Bill was mucking stalls when I walked up to his barn. He spent a considerable amount of time outside with his horses or in his garden. I knew he loved Kathy, but his tolerance for criticism bordered on nonexistent. His solution was to avoid his wife as much as possible. He didn't complain, had never said a cross word about her that I'd heard. But she treated Bill more like a hired hand than a husband. She wanted the house to remain spotless, for everything to be just so, to have money. With a sigh, she'd say, "I suppose we'll just have to do without." She didn't mean to be cruel, but Kathy was raised with different standards of living than the uncouth Parkers. She'd come from old money, and I'd always believed she'd found it hard to make the downward adjustment.

One steamy night they met at a dance. Later that same night, in the bed of Bill's truck, they conceived my nephew, Will; they were married pretty soon after. Kathy seemed to try and make the best of it, to fit in with our family. But her pearl-wearing debutante friends dropped her like handful of fire ants. Her family was cordial, but they wore their disdain for us like diamond-crusted armor. My brother worked hard but would never get rich working at the lumber mill. He'd never have the social graces she prized, so he kept himself busy and mastered the art of hiding in daylight.

Bill looked up as I approached. "Hey, bud," he said.

"How's the baby girl?"

Bill was proud of Brandy's new filly and loved to talk about her. "She gets prettier and stronger every day. I think she's going to be as big and impressive as Kitty." Dad's mare had been his pride and joy. Kitty was a fetching palomino quarter horse, perfect in every respect. Her white-gold coat fairly shone, and her brown eyes revealed both smarts and spirit. Near about broke his heart when she died from the colic.

"Kitty's prime company. That filly must be a pistol."

Bill laughed. "She has a sassy streak. That's for sure and certain."

I watched him scoop shavings and shit. He finally leaned on his fork and looked at me. "Everything all right?"

I nodded. "I wanted to talk to you about Audrey."

"All right. I need a break anyway. Come on into the office."

I followed him into the barn. He walked toward the small office next to the tack room, but he sat on a hay bale beside the door. He reached into his ice chest and held a longneck toward me.

"No thanks."

"Suit yourself." He popped the top on a nail and settled back against the rough-planked wall.

"I didn't want to bring it up at the hospital," I said, "but Audrey told Sara and me that Brad bought those drugs from our old friend, Mark Dunbar."

He shook his head. "Shit. Here we go again. We should've been a little more persuasive when we visited him in his roached-out bar kingdom."

"I reckon so. I think we should both be more watchful. He knows us now, and if he's bold enough to sell to Brad after we told him to stop, he might want to cause some commotion for us calling him out in front of his friends."

Bill looked at me with narrowed eyes. "You came over here just to tell me that, Jack? Don't piss on my boots and tell me it's raining. What did you do?"

The conversation wasn't going the way I'd hoped. "I paid him a visit a few days after we spoke to him. Encouraged him to leave us be. I gave him money for whatever might be owed him. Figured I'd put an end to it." I reached into my coat pocket and removed Dunbar's pistol and handed it to Bill. "Took this from him."

Bill looked at the gun like he had no notion what I was holding, then took it and shook his head. "He'll want some blood. You should have said something, Jack." He studied the pistol and reached to hand it back.

I shook my head. "I don't want it. Keep it, sell it, or chuck it in the fucking river if you've a mind to. Thought he was a whipped dog sitting there that night. Didn't think it likely he'd cause anymore ruckus."

He set the pistol on a hay bale. "A whipped dog's still got teeth. He's hurt our family. You should have told me, Jack, so I could protect my wife and kids." Bill's anger simmered three degrees shy of a rolling boil. "What the hell were you thinking? That how you got your face all tore up?"

I nodded. "I was thinking of the family. I thought I was doing what needed to be done. Figured I'd taken care of the problem, but clearly I didn't. I reckon he sold that shit to Brad to spite me."

"I'd say that's a safe bet. I hope you haven't poked the wrong polecat this time, brother. How much?"

"What?"

"Don't play that shit with me, Jack. How much money you give him?"

"Ten thousand."

Bill whistled long and low. "I thought they'd paid him off. Shit."

"This was new debt. Plus interest and incentive. I might as well have thrown that money in the trash."

"You think?"

"Look, I told you trading insults with him wouldn't accomplish anything. So I tried to take care of it my way."

"And what did that accomplish? What a damn mess. Let's hope him selling to Brad satisfied his need to pay you back, and he doesn't have more revenge on his mind. Our family is too big and too spread out to watch around the clock." Bill stood and paced the barn. "The uncertainty is the worst of it." He stopped pacing and looked as if he'd come to a decision, but he didn't share it with me. Seemed fair considering what I'd done.

On the drive home, I thought about how I could've better handled the talk with my brother. He was right. I should have let him know so he could protect Kathy and the kids. I figured I had the matter settled until Audrey had told me about finding the drugs. I had to worry about a threat that might never turn up—a nagging, niggling concern clouding everything I did. That conversation hadn't been a shining moment for me. And all the while, my father whispered his disapproval.

You aren't taking care of my family, Jack.

Sara had taken Mary under her wing. Shy at first, Mary was spirited and energetic once you got to know her. She asked Sara questions about childbirth, nursing, and child rearing. My wife was thrilled to answer any questions the girl might ask. The little mother-to-be became almost a third daughter to us.

After the conversation with Bill, my concern for Mary drove me to ask Sara to bring her to our house for a day or so. I wanted to keep an eye on her. Sara told Mary she wanted help sorting through the many boxes and bags of baby clothes that the Parkers had accumulated with eight grandchildren. And she could have all she wanted. Mary was happy to help, and they spent a whole day sorting and sighing and laughing—all good medicine for a weary heart.

Mama hadn't seen Mary since Thanksgiving, so we visited the Knoll after supper. As we parked and began walking to the house, Mary looked out across the field and spied the tree house. Her eyes lost focus, and a tiny smile found her lips.

Turning to me, she said, "Can we go look at the tree house? I think it's amazing."

"Course we can." I offered her my arm. She blushed and took my elbow. We strolled over to the oak grove.

"I never had anything like this when I was little," she said.

"Well, we didn't have one either. I reckon Dad was too busy with his work to build one for us, though I seem to recall Audrey asking him a few hundred times. We built our own forts and huts with scrap wood instead. But they were nothing like this. You could just about live in this little house."

Mary stared up into the branches. "That would be lovely," she said, but I don't think she was speaking to me.

Mama, who was always prepared for company, had cookies, cake, tea, and coffee ready as we walked into her house. She led Mary into her living room by the hand and glanced back at me over her shoulder. "Be a good boy and bring the goodies with you, Jack." She looked at Mary. "Now, would you like tea or coffee, dear?"

"I'm not supposed to have any caffeine," Mary said.

"I have decaf for both."

"Tea, then. Please." Another blush.

"Jack, please fix Mary a cup of decaffeinated tea."

"Yes, ma'am," I said. "It will be the pinnacle of my existence to serve you, m'lady."

Mary laughed at my foolishness, but Mama only frowned. "Please pay no mind to my son," she said. "I dropped him on his head when he was a baby." She smiled at Mary. "Several times, in fact."

Mama spent the next hour regaling her with outlandish stories of my childhood; no detail was too small or embarrassing to be overlooked. Mary laughed easily. Even though the tales had no basis in fact, it was a pleasure to see Mary without the worry lines. Finally, my mother wound down and we got ready to leave.

"Thank you for a lovely evening, Mrs. Parker." Mary stepped into Mama's waiting arms.

"You're welcome, sweetheart. And you can call me Lizzie if you like. May I?" Mary nodded, and Mama placed her hand on Mary's belly. "Take care of yourself and this precious gift."

Mary spent the night at our house. When I'd told Cassie my plan a couple days before, she had balked at first but then agreed. She didn't like the residents to stay off campus. She felt she lost the element of control when all her charges were not tucked away in Carolina House each night. After some cajoling from me, she admitted she thought it would be good for Mary to have a visit with us.

The girls bunked together in Wren's room, and Mary was sleeping in Lily's. Sara had changed the sheets on Lily's bed and made sure Mary knew where everything was. "I know everyone says to make yourself at home," Sara said, "but we want you to know we consider you part of our family and that our house is yours."

"Thank you, Sara," Mary said. Her cheeks colored once more. "Nobody has ever treated me as kindly as you and Jack. You have such a big and wonderful family. Thank you for letting me be a part of it, even for a little while. Goodnight." She disappeared into Lily's room.

In our own room, Sara said, "Mary is so precious. This afternoon, she thanked me a dozen times for letting her spend the day here with us. I can't begin to imagine what her childhood was like or her time with Mark Dunbar. Poor baby. I want to hug and protect her." She slipped into bed and pulled the quilt up to her chin.

"Cold?"

"No, I just got a sudden chill thinking about Mary with that awful man. Oh Jack, how can we do more to help those women?"

"One at a time, sweet girl. It's the best we can do."

"I pray that's good enough."

I watched her face as sleep began to claim my wife. She wanted to save every woman from their own Mark Dunbars. The women at Carolina House had become like kin to us. But there were thousands upon thousands more out there, and trying to save them all was like trying to put out a forest fire by spitting on the flames.

I realized what my father had known. It had to start somewhere: one dollar, one act of kindness, one woman.

One at a time.

CHAPTER SIXTEEN

The next morning, after breakfast and a lot of hugging all around, I drove Mary back to Carolina House. She hummed to herself as we followed the rise and fall of the hills, heading west toward Columbia. The silence between us was easy. The change in her was witness to her strength and character. I knew many women never reached their potential after years with an abusive and controlling man. Some didn't escape with their lives. But Mary had blossomed and continued to grow more confident each week. I was thankful she'd had the courage to pick up the phone that day and call Carolina House.

"Jack, I was thinking I might take a few courses in the summer or fall like you suggested. What do you think?" Mary watched me intently.

"I think that's a fine idea," I said. "What are your interests?"

"Well, I'm good at math and I'm pretty organized. I was thinking about bookkeeping or, you know, accounting."

"Bet you'd be great at that. Sara studied all that accounting but doesn't practice anymore. Of course, she takes care of the books for Carolina House when she's not painting. I'll bet she'd be tickled to help you with any studying if you needed her."

"She said that yesterday, when we were sorting the baby clothes. Sara also said she used to be a controller, but I'm not sure what that is. I was too embarrassed to ask her."

"A controller has responsibility for all the financial concerns of a company, such as payroll or bookkeeping. I think Sara enjoyed it; she was paid to tell other people what to do. Now she just tells me what to do."

Mary laughed and said, "She says she tries to tell you what to do, but you never listen to her." Her laugh was infectious and got me going too.

"It's not my fault. Mama always said I had selective hearing. She had my ears tested three times when I was five or six years old. Said I'd sit there watching Wile E. Coyote and not answer her. Turns out I'm just talented at tuning out the world."

"You're pulling my leg," she said. "She didn't really have you tested, did she?"

"She did. You can ask her yourself next time you see her."

"I hope that's soon. I like Mrs. Parker...Lizzie. She's so kind to me and so is your whole family. You and Sara are so lucky to have each other and such a big, close family." Mary grinned and turned to look out the window as we slowed down in front of Carolina House.

As we waited for the gate to swing open, she leaned over and kissed my cheek. "Thanks for everything, Jack." I pulled through and parked in the drive. As she stepped down from the truck, she turned back and said, "Love y'all." Then she was gone.

At Maggie's invitation, I met her for lunch in Columbia. I walked in and spotted her in a corner booth. She waved and I joined her, sliding into the cramped seat across from her.

"Hey, little squirrel. What's new with you?" I asked.

In answer, she held out her left hand for me. She had a thousand-watt smile, and her cheeks glowed like she'd been sun kissed.

On her finger was a diamond ring. "Mike asked me to marry him." She was near to bouncing out of her seat. "I said yes."

"You did, huh? Honey, that's really something. I didn't know you two were so serious. Had you talked about it at all before he asked?"

"Well, we did talk about it a little bit. You seem troubled, Jack. Do you think I should have said no?" Her frown was sharp as a filet knife.

"You've known Mike for a month, Maggie. That's all that concerns me. I like Mike a lot. He seems like a good man, and it's obvious he loves you."

"But?" She had me cornered.

"But why the hell do you need to get engaged so soon? I guess it makes me nervous—unless you're planning on having one of those extra-long engagements. Have you talked about a date yet?"

"We were thinking New Year's Day." She wouldn't even meet my eyes at that point. I'd screwed the pooch again, made a complete mess of a conversation. I didn't know how to fix it. First Audrey, then Bill, now Maggie. I just needed to fuck up a conversation with Lauren to go for the full set and win the grand prize—asshole brother of the year.

So, of course, I dug deeper.

"That's less than a month, Maggie. I'm sorry, but it seems as if you and Mike are rushing into this." I had a terrible thought. Maggie had inherited like the rest of us. Maybe Mike was trying to get at Maggie's money. What if he was trying to trick her, take her cash, and then disappear? My own doubt disgusted me. Maggie was a beautiful, smart woman. Any man would've considered himself lucky to have her. I tried to push the suspicion from my mind. "But, ultimately," I said, "it doesn't matter what I think or what Bill or your sisters think. If you want this to happen, then I will support you toes to nose."

"Thank you, big brother. This is what I want." She took my

hand, relief flooding into her eyes, and I was ashamed for having mistrusted her judgment.

"Then I'm all for it, little squirrel. I'm sorry I sounded doubtful, but you gave me a hell of a shock." I'd have to learn to be okay with her decision. "Now, tell me what Sara and I can do to help put this wedding together in this short window of time."

Maggie laughed and said, "You don't have to do a thing, Jack, but thank you for asking. We'll have it at the Knoll, if Mama doesn't mind. And Mike's family is paying for everything. They're sort of rich." She wrinkled her nose.

"Let me see now—Mike is good looking, intelligent, and rich. I reckon he'll have to do." I'd never been happier in my life to have been proven an overbearing idiot. And I had considerable experience with that.

Maggie laughed at my comment, but said, "There is something I wanted to ask you, Jack."

"You name it, honey. I'll set up tables and chairs, serve food, park cars, or whatever you need."

"Will you give me away?"

Maggie called our sisters and Bill to share the news. I only heard her side of their conversations, but clearly they were all happy for her. Seemed nobody else was concerned about the short courting period. Maggie wanted to tell Mama in person and left after lunch to head out that way. The one obstacle to a January-first wedding might have been Audrey and Brad's situation, but Audrey said she'd be there no matter what.

At home, I found Sara in her studio. Her hair was pinned atop her head with a paintbrush, and she was wearing an old button-down of mine, no makeup. Before entering the studio, I watched her through the glass door. Studying her canvas, she tilted her head and touched the brush handle to her chin, thinking. After a minute she smiled, dipped her brush, and made a series of strokes on the canvas. Apparently satisfied and finished for the day, she carried her brushes to the sink for cleaning as I opened the door.

"Looking good, sweet girl," I said.

"Think so?" She glanced over her shoulder at the painting. "It's coming along. I told Ellie I'd have it ready for the show next month, so I'm pushing myself a bit." The large landscape of Sassafras Mountain and its foothills seemed to rise up out of the canvas.

When I told her about Maggie's engagement and impending nuptials, Sara squealed like a child. And when I told her I was to give Maggie away, she said, "She loves you so much, Jack. That's quite an honor."

"I wish Dad could be here to do it or at least to see Maggie so happy."

She touched my chest and said, "I'm sure Tom's watching."

With Christmas around the corner, Sara, the girls, and I arrived at Carolina House with decorations and presents. There were seven or eight children staying there with their mamas. I wasn't sure of the exact number, as they never stood still long enough to get a proper count. Checking for their own names on the gift tags, the children helped carry the brightly wrapped boxes into the house. Sara knew how many kids, their names, their sizes, and their wishes. I'd suggested cash or gift cards for them. My wife and daughters had looked at me with pity, as if I'd lacked the capacity to understand even the simplest notion. They'd fought the crowds at the shopping malls and the traffic on Harbison Boulevard, while I'd relaxed at home with a hot cup of coffee and a good book.

The women of Carolina House and their children decorated the house and sang along to the Christmas songs on the radio. I was happy to see them with their minds on something other than their troubles. Bill showed up with a huge fir tree. He said, "Guess I'm in the tree delivery business now." His gruff attitude was an act. My brother was generous with both his time and whatever money he had. His anger toward me seemed to have cooled, maybe even dried up completely. He'd never been able to hold a grudge, a characteristic I envied. After setting up the tree, he winked at me and said, "It's all yours, brother. I still have our tree to set up at home." He looked around at the noisy, disorganized, chaotic, joyful group. "Thank you for including me." He touched my elbow and was gone.

Mary was decorating with the others. She seemed distracted but spotted me and flashed a mechanical smile. I walked next door to the office and found Cassie and Sara deep in conversation. I stepped inside and took a seat until they noticed me.

Cassie walked over and hugged me. "How's the tree trimming coming along, Santa?"

"Oh, they're doing a fine job, and the kids are having a big time." I wanted to see if Cassie knew what might be on Mary's mind. Maybe she was just having a bad day and needed her space. "Cassie, has anything happened with Mary? She seems upset."

She pulled a disgusted face. "I was telling Sara that Mark Dunbar showed up this morning demanding to see Mary. Of course, we didn't let him through the gate, but he was loud and caused quite a ruckus, boasting and threatening. He was drunk. But commotion like that sure doesn't help us to keep a low profile or earn us any points with our neighbors. The Columbia police came and ran him off. Said they couldn't do much else. They seemed to think he was just blowing off steam. I didn't think it worth calling you so early."

"And Mary saw and heard him," I said. "No wonder she's so fretful. The girl's terrified of what that idiot might do. He's controlling her without ever laying a hand on her. Dunbar knows what he's doing, drunk or not. And she likely feels her safety is doubtful."

"I've increased security and asked for any of the general staff to take on extra shifts if they're able. I figure the more bodies we have around here, the better." Cassie had done what she could for the short term. But we needed a more permanent plan.

Something Cassie said had stirred a half-thought. "You said he was boasting and threatening. Anything specific?"

She paused, pursing her lips. "I don't recall anything specific. He was demanding to see Mary, said she belonged to him, his typical bullshit. He did say something I found odd though."

"What's that?"

Cassie looked at me with a curious smile. "As the law led him away, he said, 'I'll rain down fire and sulfur on he who sins against me and all those he loves.'" She tilted her head as her smile faded. "Sounded poetic, almost biblical, not like him at all. Of course, the police didn't take it as a serious threat, just the ravings of a drunk. I think he sees himself as a victim—the champion of the wronged."

Before we left Carolina House, I looked for Mary again. I found her alone in the library. She had an open book on her lap, but she was staring out at the garden or maybe somewhere I couldn't see. "Mind if I join you?"

"Course not, Jack." She smiled and patted the sofa beside her.

"Cassie told me you had a visitor this morning. You all right?"

She chewed her lip for a minute, maybe organizing her thoughts. "I was a little shaken this morning, but I feel better now. It just gets so tiresome, always looking over my shoulder, worrying he might show up. I feel so happy and optimistic, and then in an instant I'm back in that house being bullied and humiliated and—well, you know. I'm sure everyone thinks my fear is exaggerated or imagined, but it's not. It's real. Sometimes it feels more real than anything."

"Nobody thinks that. Mark is dangerous to you and everyone else here. He's spiteful and unpredictable. Believe me; we're taking this situation seriously. Cassie is doing everything possible to keep you all safe."

"Oh, I know. Cassie is amazing. She's here all the time, and she never seems to relax. I do feel safe here most of the time." She smiled. "I'm a worrier, Jack. I shouldn't let him get inside my head. I know everything will turn out fine."

I wasn't so sure faith would keep that wildcat treed, but I said nothing.

CHAPTER SEVENTEEN

Christmas Day punched in cold and wet. Wren and Lily were awake before any self-respecting rooster would've considered proper. They came knocking on our bedroom door, full of energy and ready for presents. We all headed downstairs to the living room. The girls looked at their mama. Sara said, "Okay, girls. Have fun." They began to sort through the presents, looking for their own.

My daughters were too excited to care about food, but I fixed a big breakfast anyway. Sara set the table, and we coaxed the girls away from the tree long enough to take a few bites. And then they were gone again. My wife and I took our time over coffee, watching our daughters. I tried hard to concentrate on my girls, but thoughts of Mark Dunbar kept finding me like stink finds a dead cat.

The Parker clan gathered at Mama's house at noon to exchange a few presents and share a meal. Dad's absence was a half-healed wound felt by everybody, but we were far from sad. All the kids sat on the floor surrounded by spent paper and empty boxes. Their laughter tinkled like wind chimes, reminding me of warm breezes and the promise of spring, still months away. Mama quietly left the living room, returning with a bag of neatly wrapped parcels.

"Please come sit close, children," she said. "I have one more gift for each of you, from your grandfather." Mama smiled at her grandchildren and waited until they'd gathered around her. "Your Papa was so happy last Christmas; he couldn't wait to begin carving this year's figures for you." She called each child's name and gave them the last carvings they would ever receive from my father.

Mama had said that Dad was ready to get started on the carvings after last Christmas; he always loved Christmastime. But I would've guessed he didn't want to take the chance that the cancer eating away at his brain might not allow him to finish what he likely knew would be his last chance to make his grandkids happy. Whatever the reason, I was thankful. The smiles on the kids' faces were a gift to my siblings and me he couldn't have imagined. My three sisters wiped tears from their smiling faces, and Bill cleared his throat and studied the ceiling.

Maggie and Mike held hands as they watched the kids show off their carved figures to their parents. My sister's smile showed both her love for her nieces and nephews and the happiness she'd found with her fiancé. I walked over to the newly engaged couple to offer my congratulations. I hadn't seen Mike since my lunch with Maggie. Concern clouded her face as I asked him to step out onto the porch. With a wink to my sister, I led Mike away.

"I wanted to talk to you before the big day next week. We probably won't have a chance before the wedding." I sat in Dad's rocker and Mike sat in Mama's.

"Maggie told me you were troubled that I'd asked her to marry me so soon. I understand and I want to assure you and your family that I love Maggie. I knew it the first time we met. I just don't see any reason to wait." His eyes remained on mine.

"I appreciate your saying all that, Mike. I'll admit I was skeptical at first, but my sister doesn't need me to second guess her decisions. She's far more intelligent than I could ever hope to be.

I wanted to make sure you realize what Maggie's been through in these last few years. Her first husband walked out on her because she didn't give him a child. She was torn up, not because he left her, but because he suggested she was not whole because she couldn't get pregnant." I was encouraged that Mike was listening without interruption or argument.

"In the last year, she's lost her father and been diagnosed with breast cancer. A shithead boyfriend broke off their relationship because he didn't want to be inconvenienced by her disease. Of course, you know about her mastectomy and her decision not to have reconstructive surgery." Mike didn't blink or twitch.

"So what I'm trying to say is I don't think Maggie can handle another disappointment right now. Mike, you better be damn sure about this, because I will not allow my little sister to be hurt again. I'll take whatever measures are necessary to prevent any more pain for her. That's why I'm involving myself where I have no business."

"Maggie told me everything you did and more," Mike said. "She's had a tough go of it over the last few years, no question. But I'm not attracted to her because I think she's an injured bird in need of rescuing or fixing. She's not my pet project, and she's not my plaything. I love your sister because she is exactly as she seems— beautiful, talented, kind, and interesting. I can give you a thousand more adjectives, but you already know she's special." His eyes didn't move so much as a gnat's hair from mine. "And although I'm not obligated to say this, I'll tell you that I will love and protect Maggie as long as I have breath and strength. She's tough as hell, and I know she doesn't need any protection. But I will just the same."

With his ardent speech finished, Mike's shoulders rose and fell, and his mouth set itself in a hard line.

I reached out my hand to him. "Welcome to the family, brother."

I found Audrey in the living room talking to Lauren and Andy. She smiled at me and patted my leg as I sat beside her on the sofa. "I was saying that Brad was awake this morning early before I left the hospital. He isn't coherent yet, but his blood pressure is better, and the doctors are talking about weaning him off the ventilator if he shows improvement over the next week or two. He still has a long way to go, but that's something at least." I noticed she said he instead of we, but I tried not to read too much into her words.

"That sounds good, honey," Lauren said. "Is there anything else we can do to help you while he's still in the hospital?"

"You've all done too much already. I appreciate everyone taking such good care of Izzy while I'm up there. I know this is hard on her."

I smiled at my sister. "We all love having Izzy around. Fact is, I think Maggie wants to take her on the honeymoon."

Audrey laughed. "I expect Mike might have a word or two to say about that."

I was glad to see her smile for a change. Her future was uncertain. As she watched her husband make small improvements, or sometimes none at all, she must've wondered what was next for her and for Izzy. How would she support her family? How would she ever pay the mounting medical and legal bills? I believed she'd made the decision to stay with Brad and take care of him, no matter the pain and betrayal he'd heaped upon her. She didn't talk of the future past the next day, but it must've weighed heavy on her mind and heart. I suspected Audrey would choose the hard road— maybe as some bullshit self-imposed penance for the ordeal she'd put her daughter through. She'd settled for martyrdom and would carry it on her shoulders like a yoke, plowing soil laced with one boulder after another.

As we began the parting ritual of hugs and promises, there seemed a sense of reluctance to depart, as if that might be the last Christmas we'd all be together. Could be we were feeling Dad's absence more than I'd thought—the end of the Tom Parker era? But as my family scattered to other obligations, I realized it wasn't an ending for us. We'd stumbled sure as hell, but the Parkers were a determined bunch—some might've even said hard-headed. I'd make sure we took care of our own, for without family, we were lost. Maybe I had more of my father in me than I'd allowed. And maybe that wasn't so bad.

Dark had rooted out the day by the time we drove through the gates of Carolina House at ten after six. The air was frosty, the temperature plunging toward a soft freeze. The crunch of tires on gravel was the lone sound in the still night. Wood smoke from the chimney drifted through the pine boughs, settling its heady scent all around us.

Inside, the children were watching a Christmas show, and Cassie and the staff were placing dish after dish on the long dining table. The carved table was decorated with candles and evergreen garlands, its centerpiece a hand-carved wooden bowl filled with red, green, and silver glass balls. According to Mary, the table and bowl had been made by my father. "Your daddy told me he made this table and bowl especially for Carolina House so we could have these big wonderful meals. Tom was so talented, Jack." The table was far more creative than anything I'd known Dad to make, and I found it heartwarming that he shared that part of himself with Carolina House, with Mary. He'd had a special bond with her. Still, I felt a twinge of jealousy that this was another piece of himself my father could not, or chose not, to share with his son. The resentment faded into the shadows as I looked around the table and saw the lives that were changing because of my father's vision, compassion, and actions. My petty jealousy was replaced by a warm appreciation for my father.

After supper, we all gathered in the large living room for coffee and dessert. Cassie and the women in residence had made pies of both the pumpkin and pecan varieties. I had two slices of the pecan. As Cassie reached for my empty plate, she asked, "Did you get enough, Jack?"

Sara snorted and said, "Let's hope so."

"I did, Cassie, and everything was delicious. Thank you and please ignore my wife. She doesn't share my appreciation for a finely crafted pecan pie."

Sara said, "If you appreciate it any more, you won't fit into your britches."

My girls were on the floor in the midst of the Carolina House children. The oldest of the kids was a few years younger than Lily. My daughters gave them their complete attention, and I recognized a miniature Sara in each girl. With a sun-bright grin, five-year-old Olivia showed everyone a storybook she'd received and asked Wren to read it to her. My oldest looked over at me and smiled. She gathered the little girl onto her lap and began to read.

Cassie said most of the children had never received any gift in their lives. Hard, angry fathers and mothers with no financial means were a way of life for them. Fear of physical abuse, for themselves or their mothers, was a constant reminder of their plight. Receiving a toy or book wouldn't magically make everything all better for the kids. But it might begin to plant a seed in their minds that violence was not normal or acceptable behavior. Our job was to show those children and their mothers kindness and love. It fell to people like Cassie to protect them and show them that there were people who knew their worth and valued their lives.

I looked around the living room and watched the faces of the staff who gave up so much of their time for others and the women who were there because they had nowhere else to go. We all had the same basic needs. We weren't so different from one another. Food and shelter were essential, yes, but respect and the absence of fear were equally critical. In our small way, Carolina House tried to provide the environment where these women and their children could begin to discover that they too had every right to those most basic of human needs. That discovery was but the first small step of their much longer journey to freedom.

Driving home, we sang Christmas songs along with the radio. Sara listened with a smile. At a break in our caroling, Lily said, "Tonight was fun. Can this be a Christmas tradition?"

"Yes, please," says Wren. "I especially loved reading to Olivia."

"That's a lovely idea, girls," Sara said.

The dream came again, and I woke with a start. Sara stirred and then settled. That dream had hounded me so long I couldn't remember a time when I'd not had it. It had always been the same until this Christmas night. I was still running and terrified, but for the first time my father was with me. Instead of feeling relief at him being there, I was even more scared and confused. His green eyes were fixed on me, begging me to help.

As my breathing returned to normal, I stared at my wife's face. I wanted to wake her and tell her how the dream had changed, but I knew it would've been worthless and selfish. She couldn't have said anything to take away the feeling of loss and failure. I'd only have taken sleep from her. It wasn't comfort I wanted anyway. I needed an explanation for that wretched nightmare, and that was something she couldn't give. Why was I so terrified? And why was I fearful for my father? He'd been a quiet man but physically strong. He couldn't have possibly needed help from a boy. What could I have offered Tom Parker?

I'd never needed much sleep, but the lack of it, coupled with the emotional drain of the dream, left me wishing I could've returned to a dreamless slumber for a week. Instead, I got out of bed and pulled the covers up over Sara. After one more look at her face, I crept down the stairs. Lucy and Ethel met me at the foot of the staircase and followed me to the kitchen. They knew the routine and were expecting food. I had no appetite but gave them each a cookie from the treat jar. I sat on the sofa, and the dogs settled on either side.

Too jittery for TV and unable to focus on reading, I rubbed the dogs' ears, trying to recall anything that might have triggered a change in the nightmare. A random deviation? Tainted food? Could be the addition of Dad was some subconscious, unresolved father-son issue. That sounded more like psychobabble bullshit than anything concrete. But the lack of rest from the frequent interruption was real enough.

Since I couldn't sleep anyway, I dressed, wrote a note to Sara, and put the dogs in my truck. At that late hour, on Christmas night, there would be few other cars on the road. Lucy and Ethel settled on the back seat and fell asleep within the first mile. The sweet notes of Tommy Emmanuel's guitar filled my truck. I drove aimlessly, concentrating on the pluck and squeal of Tommy's strings and the thrum of tires on blacktop. The night was black as sin but for my headlights. I entered the city limits without realizing I'd been headed that way. I wasn't all that surprised to find myself near Carolina House.

I drove by the house barely above idle. By design, the tall fence gave the residents a good measure of privacy and security. All seemed quiet on the grounds. As I passed the gate a second time, a pickup parked on the opposite side of the street switched on his lights and sped away. I watched taillights in my side mirror grow smaller, then made a quick U-turn and accelerated after him. By the time I saw the truck's lights again, he was turning into Greenview Commons. If he got well into that neighborhood too far ahead, I might not find him again; the roads were like a maze in there.

I pushed the accelerator with a bit more purpose. The engine snarled, and my truck surged ahead like it'd caught its second wind. I passed the other truck and pulled ahead ten yards. I braked hard and angled my truck across the road so that passing wasn't an option. The driver skidded to a stop a few inches from my front quarter panel, and I was already out and running toward him. I slapped the tinted window with my open hand twice. "Step out of the truck now, asshole," I yelled. I stepped back to allow the door to open.

A red-headed, teenaged girl stepped down from the pickup, and she was bawling. "I'm so sorry," she said. "I know I was speeding. I fell asleep at my boyfriend's house and was trying to get home before my daddy realizes I'm not there. Please don't give me a ticket. He'll kill me." She covered her face with her hands and leaned back against the doorjamb.

I was stunned stupid, and my anger crumbled to shame. "I'm sorry, miss," I said. "I thought you were somebody else. I'm not the law." There were several paths that situation might've taken. Nary a one was what I'd have called good. Only then did I realize that truck wasn't even the same color or make as Dunbar's. "I'll move my truck so you can get on home."

Realizing she wasn't in trouble, the girl's attitude changed from repentance to annoyance and then to anger, all justified. "You're not a cop? Then why the hell did you do that? You scared the shit out of me. You could have killed me." She was still cussing and screaming when I got in my truck and drove away. I looked straight ahead and kept moving until I was far from her. Five miles down the road, I pulled over onto the shoulder and sat, eyes closed, until my pulse returned to somewhere approaching normal. Lucy licked my ear, and in my mirror I saw my dogs staring back at me, curious yet quiet—no judgment from the back seat. I put the truck in gear and put tires back onto the blacktop.

Driving home, I wondered when I'd become so paranoid. I'd been sure that was Mark Dunbar watching Carolina House and hoping for a chance to make trouble. Instead, I'd scared an innocent girl and endangered her with my bullshit theatrics. Clearly, I'd lost too much sleep over the last weeks. As exhaustion and despair fogged my brain, I understood that lack of rest was not the true problem. I needed fortification. I needed my family.

CHAPTER EIGHTEEN

Maggie's wedding day started out frosty but soon began to thaw. A cavernous tent, warmed by glowing heaters, served for both the ceremony and reception. At one end, flower-ornamented tables encircled a dance floor, and the band was tuned and ready. At the other end, family and friends sat in chairs placed in perfect rows. In front of the chairs, a dais, overflowing with sprays and vases and garlands of flowers, awaited the couple. But however beautiful everything else was, my baby sister was the star. She wore a simple white dress. Her raven hair spilled across her shoulders, unrestrained by a veil. She truly outshone the sun. On the platform, Mike waited for his bride in a gray suit. His tie matched Maggie's green eyes.

As she and I waited for our cue, just outside the main tent, Maggie stood on her toes and kissed my cheek. "What was that for?"

"For not pitying me after the mastectomy."

"I don't understand."

She squeezed my arm, smiling. "After my surgery, when my friends would stop by Mama's to visit, the pity was there in their eyes. Poor damaged Maggie. Of course, they meant well and didn't say anything so obvious. But they didn't have to. I could read their faces easy enough. I even saw some in Lauren's and Bill's eyes. But not once did I see pity in your eyes—concern for my health, yes, but never pity."

"I've never known anybody less in need of that than you. When I get confused or scared, I think about how strong you are. We have a lot of strong women in our family, but you're always the one I think about. You're my rock, little sister."

She punched my arm. "Don't make me cry and ruin my makeup, you jackass."

"You started it."

As the band started playing the "Wedding March," friends and family stood to honor Maggie. Arm in arm, we walked down the aisle, and I symbolically gave her away to Mike. I leaned in close to her and whispered, "Love you, little squirrel."

She kissed my cheek again and said, "Thank you for everything, big brother. I love you too."

There weren't any bridesmaids or groomsmen. Mama was Maggie's matron of honor, and Mike's father his best man. The ceremony was sweet and honest. They lit a candle together, creating one flame from two and recited their original vows, simple words from their hearts. With a kiss, they were hitched. I prayed Mike was a good man and their marriage would be all they wanted, but I knew that was out of my control. Disappointment, tragedy—even pure bad luck—was no stranger to any family. But with ours, bad shit sought us out and ran us down like a wolf on a wounded deer. Still, we kept fighting back. And of all my siblings, Maggie deserved to have happiness in her life the most—at least a chance. She'd earned that much.

The days began to lengthen, but the cold lingered like an old bachelor uncle after Sunday dinner. I'd just finished the tree house and stood looking up at it. I felt satisfied at finishing, but I'd miss working with Dad's tools and wood, building something he'd imagined.

The last months had connected me to him in a way we'd never been able to do when he was alive. I believed I understood a little more about how he'd reckoned the world. The beauty and proportion of that oak were how my father saw everything. To him, the curve of a tree branch was as beautiful as a woman's shoulders. His grand-children's laughter was as sweet sounding as a Martin Guitar. He saw or heard beauty everywhere because he'd looked for it. He didn't pass by a grazing horse or a flowering dogwood tree without recognizing its visual worth. He'd never said these things to me, but I had only to look at the furniture he'd built or his sketches to understand that about him. Might be if we'd had the chance to work on the tree house together, we'd have found common cause, mended the silent years.

As I touched up the paint on the interior and inspected the roof and siding, I saw not a collection of boards and shingles and nails, but I saw magic, imagined by my father and brought to life by my hands. The carefully drawn carvings, which I'd spent countless hours giving life, created an enchanted cottage covered in vines and leaves and flowers. That gift from my father would be enjoyed by generations of our family. And Tom Parker would be remembered.

I moved on to clean Dad's workshop, as he'd always done at the end of a project. I knew I'd use it for the occasional repair at the farm and wanted everything to be in place the next time I walked in. I'd felt closer to him in his workshop and in the oak's branches than ever while he'd lived.

With the lumber stacked, tools cleaned and sharpened, and the workbenches dusted, I swept the floor free of sawdust. As I pulled the carving bench away from the wall to reach the shavings I'd missed before, I noticed a dusty canvas rectangle. I pulled out the heavy parcel and set it on the bench. Cutting the twine and unwrapping the canvas, I found a carved sign. The shingle was sim-ilar to the one hanging above the shop's door, a thick slab of oak.

But the carving was far more ornate. Without question, my father had made it, but that sign was of a level of fanciful detail he'd never allowed in his furniture and cabinets. It read Parker and Son – Fine Wood Creations and Imaginings. The established date was the year I graduated from high school.

"Honey, that was so long ago," Mama said when I showed her the sign. "I think your daddy believed you would become his partner after graduation. He said you had so many ideas about design and marketing and cost projections and I don't know what all. Tom didn't realize you were leaving that day, Jack. Frankly, it caught us all off guard." She turned her head so I couldn't read her eyes.

"But he never mentioned any of this to me. He never even suggested I become his partner." I thought back to that period, trying to remember ever speaking to Dad about my working in his business permanently.

"You know he would never come out and ask. He probably assumed you would do it. Maybe you missed the signals, honey. As I recall, you were preoccupied with other things about that time. When you moved away, I suppose he just put the sign away and forgot about it."

Mama's gentle smile infuriated me for some reason.

"How could he assume something like that? Did he think I could read his mind? I don't understand at all. I was struggling to find a job to pay for college, and he still didn't say anything. Even when I dropped out he never did." But maybe Mama was right. Maybe I'd missed signals from my father. Trying to decode his intent exasperated me to my bones.

If he'd spoken his wishes out loud, or if I'd heard through the silence, everything might have been so different between us. I didn't understand how he could have simply wrapped the sign and forgotten about it. But somehow I didn't think he'd forgotten at all. I believed he'd kept it in his heart, simmering away for all those years.

Sara and the girls worked on a jigsaw puzzle, while I read a request for proposal from a potential client. The RFP was tedious, but I needed the job and was struggling to concentrate on the house plans. The client had provided the specs I needed to submit a bid along with a half dozen other builders. My eyes were beginning to glaze, and I was thinking of coffee and the long night ahead when my phone buzzed. Audrey never called in the evening unless something was wrong.

"Sorry to bother you this late," she said. "I wanted to let you know Brad's doctor says he can come home next week. He just now told us, and I wanted to tell you first."

"That's good news, honey. How's he doing?" The last time I'd seen him, two weeks before, Brad had seemed disconnected from his surroundings. He wasn't able to focus, and his response time was a couple beats shy of normal. His speech was slurred, and his motor functions were awkward and sluggish. In my opinion, Brad wasn't close to being ready for home, but I suspected the decision for them was a financial one more so than a medical one.

"Jack, there hasn't been any improvement since you visited a couple weeks ago. The neurologist says Brad will likely not mend beyond where he is now. There's a good chance he'll get much worse over time."

The damage to Brad's brain, due to the overdose and multiple flat lines, had been severe. For a while, we hadn't figured he'd make it—the machines were barely keeping him alive. Maybe it would have been a mercy if he'd not survived. I couldn't rid my mind of the image of Audrey wasting her life caring for the bastard.

"What are you going to do, Audrey?" Her options were limited, but I knew what she would do before she spoke.

"Don't start, Jack. He's my husband and I'm going to take him home and care for him. Brad has made some awful mistakes, but so have I."

"Have you told Izzy her father is coming home?"

"Yes. She's happy her daddy will be home soon but confused by his behavior. I'll have to try and explain this all to her, but I don't know where to start."

"I don't know that Izzy is old enough for the whole truth now."

Audrey sighed. She'd been through so much in the last year. "I agree. I'll say her daddy is sick, and we have to take care of him. She's so smart, Jack. That thin explanation won't hold her for long."

"True enough. If it were me, I'd tell her everything sometime in the near future. If she figures it out on her own, she'll resent you." I hesitated and then said, "If you decide to tell her now, Izzy might understand if you don't want Brad there with you. There are facilities that would take him."

"No, Jack. I couldn't do that to him. I married him, for better or worse."

"Whatever you decide, I'll be there to help. We all will." As I finished the call, I looked up to see Sara watching me.

As spring yawned and tried to wake for good, the Parker clan started spending more time at the Knoll. Lauren drove down as much as she could with the kids. Audrey and Brad spent a lot of time strolling along the fence lines or the wooded paths beyond. Brad's steps were slow as molasses, but my sister was patient, always there to steady him. They were dealing with their medical and legal and marital issues quietly but head-on, according to my sister.

The kids spent every waking hour in the tree house, sometimes pretending to be the Swiss Family Robinson. They slept in it, swung beneath it, and climbed on it. Seemed to me, it beckoned to them. They returned to it every weekend, bringing us all together as never before.

On the last weekend in April we had a cookout—hotdogs, hamburgers, and all the fixings—just like we used to. Dad had always enjoyed having his children and grandchildren all close by, within his reach. Maybe our get-togethers were an unspoken tribute to our father, our way of keeping him with us. Family was a big part of him, but still just a portion. He would sit on the porch watching the grandchildren play and listening to his own children and their spouses talk about work or family. He hadn't joined the conversations much unless he was asked. He had Carolina House, his work, and his family. Somehow he'd kept everything compartmentalized. It must have been exhausting to have kept it up for so many years.

Bill walked over to where I was flipping burgers and handed me a beer. "This is nice," he said. "I don't know why we ever stopped having these. I always enjoyed listening to the kids laugh."

I nodded toward the porch. "Dad always loved that too. Remember him sitting on the porch smiling as the kids raced past chasing lightning bugs?"

He gave me a sideways look. "Why did we stop? I don't recall."

"Oh, I don't know. I guess we all got too busy. Driving home was hard for us to do so much, and I reckon for Lauren too. Seemed like my girls always had a soccer game or birthday party on the weekends." I took a sip of beer and felt the evening chill begin to swirl around us. That early in the spring, it still got cool when the sun slid away.

"Reckon we all got busy with one thing or another." He took a pull from his own beer, his eyes never leaving mine. "I'm glad you moved back home, Jack." Bill looked over at Mama and our sisters and wives. "I wish Lauren would too. It's a long drive for her. I feel better when we're all together." He moved off into the gloaming without mentioning that the real reason we'd stopped was the bullshit between me and Dad—at some point I'd just stopped coming.

Seven of eight grandchildren were sleeping in the tree house. Kathy would sleep at Mama's to help with any late-night mind changers. Will was staying the night on the river with his dad. Bill loved night fishing. He'd asked me to go with them, but I had declined. I looked over at Sara. She was wrapped in my jacket, listening to one of Mama's stories, smiling. I loved camping on sandbars and watching the fire while we waited on a big catfish to take our bait, but Sara and I didn't often have a night when both girls were away. It would've been a damn shame to waste such a night.

With the kids all settled in the tree house with snacks, pajamas, and sleeping bags, Sara and I departed for our house. On the short drive home, Sara said, "You all right, honey?" She was still bundled in my jacket, turned toward me with her legs curled beneath her.

"Sure. Why do you ask?"

"Oh, you looked a bit sad tonight. Is something on your mind?"

"I'm fine. I was just thinking about Dad a lot tonight. Remembering how he loved cookouts."

"Your daddy loved his family. You could see it in his eyes whenever everyone was together. Tom especially loved watching you and Bill. He was proud of you two, Jack."

"It would have been nice to hear it though."

Sara sighed. "Jack, don't try to see something that's not there. Not everybody can say the things they want." Those conversations must've been tiresome to her. I didn't blame her for feeling put out.

"Bill asked me tonight why we stopped having weekend get-togethers years ago."

"What did you tell him?"

"That driving home so much was hard for us and Lauren, that we all got too busy." I glanced at her as she shook her head, a movement so slight I could've been imagining it. "What?"

"You know that's not why, Jack. You need to be honest with yourself, if not your family. You tried to hurt Tom by keeping his granddaughters from him." She held up a hand. "I'll tell you what I think. I believe it broke his heart when we stopped coming home as often. Not just because of the girls—your father missed his oldest son."

When the truth hits you in the face like a thunder clap, there's not much you can say. "Thanks for the perspective, sweet girl. You're right as usual."

"Of course I am. Now take me home and warm me up."

I pressed the accelerator a bit harder and with purpose.

For the first time since Dad's passing, our family seemed to have settled into a peaceful existence. Audrey had made her decision and seemed content to take care of her husband. Her heart was more forgiving than mine. Maggie was married to a man who was kind and decent. More than that, his love for my sister was obvious to us all. Bill was staying home more. I believed he was trying to improve his relationship with Kathy. Lauren was steady as ever. She was the pick of the Parker litter. She would always do what was right and proper. Of course, she had problems, but she took care of her own and neither complained nor made excuses.

Mama was happy because her children were finally thriving, or at least not falling apart. She wanted nothing more than to have her children and grandchildren nearby. At weekend cookouts, she was the queen; her rocking chair was her throne. She beamed as grandchildren giggled and played. She glowed when daughters or daughters-in-law asked for advice or favorite recipes or guidance on the proper depth to plant gladiola bulbs.

As I counted my family's blessings, I realized that I had more reasons than most to be thankful. Yet I worried Audrey would start with the pills again, as it sunk in that she was little better than a prisoner of her own making. Maggie's cancer could return, taking not only her breast but her life. I thought about Mark Dunbar, quiet those last few weeks, hurting Mary or my family. The unknown was always far and away more fearsome than reality.

I forced myself to stop agonizing over the might-haves and enjoy my family. Finding them in the kitchen baking cookies, I stopped and watched from the shadows of the living room. Sara had a dab of flour on her cheek, and both girls smiled as she told a story about baking with her own mama. The uncertainty and fear melted away as I watched them. In place of the doubt and angst was a new and welcome feeling. You might've called it hope. Afraid of breaking the spell and disturbing their moment, I turned and left them quietly.

CHAPTER NINETEEN

The air still had a bite in the mornings, but as the sun climbed above the pine tops, buttery warmth spread across the hills. Spring was in full throat, anxious to show off her glory. And I needed to be outside, to be a part of that awakening. Sara and I were in the habit of taking long walks most days. Sometimes we strolled around our own property, but often we drove the short distance to the Knoll and walked or rode the horses along the wooded trails behind Mama's property. We'd been wanting to try something different though.

I borrowed Bill's horse trailer and returned to Mama's for the geldings. Loading both horses up the ramp, I stored the saddles and other tack in a forward compartment. The saddle bags with wine, cheese, and other accoutrements sat on the pickup's rear seat. We drove north, toward the Foothills, to a hunt club managed by an old friend. With deer season long over and turkey season still a week away, we'd have several thousand acres to ourselves. I had a key to the gate and a beautiful woman beside me.

With the horses saddled, we mounted and chose a dirt road leading into the heart of the club's acreage. Sara and I jawed about family or our work or the next Carolina House project we were planning, but for the most part, we rode in easy silence. I told her a story about nine-year-old Bill negotiating with a classmate on a price for baby Maggie. Bill had bid his friend up to a baseball glove, a broken fishing reel, and a half-finished pack of bubblegum before Dad caught him and soured the deal. Bill had thought two sisters were plentiful. One more would've given the girls an unfair advantage over us boys.

"You two were crazy, even as little boys." Sara laughed, though she'd heard my story more than a few times. "Your poor sisters should be sainted, having to put up with you and Bill all those years."

"And they've never thanked us once. How's that for gratitude?"

Sara looked at me and grinned. "I think your mama really did drop you on your head."

The afternoon passed too quickly, and we returned to the club-house as evening gathered. Sara dismounted and walked over to me. She kissed my cheek and stepped into my arms. "Thank you for today, Jack. We needed that. I needed it."

We drove home in happy stillness. Nothing could've spoiled the day's perfection. We stopped by the Knoll to unload the horses and pick up our daughters. Mama sat on her porch listening to the night. "Did you two have a fun day?"

Sara's smiled. "We had a perfect day, Lizzie."

Mama smiled at her and touched her arm. "After all the ruckus of the last year, you both deserve a bit of quiet. The girls are asleep. Why don't you leave them with me tonight? Pick them up whenever you've a mind to tomorrow."

I looked at her and said, "That sounds like a fine idea, Mama." I hugged my mother, and we left her staring off toward the tree house.

Turning right, instead of left, out of the drive, we headed to Bill's house to drop off his trailer.

As we topped the last hill before the turnoff to Bill's place, I saw the sky was tinted orange where no orange should've been. Smoke-tainted air filled my truck's cab. Fear crept up on me as quick and silent as a panther.

I dropped a gear and slowed, just enough to keep the trailer from tipping, as I turned into Bill's drive. Fire was everywhere. The house and barn were both engulfed. Kathy and their two youngest children, Tara and Alex, stood beneath a pine tree a hundred yards from the house. Kathy hugged her children as she watched not the house, but the barn.

As I slid to a stop, we jumped out of the truck and rushed to Kathy. "Where are Bill and Will?" I had to raise my voice above the roaring flames.

"The barn," was all she could manage.

I took off at a run, calling over my shoulder to Sara, "Make sure she's called 911."

My request turned out to be unnecessary as I heard sirens bleating their way toward us. As I ran to the barn, I saw Will standing a good distance away. He was fighting to control three wild-eyed horses. I veered toward Will, but he yelled, "I'm all right. Daddy's still in the barn."

I changed course mid-stride and headed for my brother. The hay loft was an inferno. Flames spewed from the load door and roof. Rushing in through the barn's open double doors, I found the barn filled with smoke. I couldn't see Bill. Dropping to my hands and knees, I spied him backing out of Brandy's stall. Her high-pitched whinny was unnerving. Nothing on earth could curdle my blood like a horse's scream. Brandy was fighting against the rope, tossing her head, banging against the stall door. I grabbed the rope above Bill's hands. He didn't seem surprised to see me, but his eyes were desperate and he pleaded. "I've got her. Get the filly, Jack."

As Bill coaxed Brandy through the stall door and toward fresh air, a crash thundered and the barn shook. I ducked into the stall and looked around for the filly. Smoke billowed and rolled, covering everything. Again, I dropped to my knees and looked about. The filly was in the far corner, trapped beneath a burning beam.

She thrashed her head about wildly, twisting her body, trying to escape, screaming like her mama. I tried to lift the heavy timber, burning my palms but unable to stop and cursing my own impotence. Then Bill was beside me. He grabbed the beam next to me, and we both tried to lift it from the foal.

The enormous flaming pine beam defeated us with ease, yet we continued to exert every ounce of strength we could muster. I felt, before I saw, that Bill's efforts had ceased. He laid a blistered hand on my arm and leaned in close to my ear. "Enough, Jack."

"No," I screamed. "We just need some leverage."

He shook his head. "She's gone."

I saw the filly lying still in the shavings, then followed Bill outside. He walked over to help Will with the frightened horses. Will looked at his father, and Bill shook his head. Grief spilled down my nephew's soot-covered cheeks. I stumbled a few paces away and vomited, the filly's screaming still ringing in my head.

When I looked up, a collection of emergency vehicles was strewn about Bill's property, red and blue lights flashing and dancing against the distant tree line. Firefighters blasted powerful water streams onto the house with little effect. The barn was too far gone, and we all knew it. Richland County deputies stood close to Kathy, Sara, and the kids, helpless to do anything but watch. An EMT approached Bill and me. "Either of you guys hurt?"

My brother looked at his hands but said nothing.

Having been led far from the burning buildings, the horses had calmed considerably. Brandy kept looking toward the barn, watching for her foal to emerge. Will stayed close to the horses as the young EMT bandaged our burns. "They're not all that bad. Make sure you change the bandages twice a day, and everything will be fine." He winced as he realized the careless stupidity of his words. "Sorry, I didn't mean it like that."

"It's all right, son. Thanks for taking care of us." I smiled and nodded to him. "You did a fine job with these bandages." He nodded and headed over to check on Will.

A deputy walked over and asked for the property owner. Bill looked up. "I'm Bill Parker." He nodded at me and then Will. "My brother and my son over there." The deputy reached forward to shake Bill's hand. Bill held out his bandages, and the deputy retreated a step.

"I'm Deputy Louis Coleman. Can you tell me what happened, Mr. Parker?"

"We were all asleep when our smoke alarms sounded. I smelled the smoke and hustled everyone outside and away. That was when I saw the barn was afire too. Will and me ran over to try and save the horses. That's when my brother drove up and came to help." Bill looked twenty years older. Fire and smoke and death could do that to a body.

The deputy made a few notes on his pad then asked me, "Why were you here so late tonight, sir?"

"I was returning my brother's horse trailer." He nodded, more to himself than to me.

"And I see you rescued all the horses." He looked over at Will and his charges.

"Not all of them," Bill said, his voice flat.

"Sorry to hear that. Any idea how it started? Seems strange both the house and barn were burning. They're pretty far apart."

Bill looked at the burning barn. "The loft was full of hay. It would only take a spark from the house, I reckon."

"True enough. Any reason to believe somebody would do this deliberately? You piss anybody off recently?" The deputy seemed uncomfortable with his own question.

"Other than my wife, no." The deputy was ignorant of my brother's scorn or chose to ignore it. He caught up his notes then started to leave, telling Bill the fire marshal's office would conduct an arson investigation, as was standard in such cases.

"Which cases?" Bill asked.

"Cases where the cause is undetermined or not apparent. It's standard," the deputy said again, as if that explained everything.

He flipped his pad closed and walked over to stand with the other deputies.

Bill stood with his family under the pines, his arms around his wife and daughter. His sons stood shoulder to shoulder, facing their father. Little Alex peered around at the ruins of his family's home. They huddled together as if they were cold, but it wasn't warmth they sought from one another. I knew my brother was telling them they would rebuild, start anew. But more than that, he was transferring his strength to his family, who would need it, in the days and weeks to come, far more than he.

Once the fires had died to smoldering piles of memories, Sara used Kathy's car to drive my sister-in-law and the kids over to Mama's house. Will wanted to stay and help us shuttle the horses to the Knoll, but Bill was adamant. "No, son. You go on over to your grandma's house with your mama. Help her with the little ones, all right? You've done far more tonight than a boy should ever have to do. I'm proud of you, Will."

"I'll take care of them, Daddy." He stepped into his father's arms, and I walked a few paces away to afford my brother and nephew a measure of privacy. As Will walked toward the others, Bill watched him.

"That one is going to make a good man someday." Bill looked at his bandaged hands. He was right; Will had the makings of a fine, honest man.

"Let's get these horses moved," I said. "It's nearly daybreak."

We moved Brandy and a gelding first. She was Bill's main concern and at first refused to load into the horse trailer. She kept looking toward the barn, shying away from the ramp, jingling her halter. Bill led her a few paces away and spoke into her ear, stroking her neck. I wasn't fool enough to believe my brother could converse with horses, but inside of five minutes he walked Brandy up the ramp.

Since the trailer was already hitched to my truck and my hands were less damaged than Bill's, I drove. He settled back into the passenger seat and closed his eyes. We were both near our limits, and we rode in silence for a time. Without opening his eyes, my brother said, "It was him. Mark Dunbar started those fires."

"What? How can you know that?"

"Saw him. When we escaped the house and I saw the barn was afire too, he was there, behind the east paddock, his face lit up by the flames. The bastard was watching us, grinning like the devil himself." Bill opened his eyes and looked at me. I glanced over at him and then back at the road.

"You've only seen him the one time, in the bar. Could have been somebody else." But, of course, it had to have been Dunbar.

"He done this, Jack. That piece of shit screwed lag bolts through the doors into the jambs. He tried to trap us in there. He tried to burn my family alive." Bill smashed his fist against the dash, and I felt the shock through the steering wheel. He put his hands to his face. "Shit."

"This is my fault. You were right. I should have talked to you before I went after him." My desire to hurt Dunbar had nearly cost my brother his family. It had cost him his home and Brandy's filly.

"No, Jack. What you did was right. I should've been there with you. I was angry about you not telling me sooner. But you did warn me eventually, and still he got to us. That man is evil."

Mark Dunbar was evil. Poor Mary had endured so much meanness from him. Now he was coming after my family, either because I'd shamed him or because we were keeping Mary from him. His reasons didn't matter. The spiteful son of a bitch had tried to kill Bill's family. He seemed to be telling me, "See, I can hurt you whenever I want. I can rain down fire and sulfur on you and those you love."

"Wait a minute, Bill. Why didn't you tell the law any of this? Dunbar tried to kill you—the lag bolts! They need this information."

Bill was strangely quiet. He looked out the passenger window. I wondered if he would answer me at all. Finally, he said, "I can't tell them about Dunbar without getting you into trouble too. If they question him, he'll swear out a warrant on you for assault or some such. Besides, it's my word against his, and he was at a pretty far distance at night." He shook his head. "I have to work this out myself."

"Are you fucking kidding? Don't worry about me. You can't let him get away with this."

"He won't, Jack." His eyes were hard, unblinking. "I'll make sure of that."

In the east, the sun rose red and angry.

CHAPTER TWENTY

As we parked in front of Carolina House, Cassie ran out from the main residence. She wrung her hands and moved her lips without making a sound, then finally found her voice.

"It's Mary. She's gone. Not sure how long. Robin found her missing at bed check this morning. Oh, Lord." Poor Cassie could hardly breathe, she was in such a state. She twisted her fingers until I figured she'd break them clean off.

Sara put an arm around her shoulders and placed her other hand over Cassie's to quiet their restlessness. "Honey, try to calm down a bit. We need you focused and composed. Can you do that for us?"

Cassie nodded. "I can do that, yes."

"Did Robin or anybody else hear anything last night or notice anything strange about Mary's behavior?" I asked.

"One of the other women saw her talking to Danny in the library after supper. Afterward, she started acting strange. Said she didn't want to watch the movie with everyone because she didn't feel well. Then she went to her room."

"Did anybody speak to her after that?" Sara asked.

"Robin checked on her around eight. Mary wouldn't open her door, but said she was tired and going to bed early. Robin said she sounded like she'd been crying. Said she figured Mary just needed rest."

"Have you spoken to Danny?" I asked.

Cassie put her face in her hands and shook her head. "No one can locate him. His shift ended at ten last night."

Sara looked at me over Cassie's bowed head. She asked, "Can we speak to Robin?"

Cassie sniffed. "Robin went off shift this morning. She wanted to stay but had to get home and take her daughter to school. Do you want me to call her back?"

"Not right now. Let her sleep. Did you call the sheriff's department?"

I had the same question as my wife. Mary was discovered gone an hour earlier, and the law wasn't there yet.

"I called Richland County as soon as Robin told me. They said they couldn't do anything until Mary has been missing for twenty-four hours. I'm not even sure who would have jurisdiction in a situation like this, the sheriff or Columbia police or SLED."

My bet was that the South Carolina Law Enforcement Division would take the lead on something like that, especially with Dunbar likely mixed up in it. But I was making assumptions, and we still had twenty-three hours before any law would get involved. We didn't know but that Mary was fine and just off by her lonesome.

But wherever she was and whatever her reasoning, I wasn't interested in sitting around waiting on Johnny Law to get up off his ass.

"Cassie, how could Mary leave the grounds without setting off the gate alarm?" That question had been bouncing around in my brain since we'd pulled through.

"I wondered the same thing," Cassie said. "I figure she opened the gate from the control panel inside the house, and then ran out before it closed again. She might be able to do it if she ran fast— or if somebody helped her. Either that or she found one of the remotes."

"Did Mary take her belongings?" Sara asked.

"She didn't have much to begin with, but she took a few of her things, maybe some personal items. Her dresser drawers were half open. We gave her a baby shower a couple weeks ago, and she didn't take any of the baby gifts, not a single one. Her room looks as if…" Cassie went quiet. Her lips still moved, but no words found purchase.

"Looks as if what?" Sara's gentle prodding caused Cassie to focus on us again.

"I was going to say that her room looks as if she packed hurriedly, as if maybe somebody was forcing her against her will." She shook her head slowly, her eyes closed in resignation.

"We don't know that for sure," Sara said without conviction.

"Do you have Mark Dunbar's address?" I asked.

"You don't think she would—oh, no." Cassie was horrified at the thought.

"I don't know what to think, but we can't sit around waiting on the law. Do you have his address? Any other information about him? I also need you to keep trying Danny's number." I was beginning to think he was up to his neck in the whole mess, but I had a feeling he'd be hard to find.

"I have Dunbar's address and other information on him I've collected. It's in Mary's file. I'll go get it and then start calling Danny again." Cassie headed for the carriage house, more focused with a task to complete.

Sara watched her walk toward the office, then turned to me. "What do you have in mind, Jack?"

"I can't sit around for a day waiting on the law to work out whose turn it is to give a shit. I'm going to look around and ask a few questions. Maybe I'll get lucky." I'd thought I might never have to see Dunbar again, but odds were I was wrong. I didn't think Mary had gone off by herself without telling Cassie, and I couldn't think of any other explanation but that Dunbar had forced her to leave with him. How had he gained access to the grounds here without tripping the alarm? And why would Mary have gone with him without a fight? "Will you stay here with Cassie for a while? She's in a bad state and needs support. And I want to know if Danny shows up. Something isn't quite right there."

"Of course I'll stay. That poor girl," Sara said.

My brother hadn't mentioned Mark Dunbar since the fire, which puzzled me. He was busy with the insurance company and the fire marshal. The marshal had found the lag bolts and determined the fire was malicious arson, but they had no suspects, having brilliantly ruled out Bill and Kathy from trying to trap themselves in a burning house. Maybe Bill was trying to move on with life. He didn't hesitate when I asked him to help look for Mary.

"Where are we headed? I'll drive," he said, stepping down off Mama's porch.

"Let's start at Dunbar's house," I said and typed the address into Bill's GPS. Mary's ex-boyfriend rented a house in a rural neighborhood off Sandhill Road, noted for its low rent and high crime rate. For him to be living in that area, maybe the drug business wasn't as profitable as I'd allowed.

"This is a waste of time, Jack," Bill said as he pulled into Dunbar's driveway. He tapped his hands nervously on the steering wheel. "If this guy is involved, he's most likely long gone by now. We should try somewhere else."

"Maybe so, but I don't know where else to start looking for Mary."

Bill shut off his engine but didn't move.

"You coming?" I asked. He sighed and shook his head, then we stepped down from the truck and walked up to the porch. I knocked on the door harder than was necessary. Waited two seconds and banged on it again.

"Y'all boys looking for that Mark Dunbar?" The next-door neighbor sat rocking on her own small porch, watching us. She looked to be in her mid-sixties, a skinny woman with sparse hair and a face marred by little care and a hard life. She wore a house dress and a tattered robe over that. Her tone seemed friendly enough.

"Yes'm," answered Bill.

"He ain't there. Ain't seen him in four, five days. Maybe a week gone."

Bill looked at me, lifted his shoulders, and then turned to the neighbor. "Thank you, ma'am. We appreciate the help." He started toward the truck.

"Y'all the law?" she asked, curiosity overcoming any distrust of strangers she might've harbored.

"No, ma'am," I said. "Why do you ask?"

"Them SLED boys was here about a week back, asking questions and such. Weren't long afterward Mark stopped coming home altogether. Maybe y'all should ask them."

I looked over at Bill, who was strangely uninterested, not even looking at her.

"How do you know they were SLED?" I asked.

She looked at me and grinned. "It was writ on they jackets, big as you please."

"Thank you, ma'am. We'll walk around the house once and then leave," I said. "We won't disturb anything. You all right with that?"

She grinned again and chuckled. "Makes no nevermind to me. Y'all can look around till Jesus comes, for all I care. You won't find nothing more than you did the first time." She was clearly confusing us with the law still.

We walked around the house and looked in the windows. The house was meagerly furnished but neat. Inexpensive furniture and a huge television sat in a corner of the living room. We didn't see anyone or any sign of activity. I saw nothing to be gained there, so we made our way back to Bill's truck. When we drove past the neighbor's house, she was looking at us and laughing. Her teeth were discolored, melted to nubs, and I realized she was closer to forty than sixty. I reckoned hard circumstances and meth had aged her early, as if in a hurry to move her from this life to whatever might come next for her.

"Wonder what old Mark's done to have SLED finally looking for him?" I was thinking out loud and wasn't expecting Bill to answer.

"Maybe burn down one house too many, sell drugs to the wrong kid, beat another girl half to death. Take your fucking pick."

Dunbar's parents lived south and east of Columbia, in St. Matthews. Bill entered the small town at a respectful speed. St. Matthews's speed traps were common knowledge, their fines steep. We parked in front of a small white cinder-block house surrounded by a four-foot chain-link fence. My brother stayed in his truck while I knocked. A man wearing a dingy, stained undershirt opened the door but not the screen. A dog barked from deep within the gloom. The man looked at me through whiskey-dulled eyes, trying to buck himself up for fresh trouble I figured.

"Help you?" He plainly had no aim of helping me.

"I'm looking for Mark Dunbar. He your son?"

"Why?"

"I need to ask him a couple questions."

"You the law? What's the little bastard done now?" Mr. Dunbar snarled his lip and puffed out his chest. "Why y'all keep hounding me?"

"We're not the law. I'm a friend of his friend Mary. She's turned up missing, and I'm trying to find her."

"And you think my boy done something to that girl? Get your ass off my porch before I come out there and whip you both." His nostrils flared, but he stayed put behind the screen.

Bill stepped from his truck and leaned against the door, his large arms folded across his chest. Dunbar's father glanced at him, and something flickered in his eyes. Realizing his threats were empty, he lost all his bluster.

He lowered his eyes and shook his head. "Told you before. He ain't here." Mr. Dunbar turned to reenter his home but paused. He half turned to me, his hand on the door knob. "If you find him, will you tell him something for me?" He wouldn't look me in the eye.

"Yes, sir. Reckon I could do that."

"Tell him he should visit his mama. He can find her in the cemetery behind Zion Baptist. He knows where it's at."

"I'm sorry for your loss. When did you lose your wife?"

"'Bout this time, two years gone. Reckon we lost Mark long before that." He disappeared into his house and closed the door.

"You think he's telling the truth?" I asked.

"Yeah, I don't think he's seen Mark in a long while." Bill sat staring at the Dunbars' house like he was in a trance. After a minute, he started his truck and eased away from the curb.

We left St. Matthews, heading toward home on Highway 601. As we crossed the Congaree River, Bill glanced out the window. "River's low," he said.

"We could sure use some rain." Talking about the weather or the river kept us from speaking about the matter at hand. But avoiding the problem wouldn't get Mary found, and I said what we both likely were thinking. "The law won't even talk to us until tomorrow morning. If she is with him, she's in a bad spot. He's one angry man and will take it out on her sure as hell."

Bill chewed his lip and watched the blacktop. "Cassie say anything more about where he might be?"

"She said Mary had mentioned he spent considerable time on the Little River. Sometimes that was the only relief Mary had from him. But I had Carl check Deacon's Landing for Dunbar's rig, and he didn't find him or his truck."

Bill hesitated and then said, "Suppose he didn't put his boat in at Deacon's Landing. Maybe he put in from the Billy Tolar boat ramp. That'd be the closest ramp to the Little River." Bill lifted his finger from the steering wheel to indicate the boat landing still twenty minutes ahead. "It's a short trip down the Wateree, then up the creek a ways. All that land. A man could stay lost out there for a coon's age." Bill didn't take his eyes off the road.

"I doubt Dunbar's stupid enough to put in from Sumter Highway. He'd be too exposed."

"Damn it, Jack. Let's check the fucking landing."

"Okay, Bill. Let's check it."

I watched my brother watch the blacktop for a couple miles, then looked off toward the right as if I could see through miles of trees to the Wateree River. We were in the heart of the COWASEE Basin, smack dab between the Congaree and Wateree. There were thousands of acres where Dunbar might hide. We'd need to be charmed to hit on him if he were on the water.

Debris from the river at flood and trash from lazy assholes made the Billy Tolar Landing look like a county dump. There were maybe twenty trucks, with empty boat trailers, parked in rows. I spied Dunbar's truck immediately. "Over there." I indicated a pickup and boat trailer parked beneath one of the two bridges connecting Richland and Sumter Counties. The truck had been through deep mud lately. I stepped out of Bill's truck to check the plates, even though I knew the rig was Dunbar's. Hell, I'd driven the damn thing. Laying my hand on the truck's hood, I hoped for heat, indicating he hadn't been there long. A corpse would've held more warmth. I looked at Bill and shook my head. They'd been on the water for a while.

"It's him," I said as I climbed back into the truck. "He probably picked up Mary and came straight out here this morning. We'd better go find them."

Bill seemed oddly calm. "I'll get my boat."

I stayed at the landing in case Mark might come off the water. Bill left to get his boat. He wouldn't be longer than forty minutes, there and back. Down at the river, I walked out onto the floating dock. From the dock's end, I could see a good ways up and down river. Not a boat in sight.

I heard an outboard's insect-whine, but the boat was still down past a bend or two in the river. Sound slides a long way across water, and I wasn't surprised when five or six minutes passed before the boat came around the last bend. I saw two bodies in the boat, but they were too far away to tell whether it was Dunbar and Mary. Within a couple minutes, I could make out two old men. They threw a rooster tail as they carved a turn toward the dock. The driver cut the engine, and they glided up to me. I reached out and held the bow, while one of the men stepped out onto the dock, his hand on my shoulder to steady his balance. "Thank you much," he said. He tied the bowline to a dock cleat and stood to stretch his back.

"Do any good?" I asked.

"Few," he said. Those old fishermen are a closed-mouth bunch. Most would sell a grandchild or two before giving away their secret fishing holes. He looked me up and down. "How about you?"

"I'm not fishing today. Looking for a man and a girl. The girl's pregnant and might be in a spot of trouble." I looked out over the river. "Were you boys near the Little River? I think that might be where they were headed."

The old gent must've figured I was trying to trick him out of his honey-hole. "Nope. Ain't seen nary a girl on the river today." Clearly done with me, he turned his back and walked up the dock to fetch his rig.

I looked at the other man sitting in the stern watching me. "Wasn't trying to make offense. The girl could be in some trouble."

"Aw, don't mind Virgil. He's naturally ornery. Don't eat enough fiber." He smiled at me. "We ain't seen no pregnant girl. Would be hard to miss out here. I hope you find her, friend. Mind pushing me off?" He spit a brown arc over the gunnel without ever taking his eyes from me.

I untied the painter, threw it into the bow, and gave him a shove. He pulled the cord and the outboard caught. Virgil backed the trailer down the ramp until the skids were submerged. His partner made a wide loop in the river and gunned the boat directly at the ramp. He killed the motor, and the boat slid onto the trailer, slick as you please. Virgil drove up the ramp with his more talkative partner still in the stern. The old boy looked over at me as he passed and touched his hat brim.

Bill arrived with his flat bottom, swung wide, and backed to the top of the ramp. We readied and loaded the boat into the water. He parked his rig beside the others and climbed into the boat, and we headed down river.

My gut thrummed with the expectation for what lay around the next bend. Even the chop of the water beneath us, as we crossed another's wake, only sharpened the notion that we were speeding toward something uncontrollable, with violent urgency and a fragile connection to the water.

The mouth of the creek known as the Little River was unremarkable from any other creek flowing into the main river. But unlike most streams feeding the Wateree, the Little River remained navigable for miles and miles. It led deep into uninhabitable swamp and low-lying woodlands. It would've been all too easy to become confused and lost in there, with dozens of feeder creeks and flats further along. Bill sat the boat mid-river, the motor just above idle to keep from drifting.

My brother looked at me and I nodded. He throttled the boat and headed toward the creek's mouth. A low-floating log across the mouth of the Little River kept out the lazy or timid. The trick was to drive the boat directly at the mouth at a speed that would allow you to slide over the log. At the instant right before the stern left the log, you'd have to lift the motor's foot from the water. Bill performed that little maneuver effortlessly, the boat barely losing momentum. The Little River snaked its way deep into the wild on the Sumter County side of the Wateree. There were no houses or farms next to the creek, just acre upon acre of trees, wild hogs, and snakes. Twisting and turning constantly, it allowed only for slow and patient navigation. Downed trees, low across the creek, could take your head off, so any speed above a jog was ill-advised. The banks were clogged with vegetation, cleared here and there for lonely fish camps. Spent dogwood blossoms littered the water, floating toward the Wateree, as if trying to escape that oppressive landscape. The dogwoods provided the only brightness in a green and gray world. And that would be gone soon enough.

We scanned the bank mud for bow dents as we crept up the creek. The Little River was narrow, and we'd see Dunbar's boat if he was in there, but we hadn't yet met another soul. There were plentiful branches feeding the main creek, but none we'd passed was deep or wide enough for anything bigger than a canoe.

After an hour, I guessed we'd traveled three, maybe four miles up the creek. I was about to shout to Bill to kill the Evinrude when he pointed ahead. Past the next bend an outboard motor bobbed in the creek. As we rounded the bend, I saw it was connected to a fifteen-foot flat bottom—the same boat I been in before, trussed up hand and foot. The boat was tied to a cypress knee, and on the high bank above sat a fish camp. All we could see from the creek below was the shack's tin roof. Bill eased up to the muddy bank beside Dunbar's boat. I folded a couple half-hitches at the bowline's bitter end and tossed them over the knee. A quick tug held us fast.

We climbed the steep bank and stared at what was left of the camp. Somebody or some animal had ripped through it and scattered food and gear every which way. From a tree limb hung a buck, gutted, long bled out, and black with flies. Right in the ruined camp's center was Mark Dunbar, flat on his back, a pump shotgun beside him. His head was turned to the left, and I saw the surprisingly small hole beneath his right eye and larger one on the back of his skull, where the bullet had found its way out.

Only a hollow-point could've destroyed the flesh and bone with such authority—that was no scattergun wound. He was likely dead before he hit the ground. Animals had been at the body too; he was chewed up something fierce. A possum ignored us and nosed around Dunbar's face. Bill threw a stick at it, and the possum hissed its irritation and waddled into the brush. More flies covered the bastard, and the buzzing was enough to drive a man mad. The possum's commotion made them lift, but they settled back on him once more.

"Jesus God Almighty," I said.

Bill said nothing. He just stared at the body.

I took a step toward Dunbar, but Bill laid a hand on my arm. When I looked at my brother, he held my gaze without speaking, then calmly turned back to the boats.

I couldn't reconcile the sight of Dunbar lying on his back with that bullet hole in his face. Someone had made a statement. I thought to ask my brother, but the growl of the motor and his eyes focused on the creek kept me silent.

We entered the Wateree an hour later. Bill beached his boat on a sandbar on the far side of the river. I looked at him from the bow. He sat the stern without expression, staring out over the river. He nodded once, reached behind the boat seat, and pulled out a large caliber pistol—the .45 I'd given him in his barn. He walked the few steps between us and handed the gun to me. I didn't need to check to know the magazine was one hollow-point shy of full.

"What should we do?" Bill asked. His voice held not a trace of fear—only acceptance of whatever fate awaited.

"Find me the deepest fucking hole in this river."

By the time we got the Sumter Sheriff's Department out there, and they called SLED and the Department of Natural Resources, dusk was knocking on the door.

Special Agent Talbert Cantrell, of the South Carolina Law Enforcement Division, was the last to talk to us. He was skinny as a hoe handle and kept hitching his belt up as the Glock on his side threatened to drop his britches to his ankles. "So you boys just happen to find a dead man way back yonder up that creek?"

Bill sighed. "Like we told the sheriff and game warden…"

He glanced up sharply at my brother. "I believe they prefer the title conservation officer."

"I don't give a shit what they prefer. We told them we were looking for a friend of ours who used to go with that particular dead man." That fellow had got Bill's short hairs up, and I was concerned what my brother might say next.

I said, "The girl, Mary, is a resident of a women's shelter in Columbia. She turned up missing this morning, and we've been looking for her." I nodded to the DNR boat tying up to the dock, with a black body bag on the bow deck. "Mark Dunbar was her ex-boyfriend. We knew he fancied the Little River, so that's what took us there. We figured maybe he'd taken her." I glanced at Bill. He had his arms folded, staring out over the river.

"Why didn't you call the authorities about the girl?"

My turn to sigh. "We did. Richland County and Columbia law told us to wait twenty-four hours and give them a shout, only then, if she hadn't turned up. We were out here doing your fucking job."

Bill turned from the river and curled a lip at Cantrell. "Any more questions, Special Agent?" he asked.

Cantrell hitched his belt again. "Make sure we can get in touch with you both."

After we'd answered all their questions, the officers wrote down our particulars and let us go. We watched as they loaded the body bag into the back of a county utility van. At the top of the parking lot, they headed east toward Sumter, and we drove west toward home.

Bill dropped me at my house. He hadn't said a word since we'd left the river. I stepped down from his truck and turned back to speak, but before I could say anything, he said, "Whatever you decide, Jack, will be right—I won't hold anything against you. You're like Dad. You always do what needs to be done." I knew my brother didn't mean it as such, but to me it sounded like an accusation.

Sara listened, without comment, as I told her about finding Dunbar's body. My wife's not squeamish, so I gave her the unabridged edition, bullet wound, possum, flies, and all. He was the man who'd threatened Audrey and Brad and who, among other crimes, had beaten a pregnant woman half to death. Sara would never have said it, but I figured she felt a certain justice had been served, a balance restored. She asked no questions and offered no opinions about him or the manner of his death. And I stopped short of telling her about the gun buried in the Wateree's muddy bottom.

Mary, of course, hadn't been at the camp and was still every bit as gone as she'd been that morning. Sara had spent the day at Carolina House, comforting the others, working the phones, and trying to uncover any clue as to where the young mother-to-be might've got to. She was disheartened we hadn't found Mary but relieved that Dunbar hadn't taken her or worse. I'd call the law in the morning, but we no longer even had a suspect for them. We had to hope they would be genuinely interested in finding Mary and not just her connection to Dunbar as a means to find his killer. I knew I couldn't sit idle while they conducted a careful and slow investigation. Tomorrow morning was too late to wait, and I wouldn't sleep anyway.

CHAPTER TWENTY-ONE

"**W**hen do we start?" Bill asked when I called to tell him my plan. He sounded relieved to have something to do. "Now," I said. "We can't wait on the law. Let's go pick up spotlights from Dad's shop. Then we can round up some folks to help look for Mary. We'll start in Columbia, at Carolina House." It seemed impossible to find her, but other than sitting on our asses, searching was our only option. Mary didn't have a telephone, so unless she contacted us, we'd keep searching.

Full-on dark had blanketed the Knoll by the time we parked at Mama's house. Bill went to tell her what we were doing and begin calling friends to help. I walked to Dad's workshop to gather as many spotlights, flashlights, and lanterns as I could find. On my way back to the house, I heard a commotion coming from the direction of the tree house. A weak light glowed through the windows. Setting all but one flashlight down in the grass, I sprinted to the tree house and began to climb.

A tortured cry caused me to scramble up the ladder like the devil was on my tail. I pushed open the trap door and looked into the room lit by a single toy lantern, likely left by one of the kids. I found Mary sitting in a corner, soaked in sweat and birthing fluid.

She was breathing hard and fast, well into labor I figured. I climbed down two ladder rungs and hollered for Bill. He was already inside the house, so I climbed up into the tree house and knelt beside Mary. She looked at me with trapped-rabbit eyes and said, "Help me, Jack. Please."

"I will, honey. Let me get myself some assistance out here, all right?" I called Bill and gave him the state of affairs. He and Mama were there in seconds. They had sheets and towels. "Did you bring hot water?" I asked.

Mama smiled as she took Mary's hand. She said, "Jack, honey, try not to think too much." Bill laughed. In my defense, that was my first emergency delivery situation.

Mama arranged Mary on the sheets so she was more comfortable and in a better position to deliver. She instructed Bill and me to get more lights. We climbed down and retrieved two gas lanterns from the field where I'd left them. With the lanterns lit, the space was both brighter and warmer. Having accomplished that important task, Bill and I sat down to await further instructions. Mama said, "One of you boys will have to deliver this baby. My eyes aren't strong enough."

My brother and I looked at each other, and Bill said, "You do it, Jack—you're older. I'll be right here to help if you need me."

"Thanks a lot," I said. Duly nominated and somewhat elected by questionable means, I asked Mama, "What do I do?"

"Check to see how much she's dilated," Mama said.

"Not her pupils, Jack," Bill said, grinning like a damn fool.

Mama explained how to go about it. Bill's wide eyes and open mouth about summed up how I felt about the whole procedure. But I did as my mother told me and held up my right hand, my finger and thumb a couple inches or so apart.

"About five to six centimeters," Mama said. "We have a little while to go."

"Do we have time to get her to a hospital or at least into the house?" Bill asked. Why hadn't I thought to ask that?

Mama looked at Mary, and then said, "I don't believe that's an option. How would we get her down the ladder? And she could deliver in fifteen minutes or twelve hours. There's no way to tell how long, but her labor is already active." She shook her head. "We'd best stay put."

"Maggie," I said. "Get Maggie here. She's a nurse."

Bill called Maggie and spoke to her briefly. "She and Mike are on the way," he said. I felt a flood of relief at that. I was almost in the clear.

Mama mopped Mary's forehead and spoke quietly, telling the girl how proud she was of her. Each contraction was closer to the last, getting more and more intense. A short time later, Maggie arrived, and she and Mike climbed up to join us. Although the tree house was plenty large enough, Bill and Mike climbed down to the ground mumbling something about tight spaces and claustrophobia.

Maggie checked Mary's progress and smiled at her. "Doing great, Mary. I believe you're going to be holding a beautiful baby before the sun rises." She held Mary's right hand and Mama held her left. I was squarely between Mary's legs and wished to God that I was not.

"So, you've got this, little squirrel, right?" I asked my sister.

"You're doing a fine job, Jack. Stay right where you are. We need you here." Maggie winked at me.

We did our best to comfort and encourage Mary. I was curious as to how she'd ended up twenty miles from Carolina House, in labor, in the tree house. But in a rare bout of common sense, I realized that wasn't the right time to ask her. Instead, I sat quietly, checking Mary when told and gritting my teeth each time she had a contraction and screamed.

Bill stuck his head up through the door to ask for updates every so often. He told us he'd called Cassie and the rest of the family to let them know what was going on. I heard muffled conversation below and figured Bill was updating Mike. And we settled in for a long night.

As dawn lit the eastern treetops, Mary delivered seven pounds, three ounces of impossibly small humanity into my waiting hands. Mary's boy was red and wrinkled, his face was pinched, and he was loud as a jackhammer. And he was perfect and beautiful. He was the common miracle that happened so often we sometimes forgot how truly miraculous it was.

Maggie cut the cord and began to clean and inspect the baby. Mama soothed the new mother, telling her how well she'd done. Mary couldn't take her eyes off the baby and, though she was exhausted, smiled the smile of the blessed.

"Have you picked out a name for your son, honey?" Mama asked while she helped Mary onto fresh sheets and covered her with a blanket.

"I have," Mary said with a sweet smile, as Maggie placed him into his mother's arms to hold for the first time. Mama continued to fuss with Mary's bedding, needlessly keeping busy. I saw tears trace down her smiling face.

I held the baby and made my way out onto the deck. As I exited the tree house, I noticed the sunlight reflected on the dogwood blossoms below. The oak grove's understory was alight with white flowers, the essence of spring, of new life. I looked down, expecting to see Bill and Mike pacing or sleeping in lawn chairs. Instead, I saw Sara and my daughters, and I saw Audrey and most of the Parker clan. Lauren had driven down in the middle of the night. Even Miss Ida Mae was there. Everybody stared up at me. I caught Sara's eye, and for a brief moment I was in the hospital holding baby Wren, looking at my beautiful, exhausted wife. Seemed a lifetime before.

"I'd like y'all to meet Mary's son," I said, "Thomas. His mama says you can call him Tom."

As I drove Mary and her baby into Columbia to see both her obstetrician and pediatrician, Mary told me how she'd come to be in the tree house. "Mark had Danny give me a message that he was picking me up yesterday morning before the house was awake. He was taking me away, somewhere in North Carolina, where he has family land and a cabin. If I refused to go with him quietly, he'd hurt anyone he had to and take me by force. I think he was hiding from the law somewhere and needed to leave the state soon." Mary looked at me and then out the window. "I know I should have told you or Cassie, but it scared me that he was able to get to somebody on the staff. And I was terrified he'd hurt one of the ladies. I panicked and I ran."

Mary had triggered the gate open from inside the house, as we'd suspected, and slipped out in the early morning hours. She'd walked to the Piggly Wiggly, two blocks away, and taken a ride on a dairy truck from an old route man bound for Sumter. He'd let her off a mile from the Knoll, and Mary had walked right past the house as Mama slept. "Your family's farm was the only place I could think to go, Jack."

"Why didn't you wake Mama? She would have welcomed you into her house."

"On the drive there, I began to have contractions. I tried to hide the pain from the old man so as not to scare him. By the time I'd walked to the Knoll, I was in a terrible panic and not thinking straight, I guess. Once I'd climbed into the tree house, the pain stopped and I fell asleep. I didn't wake until the contractions started again, right before dark."

I decided to wait and tell Mary about Mark another time. He couldn't hurt her anymore, and his death was one more burden she didn't need. We'd concentrate on making sure Mary and little Tom got the medical attention and support they needed. She'd likely find out about him through the news or word of mouth soon enough. Couldn't protect her from the world forever. That came as a hard truth to swallow.

CHAPTER TWENTY-TWO

I'm running through the woods, on the path between the neighbors' farm and ours. Running for home. I'm eight years old. I know this because the sheath knife my father gave me for my eighth birthday slaps my leg after each step, calling to me in a heartbeat cadence. Run. Jack. Run. Jack. My lungs burn, and each drawn breath is a torment. I run fast, my bare feet bouncing on the path's springy layers of pine needles.

I'm standing before my father with my head bowed, hands on my knees. He waits patiently, holding the horse's halter with his left hand, stroking its nose with his right. Finally, I can speak and the words pour forth in a rush, a confusion of syllables, a secret language my father understands.

Before I finish, he lets go the halter and turns toward the house. I begin to follow, momentarily forgetting the horse. When I look back, it's gone. He's already coming back down the porch steps, before I can move, and runs past me, vanishing into the woods from which I'd just come. I run, trying to catch my father, but my young legs are no match for his.

As I approach the neighboring farm, I hear shouts and curses. At the woods' edge, I crawl beneath a holly tree and peer out into a clearing surrounded by shimmering white blossoms. The old holly leaves are painful to my bare arms and legs; hundreds of pricking needles pluck at my limbs. The scene is the same I'd witnessed earlier. A woman's raven hair is held savagely twisted by a man's left hand. He wears no shirt or shoes. She's in a simple cotton dress. In his right hand, he holds a hickory axe handle. He's wrenching her hair, screaming at her, cursing her with words I don't understand.

Now, my father is here as well. Instead of feeling comforted, I'm terrified. I'm afraid not for myself, but for him. His back is to me, and he stands twenty feet away. His body is transparent, pulsating with light. He's pointing at the man with his right hand. His left hand supports the right, as if he doesn't have the strength to continue pointing. The man is staring at my father, his eyes narrowed, his mouth set in a hard, straight line. The woman is sprawled upon the ground, supported by his fingers clutching her hair. Her eyes are closed, but she opens them for one fleeting moment and looks at my father. I see eyes the deep green of a magnolia leaf bathed in dew. I see surrender.

The woman seems, at first, covered with mud and filth. Then I realize it's not dirt. Her pale skin shines through in patches untouched by black, metallic-scented blood. One hand rests on her swollen belly, the other touches the silver cross at her white throat. The delicate cross twinkles as light plays across its polished edges. She ignores the gash on her cheek.

My father says, "Put down the hickory. Let's talk about this."

"Go to hell. This ain't your business," the man replies.

"Please. She needs a doctor. She's hurt."

The man squints his eyes at my father. "Hurt? She ain't hurt. But she's going to be. I'll be damned if I don't teach her a good lesson this time." He raises the hickory handle high above his head, and his eyes widen as he returns his gaze to the woman at his feet.

"No. Please," my father says. With my heart thundering in my ears, I can barely hear his plea.

The man's shoulder muscles bunch as he brings the hickory down. I hear a sharp crack, like a bullwhip. A black spot appears above the man's right eyebrow, and for one moment, he looks confused. The axe handle slips from his grip, and he crumples to the ground beside the woman.

My father runs to her. He's holding her, and blood now covers them both. He keeps repeating, "They'll be fine. They'll be fine," over and over as he rocks her, touches her swollen belly. He looks up at me, now standing in front of the holly tree. "Go get your mama," he says. "Run, Jack."

I woke with a start, gasping for breath, my face wet with tears. The dream didn't fade, nor did my heart's quick-tick hammering wane for a considerable time.

No chance in hell I'd sleep again, so I pulled on jeans and a button-down and slipped downstairs to make coffee at three o'clock. I took my cup into the family room and sat on the sofa. An old film played silently, while Lucy and Ethel slept beside me. My right hand rested on Ethel's head, my left held the cooling coffee. I needed to speak to my mother, and I watched the mantle clock. I knew she'd be up by five, so at ten after, I called. "Hey, Mama. Sorry to call so early."

She sounded like she'd been up for hours. "It's fine, son. I'm on my second cup already," she said. "Everything all right?"

"Mama, did something happen with our neighbors to the east when I was eight or nine? I had the most disturbing dream."

No sound, no breathing, no voice from the phone. I began to think we'd been cut off, when she said, "Jack, you need to come on over here. We'd best talk."

As I walked up the steps to Mama's porch, Hemingway began to crow and then stopped, as if in deference to my lack of sleep. Mama rocked gently, her eyes on me. There were two steaming coffee cups on the table between her rocker and Dad's. I kissed her cheek then sat in my father's chair. As she reached for her coffee, I noticed a tremor in her hand I'd not seen before.

"Tell me your dream, son," she said. "Please."

I told it to her carefully. The terror was still fresh and full in my mind, and my story flowed like a cresting river. She listened with her eyes closed. When I'd finished, she opened them but stared in the direction of the barn, the woods, the path beyond. After a minute, she looked at me and said, "Everything you dreamed is true, Jack. It happened just so. But there is a lot you don't know."

"Then tell me." I'd been haunted by that dream for so many years, and I leaned forward, eager for my mother's words and dreading them every bit as much.

"Tom's sister and her husband, Ed Martin, lived on the adjoining land to the east of Parker's Knoll, connected by a half mile of woods. Both farms had belonged to your daddy's father, Rudolph Parker, who owned hundreds of acres east of Columbia and gave large plots to his two children upon their respective marriages.

"Ed Martin was abusive to your aunt in every conceivable way. Tom tried to convince her to leave her husband, but divorce wasn't done much back then, at least not around here. Typically, a woman stayed with the same man no matter how much of a monster he was or became. Still, your daddy begged her to leave and threatened her husband if he didn't stop. But Ed was a stubborn, prideful man. He believed nobody had a right to tell him how he could or couldn't treat his wife. One day Tom had had enough and beat him half to death. The man was laid up for three weeks. We all figured Ed had learned his lesson. He did behave himself for a time.

"But that particular day, a Saturday in April, you were playing in the woods between our houses when you heard a commotion and saw Ed thrashing your aunt. And so you ran."

Images and memories began to flood my mind, until I thought I'd drown. I remembered I'd never seen anybody so angry or violent, never experienced such rage directed from one person to another.

One thought had taken root—run. So I ran for my father. When Dad had entered our house, before running to their farm, he'd taken his revolver from the closet in his bedroom. He had killed Ed Martin with a single bullet before Ed could bring the hickory handle down again.

"Although Tom's sister survived the brutal beating, her baby didn't. When she came home from the hospital, she slept for two days. We tried to convince her to stay here with us for a bit, but she wouldn't. When the sedative's effects faded, she walked outside in her nightgown and bare feet and hanged herself beneath the tree house your grandfather had built for the child in her belly. Tom found her that evening when he carried supper to her. The next day, he tore down that tree house and the one your grandfather had built for you kids on our farm. He couldn't bear to look at them."

And Dad had carried her silver cross and the image of her swaying body with him every day, until his own death.

"I have vague memories of him having a sister who died many years ago, but I thought she died in an accident or from an illness. What was her name?" But, of course, I knew.

"Her name was Evangeline Carolina Parker Martin." Mama placed her hand on mine. "We called her Carolina."

I felt the world expand and then contract, choking off my breath.

"Son, are you all right? Do you want to take a break?"

I shook my head as I recovered, and my breathing returned to somewhere close to normal. "No ma'am. I'm fine." But I wasn't.

A few weeks after my aunt's death, I'd apparently begun to believe the incident had been a dream. My parents had encouraged it, believing denial best for me. Our family never spoke about that day. For me it didn't exist, except as a nightmare with no context and no end. As the weeks became months, the horror faded into the dusk, and lies became Parker reality.

Dad had quietly gone about his life, carrying his burden, unable to forgive himself, unable to talk to me.

"Tom blamed himself for not being able to help Carolina or her baby, either before or after the incident. His belief in God never wavered, but his faith in himself suffered for many years. You probably don't remember this, but whenever one of you kids would ask him to build a tree house, he would give some excuse why he couldn't do it then, always promising to build it someday. He just couldn't do it for so long a time."

"Mama, how could he blame himself for any of this?" I asked.

"Son, I don't know. He was never charged or arrested for killing Ed, but he felt he was responsible for all three deaths, as if he could have prevented them, as if that was ever possible. I tried talking to him, but he kept repeating that he couldn't save Carolina and the baby. Tom adored his sister. Oh, Jack, she was such a gentle soul. She loved animals and all manner of plants. Carolina had beds and beds of beautiful flowers and dozens of dogwoods, beautiful trees she'd planted. In a rage, your grandfather chopped down all Carolina's dogwoods before he sold her farm. I guess he figured if his daughter couldn't enjoy them, no one ever would. That's why your daddy planted all those dogwoods beneath the live oaks out there years ago." Mama gestured toward the grove, where Dad had begun to build the tree house before his death.

"Did he ask for any help?"

"No. I tried to get him to speak to our pastor or a counselor or a friend, but he wouldn't." She held up a hand. "A different time, Jack. In those days, men didn't speak to therapists or speak at all about what they felt, especially Southern men." Mama set her tepid coffee on the table. "Your daddy and I agreed not to speak to you kids about all this, and eventually we stopped talking about it altogether, even to each other. I thought you'd forgotten that day or at least believed it to be a dream. I'm not so sure Tom felt that way. I think he believed you blamed him."

"Dad never talked to me about it."

"He wouldn't, would he? Tom kept his thoughts to himself. It wasn't just you, Jack. He had a hard time talking to me as well.

Right or wrong, I accepted his silence as part of who he became after Carolina died."

I studied her face. Although my mother was quiet and unassuming, she had courage and strength. She'd been through so much, and her loyalty to my father had never wavered. She'd stood by him for all those silent years, trying and failing to help him. She and women like her were the reason battle-hardened soldiers called out for their mothers while their life's blood spilled out upon the battlefield. Only a mother could balance strength and compassion with what seemed so little effort. She hadn't failed my father. I believed she was the lone reason he hadn't chosen to join Carolina. But Mama had held all that in her heart for many years. How she must have wanted to talk to someone about what she couldn't say to her husband, what he wouldn't allow her to say. How alone she must have felt.

EPILOGUE

I was working in my office when my phone buzzed. "Jack? Larry Ramsey here. I was wondering if you could stop by the office next Wednesday. Say 5:30?"

Once again I was sitting in Larry's waiting room. I found it peculiar to see a twenty-something young woman sitting at Mrs. Tillman's desk. Larry's receptionist had retired the month before, and strangely enough, I missed seeing her. She'd run a tight ship for Larry's firm and received grief and jokes from idiots like me in return. She'd deserved better.

The receptionist ushered me into Larry's office. He was on the phone but motioned me to a chair across his desk. Finishing his call quickly, he greeted me and made small talk. My father's attorney and longtime friend looked at me over the top of his glasses, sighed, and reached into his middle drawer. He pulled out a white envelope and slid it across the desk.

I stared at it but didn't reach to take it. "What's this?" I asked. "Did I forget to sign something?" It had been exactly one year since Dad had passed, and I knew no document needed my signature.

"It's a letter from your daddy, Jack." Larry raised his eyes from the letter to my face. "He gave it to me a week before he died. He asked me to hold it and give it to you one year after his death."

"But he didn't know when he would die, and he certainly didn't plan on having a heart attack. He could have lived a long time with treatment and drugs." Even as I said it, I didn't believe Dad would have tried to prolong his life with the agony and pain he was certain to endure, as cancer plowed its way through his brain and body.

"Jack, I don't know what Tom was thinking or why he did this, but I think he knew he wouldn't live much longer. I hope this doesn't sound cruel or insensitive, but I believe his heart attack was a blessing. Perhaps he even..." Larry's face contorted with sadness. "I'm sorry, Jack. I'm old and full of hot air. I should keep my thoughts to myself."

"You were going to say that maybe he took his own life, worked himself into a heart attack, to avoid the pain and to spare Mama and his children from watching him wither away to nothing, going mad all the while." I waited for Larry to meet my eyes. "I think you might be right, Larry. I don't think Dad would have wanted to hang on to life just for the sake of breathing. Maybe he accomplished all he'd set out to do. Maybe he was ready to join Carolina."

I took the letter from Larry and drove away from Columbia, the sun at my back. The sky was cloudless and blue, a day for remembering and maybe forgiving. I drove to Parker's Knoll and sat in my truck watching the horses crop new grass. Bill's mare, Brandy, lifted her head at the crunching gravel and then continued grazing. I opened Dad's letter, written in his neat, spare script.

> *Dear Jack,*
> *I don't have suitable words to express my love for you.*
> *You were my joy and my salvation. That may sound*
> *strange coming from a father who seemed indifferent*
> *or uncaring at times to his oldest son. I'm fully aware*
> *that our relationship was unsatisfying to you, that I was*
> *unavailable, even cold. You see, I could never rid my mind*
> *of the image of you standing there watching as I killed a*
> *man, then held my broken sister. Though we never spoke*

of it, I always felt as if I'd failed you that day, not just
Carolina and the baby. I could see no path to redemption,
and I did nothing while all the unsaid words festered and
rotted between us, widening the rift with each new slight.

Even so, I watched you grow into a devoted husband
and father. Your family loves and respects you, Jack—not
just Sara and your sweet daughters, but your brother and
sisters and my darling Lizzie. I know, as surely as I know
God is watching over us, you are doing everything you
can for those we love. You're keeping them safe, and more
importantly, you're keeping them together.

How I wish I could be there as my grandchildren grow. I
know you finished the tree house, and my angels are enjoying it. I regret not being there to watch them at their play. I
know too you figured out why I founded Carolina House.
I knew you would finish the tree house, become involved
in the foundation, and understand their significance—the
tree house to fulfill a promise to my children and Carolina
House to honor my sister. Understand this, son: knowing
in my heart you would do these things, I am at peace.

I have but one wish, Jack. Please forgive me. I understand the pain I've caused you, but search your heart and
try to understand why I had to take a life the summer you
were eight. I pray you are never faced with such a choice,
but above all else, we must protect those who can't protect themselves.

Thank you, son, for taking care of our family.

With a father's love,
Dad

Later that day, I stood below the tree house listening to Tom
Parker's grandchildren laugh and play within. I smiled at the simple beauty of a child's laughter. To our kids, the tree house was a

playhouse their grandfather had designed and I'd built for their enjoyment. Someday they would know it was so much more. When they were old enough, the Parker grandchildren would know about their great-aunt and their grandfather's love for her. The secrets and half-truths would finally stop. But I thought about Bill and realized that wasn't quite right. Some secrets had to be kept. Sometimes the truth is far worse than a lie.

Maggie walked up and put her arm around my waist, her head on my shoulder. I placed my arm around her and squeezed gently, our familiar and cherished ritual. "What's happening, little squirrel?"

"I was inside playing with little Tom. He's cute as a button and so smart. Mary sure is doing a fine job with him. I think she was born to be a mother."

"She's a natural for certain."

"And she seems to like living here with Mama."

"I think she enjoys being a part of the family," I said. "But you can rest assured Mama is enjoying Mary and the baby too. She'll be sad to see them go." I looked at Maggie and could see marriage agreed with her. She carried a glow about her, a serenity, as if she'd found the answer to a particularly difficult question. "I think it will do us all good to have a little one around, even if it's just for a while, until Mary finishes her classes and moves to Greenville to manage the new Carolina House. At least she'll be close to Lauren."

Maggie grinned at me. "Having little Tom around will give you some much needed practice at changing diapers."

I pulled a face. "No thank you. I don't intend to change any diapers. I'm sure Mary and Mama have that little chore covered for the near future."

"I was thinking more about seven months from now." With that, Maggie turned and walked back toward the house, her hand resting easy on her belly.

ACKNOWLEDGMENTS

Thank you to Hub City Press—especially Meg Reid, Betsy Teter, and Kate McMullen—for such fine attention to the cover, editing, book design, and all the many steps that go into the crafting of a book. Thank you to all the partners of the South Carolina Novel Prize for their support of this award.

Heartfelt appreciation to Jill McCorkle for selecting this novel.

Thank you to Sandra E. Johnson for all the support and advice—and for our long lunches at Panera Bread, which always leave me recharged and inspired.

A special thank you to Erica Studer for reading an early draft of the novel and providing brilliant feedback—and for always making me feel like family. I am forever grateful.

Most of all, thank you to my best friend and partner, Patty Mattson. Thank you for reading the never-ending drafts without complaint. Your compassion, insight and honesty are found within these pages. Without your love and support, this novel would not have been brought to life—it's as much yours as it is mine.

PUBLISHING
New & Extraordinary
VOICES FROM THE
AMERICAN SOUTH

HUB CITY PRESS is a non-profit independent press in Spartanburg, SC that publishes well-crafted, high-quality works by new and established authors, with an emphasis on the Southern experience. We are committed to high-caliber novels, short stories, poetry, plays, memoir, and works emphasizing regional culture and history. We are particularly interested in books with a strong sense of place.

The biennal South Carolina Novel Prize recognizes exceptional writers who are residents and natives of the state. The prize is conducted, sponsored, and supported by Hub City Press, the South Carolina Arts Commission, the College of Charleston, the South Carolina State Library and South Carolina Humanities.

PREVIOUS PRIZE WINNERS

Ember • Brock Adams

Minnow • James E. McTeer II

In the Garden of Stone • Susan Tekulve

Mercy Creek • Matt Matthews

Through the Pale Door • Brian Ray

Sabon MT Pro
11.5 / 15.6